All I ever wanted was a baby, but not like this

A baby. Oh God. But just like all the others, I'll probably lose her. Him? I simply can't let myself start thinking about this baby as real.

Writing in this journal isn't helping—I've got to talk to somebody. I'll die if I don't. Now. Today.

Robbie's outside the door. I can't lay this burden on her on her wedding day.

Markie! She's been in this predicament herself, albeit as a teenager. Maybe she can help me sort this out.

A baby. Luke Driscoll's baby.

Dear Reader,

Frankie is the eldest of the McBride sisters, but she's the last to find true love...and to have the baby she's always dreamed of. In Book Two, *Lone Star Rising*, Frankie separated from her cheating husband, and her affluent, carefully controlled life in Austin was shattered. But I think any woman as spunky as Frankie deserves a second chance, don't you? And if anyone can make Frankie believe in love again, it's Texas Ranger Luke Driscoll.

When Frankie and Luke go on their first date, she buys the pie. I've already had reader requests for Parson's famous recipes from The Hungry Aggie. People tend to forget I make this stuff up! If you'd like the recipe for Texas Cream Pie, please check out my Web site at www.darlenegraham.com.

Thank you, dear readers, for all your encouragement as I wrote this trilogy. I had a blast!

My best to you,

Darlene Graham

P.S. I love to hear from my readers! Drop me a line at P.O. Box 72024, Norman, OK 73070 or visit my Web site and send an e-mail.

LONE STAR DIARY
Darlene Graham

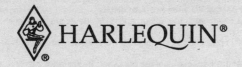

TORONTO • NEW YORK • LONDON
AMSTERDAM • PARIS • SYDNEY • HAMBURG
STOCKHOLM • ATHENS • TOKYO • MILAN • MADRID
PRAGUE • WARSAW • BUDAPEST • AUCKLAND

ISBN-13: 978-0-373-71377-6
ISBN-10:   0-373-71377-0

LONE STAR DIARY

Copyright © 2006 by Darlene Gardenhire.

Printed in U.S.A.

ABOUT THE AUTHOR

Reviewers say it's Darlene Graham's suspense that "grabs hold of her readers' attention and never lets go." But Darlene insists her writing is all about the *love*. "I'm not satisfied with my story until I've shed a few happy tears." When she's not sobbing into a tissue, the former nurse and mother of three grown children teaches writing classes at the local university and conducts workshops throughout the U.S. If she makes you cry, she'd love to know. Contact her at www.darlenegraham.com.

Books by Darlene Graham

HARLEQUIN SUPERROMANCE

I have been blessed with a large and wonderful extended family. This book is dedicated to all those precious relatives, *especially* the ones in Texas. I never take any of you for granted.

CHAPTER ONE

LUKE DRISCOLL fought down a clutch of nausea as his boots thudded along the dusty moonlit path. Even with the desert's cooling night breezes, the landscape around him reeked like an outhouse.

Little wonder. The place was a virtual garbage dump. His flashlight illuminated an arid terrain littered with bottles, cans, trash bags, soiled disposable diapers, sanitary napkins, discarded clothes, ripped backpacks, even used toilet paper and human feces.

But it was the sight of a syringe with an exposed needle near his boot that disgusted Luke the most. The Coyotes and drug runners shot their veins full of stimulants, staying high to endure the torturous journeys. Their human cargo got no such chemical help.

Out of the moonlit shadows a figure wearing a U.S. Border Patrol uniform emerged and flicked a flashlight up into Luke's face as he strode toward him.

Luke squinted at the glare as he fished his badge out of the hip pocket of his jeans and flipped open the cover. "Luke Driscoll."

The light flashed off the badge, then the guard aimed

the cone at the ground. "Nobody said anything about you being a Texas Ranger."

"More like former." There was no *former*, truth be told. In Luke's mind, once a Ranger, always one. But these days Luke kept his badge in his pocket instead of pinned to his shirt for all the world to see. He no longer covered the span of a couple of Texas-sized counties the way most Rangers did. These days he worked indoors with the hard-bitten crew of the Unsolved Crimes Investigation Team out of Austin, where, he imagined, it had been quietly arranged for the powers-that-be to keep an eye on him. Long-Arm Luke had become Loose Cannon Luke after his wife and daughter were killed.

"Chuck Medina." The border guard extended his hand and the two men shook. "I'm in charge of this case, at least for now." The youngish agent, who looked part Hispanic, studied Luke's face in the off-glow of his flashlight. "Driscoll? Where have I heard that name before?"

"Beats me." Luke kept his expression impassive and his tone a careful neutral. He had long cultivated the habit of sidestepping his history. "Thanks for meeting me."

"No problem. But I'm confused. What does the OAG want with this?"

"Nothing." And Luke was glad of it. He preferred to work alone. While the Office of the Attorney General would tackle most anything—murder, money-laundering, child porn—they would never step on local law enforcement's toes. And Luke had a feeling some pretty big toes were going to get stepped on in this deal. He had already delved into one murder that appeared to be part of some linked criminal transactions. "This one's my personal deal."

"Personal?" Medina studied him so closely that Luke decided he'd better throw the kid off the scent.

"I'm sort of like a cold-case investigator." He made his involvement sound detached, remote. "We think this murder is related to some old trouble up north." He started walking toward the crime scene tape stretched between two mesquite bushes.

The guard kept pace with him. "Whereabouts up north?"

"The Hill Country." Luke had already made two trips down the winding back country roads to Five Points, Texas, a town that was beginning to devil his mind for a lot of reasons.

"How'd you get wind of this?" the guard asked as Luke raised the stretchy yellow tape to duck under.

"A couple of brothers came to me." Luke had been surprised but gratified when the Morales boys had talked to him. He supposed the fallout from his history wasn't all bad. "The young woman you guys found out here in this dung heap—" he straightened and surveyed the area "—was their sister."

Medina shook his head. "Oh *man.*"

Far back in the mesquite bushes, they came to a shallow depression, freshly dug in the hard-packed desert. "The guy buried her?"

"Yeah. In a shallow grave. Very shallow. Almost like he didn't care if she got found. I guess even if she was, he knew he'd never get caught. The Coyotes aren't scared of us."

Luke's own words, recently spoken to a most feminine woman with a somewhat unfeminine name—Frankie—echoed in his mind now.

These are very dangerous men, ma'am, he had warned the hauntingly beautiful brunette.

He shook off the distraction—the weird sense of enchantment—that overcame him every time his thoughts strayed to this Frankie woman. Right now he didn't have time to dwell on unbidden feelings.

He panned his flashlight over the area, which was unnaturally clean, stripped of all debris. "I see you boys got everything."

"Every last little bobby pin. A freaking waste of time."

"Ah, now," Luke drawled, "I've never found catching a killer a waste of time."

Medina grunted. Luke figured he knew what the guy was thinking: if these illegal aliens wanted to break the law and trust their lives to Coyote-types, they got what they paid for. After an uncomfortable silence, in which the two men adjusted to the likelihood that they stood on different sides of the issue, Luke said, "Tell me about the victim."

The guard shrugged. "One more pretty Mexican girl on the run."

Maria's brothers had told him, tearfully, that their sister was pretty. And the Texas State Police officers Luke had talked to before he came out here had confirmed that, indeed, the victim had a pretty face—what was left of it. Sixty-five stab wounds. Coyotes—rightly named—were no better than mad dogs, vicious animals that devoured the innocent.

When the local sheriff had shown up at a humanitarian compound called the Light at Five Points looking for

Maria's brothers, Luke was already there talking to Justin Kilgore, the man who ran the relief organization and—this interested Luke more than it should have—Frankie McBride's brother-in-law. Kilgore said the Morales boys— the same Morales boys, it turned out, who had originally come to Luke with a bizarre story about some Mayan carvings—had disappeared.

The brothers would never come out of hiding, Kilgore told the cops, even to claim their sister's body. Luke knew that was right. And he suspected whoever had killed the sister did it for exactly that reason—to draw the brothers out.

Luke had convinced the Moraleses to tell him about Maria, about their home town in Jalisco, about their family history, but he couldn't convince them to come down here to the border, though they had begged *him* to. Luke was the only Anglo they trusted, they said. Luke intended to keep that trust.

The crime scene tape, looking defeated as it sagged in the sand, was about all that was left to indicate a murder had occurred here yesterday. Maria's body, after a routine autopsy, would be sent back to Mexico, back to her aging, widowed mother. The men who killed her were long gone too, possibly to Mexico as well.

Maria Morales's murder would lie unsolved, lost in a morass of paperwork and legalities. Of no more conse- quence than the litter on this desert. Something ugly, some- thing to wash your hands of. Waste. But for reasons all his own, Luke wouldn't rest until he'd hunted down the dog who killed this girl. Nor would he rest until he had an answer to the ultimate question in this whole deal. *Why?*

"The girl we took in for questioning described the killer. Turns out he's a known Coyote in his early twenties." The guard dug something out of his flak jacket. "We mooched this picture off the Houston police. The guy operates over that way as well."

They were standing just inside the border, on the U.S. side of the Rio Grande River, south-southwest of San Antonio, far, far away from the Houston side of Texas.

"Busy hombre," Luke muttered.

"Yeah." The Federal handed Luke a grainy black-and-white photo that had obviously been downloaded off the Internet. "According to our sources, the guy has relatives on both sides of the state, *and* in Arizona, *and* as far south as Chiapas. He could be anywhere between here and Central America."

Luke lifted his flashlight and examined the picture. A young Hispanic man with a buzz haircut and a smudge of mustache shadowing his upper lip looked out with a cold, reptilian gaze that would halt the blood of an ordinary person.

Luke studied the heavy-set face as dispassionately as a geologist studying a rock. It was a skill—the reading of faces. This particular one would have set Luke's instincts to strumming even if the guy hadn't been an alleged murderer, even if Luke hadn't seen this face before—in person.

Izek Texcoyo. Known in the border underworld as Tex. The cynical mouth that refused to smile, the dark scar that rose from the corner of that unsmiling mouth clear to one eye, as familiar to Luke as his own trim goatee and crow's feet.

The young man was surprisingly handsome despite his disfigurement. "Can I get a copy of this?"

"Keep that. Here's another." He dug around in the jacket. "You know, it's a damn shame. The more the illegals come, the more the Coyotes prey on them." The guard explained what Luke already knew. "Sometimes it's like we're spittin' on a fire. They're like roaches, you know? Scuttling across in the night. But we have to try, right?"

"You in your way, me in mine," Luke said. He had heard another agent compare crossers to ants. If you smashed one, twenty more took his place. He gave the skinny guard a pitiless glance, but he couldn't find it in his heart to judge him too harshly. So young. Seemed like they all were. Luke himself was only forty-three and yet he always felt like an old geezer in the subterranean world of the border.

Whether it was the crossers or the patrol or the Coyotes, the people down here seemed like scared children caught up in a dangerous game. This one was no exception, no older than your average college student, doing the best that he could. Patrolling miles and miles of impossibly vast terrain, vainly rounding up illegals that flooded across in numbers that staggered the imagination.

Medina finally produced a paper and handed it over.

Carrying around obscene photos in his flak vest.

It was a body. A female form, half-dressed in a ripped T-shirt. "Did she have any personal effects on her besides the T-shirt?" Luke asked as he looked at it.

The border guard gave him an annoyed squint. "You're kiddin', right?"

The Coyote who killed her had, of course, robbed her blind as well.

"The brothers believe she was wearing a vest with Huichol beadwork. It had great...*sentimental* value. She was also supposedly carrying an object in her backpack. Did anybody find said backpack, or perhaps a chunk of carved stone in the vicinity?"

Luke suspected there was more to this chunk of rock and this vest than sentimental value. The Morales brothers were withholding something here, but they would eventually come straight with him or find themselves hugging jail bars.

"No backpack," the kid said. "No carving. But I know exactly the kind of thing you're talking about. Occasionally we'll hear tell of crossers smuggling over artifacts. Mayan stuff, mostly. My guess is they sell them in El Norte for a fortune. And a beaded vest?" The guard eyed Luke sarcastically. "These crossers wear rags. And knock-offs of Nikes when they can get 'em."

Indeed. No one in their right mind would wear precious ceremonial garb for this journey. Crossers snaked along in unbroken lines over dusty, well-beaten paths like this one, hacking through the underbrush, scooting on their backsides down canyon floors, crawling along muddy arroyo bottoms.

Luke pushed his Stetson back on his head and rubbed his forehead, thinking for the millionth time that there had to be a humane solution for these people. Did Maria's brothers blame themselves for not going back to Mexico to get the vest themselves instead of having their sister wear it on her person? But it was Luke's understanding that no man was supposed to touch the feminine half of the pattern. He wondered if evil would befall the Coyote who'd stolen it, part of him longing to believe these ancient superstitions were true.

"Maybe her friend knows something about the backpack, but my guess is it's long gone, down the trail with that Coyote."

"Her friend?"

"The girl traveling with her. Scared to death. She burrowed down in the sand behind the bushes while they killed this one."

"Can I talk to her?"

"She's back in Del Rio, in jail."

Luke sighed. Ever since he'd gotten involved with these people, it seemed like he was forever springing somebody out of jail. Out at the Light at Five Points he and Justin Kilgore had shared the frustrating similarities in their work. Financial problems. Medical problems. Problems with the law. And lately, even political problems.

"Thanks a lot, Dad," Justin had muttered as he told Luke about the trouble his father had stirred up. "Dad" to Justin Kilgore was none other than Congressman Kurt Kilgore. For the life of him, Luke couldn't figure out why the congressman was so dead set against his son's humanitarian work.

"What's her name?" Luke dug in his jeans for his little notebook.

"Yolonda Reyes. I can have one of our guys go fetch her." The guard reached for his shoulder radio and spoke into it.

And then what? Luke thought. Luke wasn't about to send the child back to jail or to Mexico into the hands of the border *judiciales*.

An engine whined and the single headlight of a quad runner appeared out of nowhere, hurtling down the path in a cloud of dust, another young agent jostling high up on the narrow seat. The kid gave a two-fingered salute as he flew past. Medina saluted back as he hopped out of the way. Luke stepped back too, twisting his ankle as the heel of his cowboy boot rolled off a soggy diaper.

"Sorry," Medina hollered as the roar of the quad faded into the darkness. "Joe flies around like a maniac."

Luke knocked the dust off his sleeves as he regained his footing.

"You been at this awhile?" The guard gave Luke a wary once-over and Luke imagined the kid was noting the threads of gray in his hair and goatee, a certain cynicism around his eyes. But Luke's weathered looks weren't the result of age or even too many dangerous scrapes and long hours as a Ranger. If he had a hard-bitten look, it came from brooding too long. From seeing his dead child's face in all its sweetest, most innocent poses every time he closed his eyes. He was acutely aware that this festering anger wasn't healthy. He just didn't know how stop it.

"Long enough." Four years studying law enforcement, four years as a DPS trooper. A dozen or so as an active Ranger. Too much of it undercover in Mexico. Somewhere in all of that, he and Liana had managed to forge eight years of bliss before those little creeps had killed Liana and Bethany. It struck him that he hadn't dreamed a good, clear dream about his wife and daughter for a while now. "Let's get back to Maria's case," he said. "The family would like to have her stuff."

The guard flipped up a palm like a traffic cop. "Since you've been at this so long, you ought to know everything from the crime scene is in police custody and staying there. And you know not to get your hopes up about ever getting it back…or catching this creep for that matter."

"Haven't let a creep go yet," Luke stated flatly. Because he hadn't. Medina still hadn't figured out who he was. "In the meantime, I'm just trying to help this family obtain what's rightfully theirs. They don't even speak English."

"Nobody does, man." The agent said it with that sarcastic edge in his voice that was beginning to annoy Luke.

"They need an advocate," he said calmly. "Right now, that would be me." He dug a business card from the hip pocket of his Levi's.

Medina took it and flipped the beam of his flashlight on it, thumbing the embossed seal of the Lone Star State. "Nice. I'm fresh out. Budget cuts." Again, the guy's voice was sarcastic.

Luke didn't respond as Medina stuffed the card away in his flak vest. His silence seemed only to encourage the kid. "What, exactly, do these brothers expect? Last year over a million and a half of these types crawled up into the States." Apparently Chuck Medina was determined to vent his spleen. "It's like an *invasion,* man. This so-called border is a freaking sieve. The narco-militarist types, drug runners, Coyotes run the show down here. And they're using assault rifles to do it. It's a war zone." He fanned an arm over the abandoned desert as they started making their way back to the main path. "Fear keeps the locals locked away, peering out of their houses over the barrels of their shotguns. And that's just so they can keep the crossers out of their own front yards. They've given up on the outlying ranch lands. The few times a rancher had the guts to detain illegals for trespassing, the press crucified him as a racist vigilante. Some have even been sued. See all this crap?" The guard kicked at the trash, raising a plume of moonlit dust.

"It's like this on practically the whole four-thousand-mile border. In the meantime, we're caught in the middle. The Coyotes are making a killing off these poor people and nobody's doing a thing about it. The illegals don't trust anybody but the Coyotes until it's too late. Until something like this—" He jerked his head back toward the crime scene. "Even if somebody had called 911, how could we get close enough to protect that young woman when the Coyotes let loose with a spray of bullets at the slightest sound and her rock-chucking compadres are ready to ambush us from behind every mesquite bush? And now we've got to worry about terrorists." He finally stopped long enough to draw a frustrated breath.

Hoping Medina had talked himself out, Luke said, "It's hard to sort out the good from the bad. I've gotten the same treatment." So had Justin Kilgore. Crossers came in all shapes and sizes, all ages, all nationalities. But they all had one thing in common. Fear. Fear of getting caught. Fear of going to jail. Fear of authority. Fear of the gringo. Luke had worked hard to break through that fear and be one Texas Ranger they trusted. "You can't blame them for being mistrustful, even when people are trying to help them."

"I'll tell you what's sad," the young border guard said,

calmer now. "It's the way these people accept their fate. Like they have no hope of anything ever getting better."

"That's the problem. They do have hope." Luke sighed. "Otherwise they wouldn't even attempt these crossings."

The quad runner roared back up the rutted path, this time with a tiny young woman hanging on for dear life on the back. The driver got off and helped her dismount. She was so thin it hurt to look at her. Great, Luke thought, now he had a skinny teenager to deal with. "Her name's Yolonda?" he clarified.

"Yeah. That little *chica's* lucky she's alive." The guard spat in the dust, then hurried to follow Luke. "You know what she said? She said at least this time the Morales family would have a body."

Luke stopped, turned, frowned. "This time?"

The guard hitched at his belt, suddenly self-important with information the Ranger didn't have.

"The Morales' father disappeared years ago."

"Their father?" Luke processed this.

"He sent their mother the sign, but they never heard from him again."

"The sign?" Luke squinted at Medina.

"The Lone Star. They'll send it on a postcard or a trinket or something back home to Mexico. It shows that they've made it as far as a place called Five Points. I do not know why these people bother with such secrecy." Medina shook his head. "Everybody knows Five Points is a key stopping place for crossers. Five highways going in every direction. Just a hop-skip to I-10."

"I see," Luke said. Five Points. He could practically see

a puzzle piece locking in place. The Morales boys had failed to inform him of this little detail. Suddenly he knew exactly what he was going to do with this Yolonda girl: offer her asylum if she would tell him everything she knew. He could take her out to the Light at Five Points.

Luke thought of the people there and others he'd met when he'd gone to check out another murder in that small town, and like a rubber band, his mind snapped back to the woman named Frankie.

She'd given her full name, Frankie McBride Hostler, although the last name hadn't rolled out as evenly as the first two, as if she'd choked on it. He had checked her left hand then, its slender fingers entwined with the other hand around the grip of a heavy revolver. A diamond the size of Dallas had winked at him in the blazing Southwest sun.

He'd never met a woman that way, while she held a gun on him in a firm firing stance. When she shot the head off the copperhead snake coiled less than a yard from his boot, he had decided this particular woman was something else.

Too bad this Frankie McBride…*Hostler* was married.

Five Points. He was headed back there for sure. Back to the home place of Frankie McBride.

CHAPTER TWO

My birthday. And I cannot believe I am actually writing these words in this journal: I am divorcing Kyle. I signed the papers yesterday. The weird thing is, ever since I made my decision, I've felt this enormous sense of…peace. Well, relief at least. And the strangest…*euphoria* from facing the truth.

My sister Robbie was right about one thing. Writing it down in this journal has clarified the hell out of things. I guess keeping a journal runs in our blood. Great-grandmother McBride started that tradition back in the territory days. I've been scribbling the most atrocious stuff in here, mostly about how I'd like to murder Kyle, but I couldn't believe how seeing what Kyle had done written in black and white helped me face up to what I had to do.

I caught a glimpse of Robbie's journal once. A cheap thing from Wal-Mart with a picture of a puppy dog on the front. That's the main difference between me and my younger sister. She takes life as it comes and I manage it to death.

But I doubt I'll change my ways. I'm turning forty

today, and being fastidious and organized is in my blood, too. Like Mother.

I am terrified that I'll end up like her someday. I seem to be well on my way. Fussing over another woman's children, starting up another woman's business, living in another woman's house, a nineteenth-century rattletrap that would be condemned if not for the improvements Zack Trueblood has made to it.

Soon Robbie and Zack will be getting married and they'll move the children out to the farm. The Tellchick-Trueblood Farm, Zack renamed it.

Then what? Will I become a boring little drudge? Fussing with the displays in the shop, lunching with lady friends, buying extravagant gifts for my niece and nephews? Will I fall into a sad little rut, a childless divorcée piecing together a half-life around her extended family, but in reality, so alone.

But even with all my fears, I can't shake this feeling that I'm alive again for the first time in years. As if I'm breaking free. As if I could conquer the world.

And speaking of the world, time to get out in it. The sun's up, and I want to get down to the store early. We're putting up wallpaper today. Robbie's coming in right after she drops the boys at school.

FRANKIE MCBRIDE inhaled a bracing dose of icy January air as her numb fingers worked the key in the lock of her sister's craft shop. It was cold enough in the Hill Country to freeze a Yankee's behind this morning, but Frankie felt full of unaccountable excitement and purpose. The littlest things seemed to make her happy lately. Her baby niece. This store. Fresh coffee in the morning. It all seemed so vital, so far removed from the sterile life she'd left behind.

She glanced up and down Main Street. Except for a half dozen antique stores, a handful of upscale art galleries and a general spiffing up for the ever-increasing tourist trade, the main street of Five Points, Texas, had not changed since Frankie's high school days.

The store sat nestled where the narrow brick avenue made a gentle S half-way through town, visible to tourists who left the beaten path where five highways converged. Frankie's dad and Zack Trueblood had done an excellent job of making the shop stand out, with its turned posts and gingerbread trim, painted in authentic Victorian shades of pumpkin, teal and cream. Robbie had insisted that the front door be painted true Texas red, and had carried the signature color over in a stenciled Lone Star design high on the front window and again on the doors of the antique display cabinets.

Frankie loved this place. She took a second to delight in the familiar—the lavender curves of the Texas Hill Country touched by a golden sunrise, the aroma of Parson's pancakes wafting from the Hungry Aggie, where a cluster of pickups gathered like cattle at a trough, the whine of the school bus engine, the firefighters raising the single door on the old limestone firehouse that sat in the other curve of the S.

She jiggled the key as she wondered if Zack was on duty

today. Ah. Here he was now, headed for the tiny bakery where the fluorescent lights were glaring and the pastries were hot.

Zack waved. He was a handsome man, virile and fit. And genuinely kind. Her sister Robbie was so lucky.

Which reminded Frankie that she was…not so lucky.

Right on the heels of that deflating thought came guilt. How could she envy her sisters for the love they'd found? Her problems were nothing compared to theirs. Robbie's husband had been killed in a tragic barn fire only a year earlier. Markie had endured the pain of giving a child up for adoption when she was a mere teenager. She admired the way her sisters had triumphed, had found happiness despite their setbacks.

Still, Frankie couldn't help but think that at least Robbie had her children, whereas Frankie had lost all her babies, one after another. Four wrenching miscarriages. She studied Zack's back and decided it was easier to think about the contrast between solid, generous-hearted fire-fighter and her own tightly wound, bone-selfish husband. Immediately on the heels of that thought came the memory of meeting that other man, the Texas Ranger, the one with the broad shoulders and piercing eyes. This memory had been deviling her, off and on, for weeks. Her attraction to the man had been immediate, electric, and, to Frankie, thoroughly shocking.

At first she'd thought it was some kind of rebound thing, being drawn to an attractive man out of sheer loneliness. But her preoccupation with him persisted, and she began to wonder if there had been something special about him after all. Mercifully, the memory faded over the weeks, as if the whole meeting had been some kind of fantasy, and ultimately she was back to her sad reality—divorcing herself from an unfaithful husband.

Tears stung her eyes, as they did every time she thought about Kyle's betrayal, but Frankie was quickly learning to shake off self-pity. Work, she had decided, was the answer to her woes. Her sister needed her help, and even with a substantial settlement in the offing, Frankie knew she couldn't live on Kyle's money forever. Getting this store up and running was going to solve both of their problems.

The lock finally clicked open and she bent to pick up the plastic storage tub she'd carried from the trunk of her Mercedes.

"The Rising Star is looking real good," a chiming female voice called out. It was Ardella Brown, the proprietor of the flower shop down the walk. "Getting things all organized over there, are you, Frankie?" Ardella nodded at the plastic bin.

Frankie smiled. "Trying to."

"Good girl!" Ardella's smile was as bright as the eastern sun that glinted off her spectacles. Ever since Ardella and Frankie's mother had been young women, they had passed each other bits of juicy gossip as if trading sticks of gum. Ardella made no secret of her feelings about the McBride sisters. She liked Robbie, didn't like Markie, and was carefully respectful, even a tad admiring, of Frankie.

But Frankie didn't know how to take Ardella's new attitude about Robbie's shop. Marynell had reported back every sniping thing Ardella had said about the beginnings of their enterprise. But recent events made Frankie wonder if Ardella had actually said those things or if Marynell had conveniently inserted words into someone else's mouth. It was going to be hard to trust their mother ever again.

One thing was sure, her sister Robbie had been much warmer toward Ardella since Ardella had been alert enough to report smoke on the night of the shop's fire, saving baby Danielle's life.

"Have a good day!" Frankie shot Ardella a smile, scooted inside, plunked the bin down with a thud and hurried back out. She was reaching into the trunk to pull out the short stepladder they'd borrowed from Zack when she had a sensation of being watched. She straightened and noted two paunchy old guys in overalls looking her way. "Morning!" she called.

Living in Five Points was going to take some getting used to. In a big city like Austin, even a woman of her social standing could be anonymous. But here, everybody and everything got noticed.

She wrestled the ladder inside, turned the deadbolt, fastened the chain. Bright morning sun backlit the frosted oval glass that had graced the entrance since territorial days. Thank God the front half of the store, with its antique charm, hadn't been damaged by the fire. On a sideboard where Robbie had set up a charming coffee service, she started a carafe of her favorite blend. Frankie had convinced Robbie that elegant touches like candy dishes and demitasse-sized cups of flavored coffee would encourage shoppers to linger.

With the coffee dripping, she hurried to the storeroom. She was pulling out rolls of wallpaper when a loud rapping on the front glass made her jump.

She frowned. Had Robbie misplaced her keys to the store yet again? Living with Robbie was starting to tax her patience.

"Coming!" she snapped, trying not to be annoyed at the scattered ways of her sister.

The flotsam and jetsam of moving lay everywhere, as it did at Robbie's house. Frankie determined anew to help her sister get more organized. *Starting with her keys,* she thought as the rapping ricocheted through the store again.

She came up short when she saw, framed in the oval frosted window, the silhouette of a tall man in a cowboy hat. Her stomach plunged when she recognized Luke Driscoll's profile. Memories rushed back. His handsome face, piercing eyes, laconic manner, broad-shouldered physique. She even remembered the sound of his voice—low, gravelly, emotionless.

"Mrs. Hostler?" that very voice now caused a flutter at her core.

She opened the door a crack, kept the chain lock on.

He actually touched the brim of his Stetson. "It's me, Mrs. Hostler. Luke Driscoll."

She hated the very sound of Kyle's last name now, but that was not the Ranger's problem.

"Mr. Driscoll. Of course I remember you." She undid the chain and opened the door wider. You didn't forget a man you'd shot at with a revolver, though she had certainly never expected to see, much less speak to, this one again.

"Just Luke. Remember?"

"Yes. I do…remember. What…what are you doing here?" Despite the cold air, she could actually feel her cheeks heating up.

"I saw you unloading the car while I was in there getting her something to eat," he said, jerking his head in the direction of the Aggie.

Her? Only then did Frankie notice a painfully thin girl with dark Hispanic looks, cowering behind Driscoll's big shoulder. The teenager was wearing filthy sneakers, threadbare jeans, a baggy denim jacket and a thin shawl clutched tightly about her head. Probably an illegal. There were plenty of them around here.

But before Frankie addressed the girl, she had to ask, "You...you were watching me?"

"Yes, ma'am," he said unapologetically. "Um..." He looked around. "Can we get in off the street? Yolonda's a little skittish."

The young girl, maybe fifteen or sixteen, did indeed look frightened. She mumbled something in Spanish while her wide black eyes pleaded with Frankie in a way that needed no interpretation.

"Of course." Frankie stepped back to allow them in. Driscoll's boots clumped loudly on the hardwood floor. "This your sister's shop?" he asked as he steered the girl inside.

"Yes," Frankie said as she closed the door. Although she had developed proprietary feelings about the place lately. "I work here."

"Oh?" He gave her a curious frown. "I thought you said you were just visiting. Remember? A while back? When we met out at your parents' farm?"

How could she forget? Frankie felt her color rising higher. She'd pointed a gun at a Texas Ranger, shot a snake, then gotten all flustered and teary. She did recall saying something about going back to Austin. But now she had no intention of reconciling with her husband. She sighed. One day she said one thing, the next she did another.

Why she cared what this man thought of her was a mystery. Maybe it was the way he was looking at her—as if *he* cared. Or maybe it was because he came across so…pulled together. From the top of his tan Stetson to the muscular, relaxed way he moved, the man exuded an air of strength and competence.

"I…uh…" she stammered, realizing he was still waiting for her answer. "I never went back to, uh, to Austin. I stayed on to help my sister." Not strictly true. She'd stayed to sort out her messy life.

"As you can see—" she swept around in front of his imposing frame, leading the way through the piles of clutter on the floor "—we're still getting organized. We had a rather unfortunate fire. We've fixed the damage, but…" She looked back and he was regarding her patiently. "We can sit down back here in the storage room."

"I know about the fire," Driscoll's voice came calmly from behind her. "I interviewed the arsonist."

Frankie spun around, surprised. "Really?"

"Old guy named Mestor. Interrogated him at the jail."

The day they'd met, Frankie thought this Texas Ranger had told her he was looking for some Mexican Coyotes. Was this related? "Why ever did you question *him?*"

"I'm working on a string of events. But that's not why I came over here this morning." He pushed his Stetson back on his head. "I need to take Yolonda here out to the Light at Five Points."

"My sister and brother-in-law's place. You need directions?"

"No, ma'am. Already talked to Justin Kilgore."

Goodness. This man seemed to know everybody. "So, is Yolonda an…an illegal alien then?" Frankie tried not to cast any wary glances at the child and prayed the girl didn't speak English.

"Yes, ma'am. Crossed two nights ago. Not under the most ideal circumstances."

"Are circumstances down there ever ideal?" Frankie frowned, but again, not at the girl. In Frankie's world, undocumented aliens were never acknowledged as such, even if they were cleaning your house or doing your yardwork. She hoped this Ranger wasn't going to ask *her* to take charge of the girl.

"Her case is even worse than most," Driscoll went on dryly. "And now she needs protection." A glance from the Ranger caused the girl to adopt that big-eyed, fear-filled look again.

Quietly he said, "*¿Estás bien?*"

It was then that Frankie noticed that the jean jacket the girl was wearing was way too large for her, a man's size in fact, and that Driscoll was wearing only a Western-cut denim shirt. Running around in January weather in his shirtsleeves? Likely because he'd given his jacket to a freezing child.

The child gave him a quick nod, but Frankie didn't think this girl looked *okay* at all. "Mr. Driscoll—Luke—I can't…I'd like to help, but…"

"Yolonda's not the reason I'm here. I hate to interrupt

your work, but I didn't have a number where I could reach you. It's a pure stroke of luck that I saw you. I need a favor."

"Of course." Frankie reasoned she should cooperate with the law, but she suspected it would be closer to the truth to admit that doing a favor for this handsome man would be no hardship.

"Would you care for some coffee?" she said. The aroma filling the cozy store was suddenly working on her.

"No, ma'am. Thanks anyhow," Driscoll drawled.

But when he said something to Yolonda in Spanish, the girl mumbled back, nodding. "She'll have some, if it's no trouble. Black."

Frankie smiled and went to the sideboard. She poured two foam cups of coffee, handed one to Yolonda, quickly added cream to her own.

She led the girl to an old wrought-iron park bench—one of Robbie's finds—while Driscoll took a nearby lawn chair that Zack had left behind.

Frankie sipped the coffee, then said, "What can I do for you?"

Again, the corners of Driscoll's mouth turned down in that grudging way. It wasn't an unpleasant expression. It was actually kind of sexy. Frankie almost rolled her eyes at her own errant thoughts. *Behave,* she told herself, *the man is probably married.* And so, incidentally, was she. Though not for much longer.

"You need help with the girl?" Frankie adopted a kindly mien, as if she were some social worker handling a case. She also surreptitiously checked out the third finger on Luke Driscoll's left hand. A gold band.

When she looked up, their eyes met and the collision sent another tremor to her core. Luke held her gaze only a millisecond before he spoke in a flat monotone. "No, Mrs. Hostler. I was wondering—"

"Call me Frankie." *Please. Anything but the name of that little prick I married.*

"Okay. Frankie. I wondered if you could show me the way back to those caves we saw the day we met. On your parents' land?"

"We were actually on my sister's land that day. The farms are adjoining. Well, it's not my sister's land anymore, or at least it isn't hers until she gets married again. It belongs to a man named Zack Trueblood now. The man she's going to marry this spring. She's a widow, you know."

"I know." Luke's tone was long-suffering. "I met Trueblood, and your sister." Then he frowned. "So, would you prefer that I contact Trueblood about the caves?"

"No," Frankie said a little too quickly. "I'd be happy to take you out there myself. I'm sure Zack wouldn't mind." She already knew *she* wouldn't mind spending time with this man. "When do you want to go?"

"Now, if possible. We could drop Yolonda on the way."

"We can call Justin and my sister once we're on the road." Frankie jumped up, ditched the coffee, and marched into the main store, feeling Luke Driscoll and his charge close behind. Why was she doing this?

When Luke came up alongside her and she smelled his aftershave, she knew why. "I hope her cell phone works. It's so remote out there. The Kilgore spread doesn't even have electricity in places, you know. Over eighty thousand acres. Parts of it only accessible on horseback."

One of Luke Driscoll's dark eyebrows had arched up when Frankie mentioned the size of the ranch, but he had said nothing, which had the effect of making Frankie all the more nervous. Why was she babbling? Why was she running to fetch her purse, gathering up her coat? Why? Because she was ripe for adventure, for any distraction? Especially a good-looking one in boots and a Stetson? What about the wallpapering?

Oh, to hell with it, Frankie thought as she snatched her purse and leather jacket off the coat tree and jammed her arms into the sleeves. She'd figure all of that out and call Robbie on the way, as well.

Outside on the sidewalk, Ardella was dragging some large pots out for display. She smiled and gave the trio a little nod, and Frankie thought, *She'll report to mother that she saw me leaving the shop with a poorly dressed Mexican girl and a tall man in a cowboy hat.*

But again, Frankie didn't care. When had she stopped vying for the whole world's approval? The sun hit her eyes and she rummaged in her purse for sunglasses.

A bright, beckoning January day waited out there in the remote, mystical Texas Hill Country. And Frankie McBride—strike the Hostler part, strike it *for good*—was going to go out into those hills with this compelling man. For once in her anal-retentive, play-it-safe, carefully measured, hideously sterile life, she was going to take her chances and just go with her gut.

Or…would that be her heart?

YOLONDA REYES pleaded with her wide obsidian eyes and whined something in Spanish. Something about not going to *La Luz,* the name the illegals used for the Light at Five Points.

But Luke Driscoll's response, also in Spanish, sounded firm. Frankie caught the last words: *y no más problemas*— and no more trouble.

"Yolonda here," Luke explained to Frankie, "tried twice to escape back to Mexico. Because I didn't let her, she's plenty upset. But this girl is the lone witness I have."

"A witness? To what?"

"Murder."

Frankie gasped, but Luke cut off her next question. "She doesn't need to relive it now, even in English."

The girl sat hunched in the small back seat of Driscoll's crew cab on the long drive from town to the Kilgore ranch, her face growing as sullen as a storm cloud.

"Why do you need to see those caves?" Frankie broke the tense silence.

He answered her question with a question. "What do you know about Congressman Kurt Kilgore?"

That name surprised Frankie. "Nothing except for what I read in the paper, what I see on the news. Why?"

"He's your youngest sister's father-in-law now, correct?"

"Yes, but Markie and Justin don't have much of anything to do with him. Justin and his father are…estranged. They had a run-in. He didn't even come to their wedding."

"Yeah. They recently got married, too—when was it now?"

"Last fall, right before my niece was born. Zack deliv—"

"Yes. How is Mrs. Tellchick doing these days?"

Frankie wanted to say that he had a habit of interrupting, but she thought better of it. She didn't know him well enough to point out his shortcomings yet. *Yet?* Was she planning to get to know this man better?

She moved a little closer to the passenger door of his pickup to mull that one over. His...*aura* felt overwhelming in the confined space of the cab. An XM country station played softly on a high-quality sound system. The lyrics made her nervous. "Islands in the Stream" by Dolly Parton and Kenny Rogers. *No one in between,* the duet sang. *Islands in the stream.*

The immaculate interior, glowing with hot-red dash lights, smelled like leather and aftershave, rich and masculine. The scent seemed to permeate everything. The cologne was one she was sure she had sniffed in some high-end department store. One that Kyle would never wear.

"I started to say that Zack delivered Robbie's baby." She strove to resume the conversation as the singers wailed, *Sail away with me,* and she felt something shifting, some emotion taking wing inside her.

"He and Robbie knew each other in high school. Actually, Markie and Justin knew each other before, too." She was jabbering again. "High school sweethearts. Well, Markie was in high school. Justin was already in college."

"What about you and your husband? You guys go way back, too?"

Frankie felt her color flare up again. She was going to blush herself to death around this man. "No. We...actually,

I'd rather not talk about him. I'm in the process of getting a divorce."

His eyebrow slashed up again. Frankie wasn't sure if that was good or bad. This man might take a little getting used to. Why was she thinking about things like knowing him better and getting used to him? But as they hurtled down the highway, she had to admit that she was already thinking about where this would lead, this hopping in a pickup and taking off into the Hill Country. She studied his profile, his expression inscrutable behind the shades. He was handsome as hell.

It would be several more miles over a winding highway before they would reach the McBride farm where Frankie had grown up. That farm and the Tellchick-Trueblood farm sat tucked into a bend of the Blue River, surrounded by Kilgore land. As they approached the turnoff, Frankie worried about explaining herself if one of her parents passed on the road. Unlikely, since P.J. seldom left the farm, and Marynell never acknowledged people on the highway.

"Just plain un-Texan," P.J. had once kidded his wife about her standoffish behavior.

"Un-Texan?" Marynell had snapped. "That's all you think about, isn't it, P. J. McBride? Fitting in? As if giving a two-fingered salute to some good old boy means you really belong?"

Frankie remembered how unwarranted it was, like all of Marynell's attacks. Her father simply loved his neighbors, loved Texas. His friendliness wasn't some sycophantic effort to *fit in*.

"This it?" Luke's deep voice interrupted Frankie's sad memory.

They had come to the turnoff, where a cluster of live oaks with gray-green limbs dipped low to the ground. The foliage remained attached in winter, waiting for spring when new leaves would push off the faded ones. Maybe, Frankie thought, she was like those trees, stuck with the old. Dormant until something new pushed it aside. She looked at Luke Driscoll as he slowed the truck and the sun reflected off his shades. "Yes. Turn here."

He steered the pickup off the highway onto a gravel ranch road.

For three miles, a straight and dusty path led past first Frankie's parents' white-frame two-story, with its gray-metal windmill and neat outbuildings, then past her sister Robbie's squat old farmhouse, in much better condition these days thanks to Zack Trueblood, until at last they were arrowing across Kilgore land.

The truck strained into a gentle climb as the rock-strewn landscape grew higher, drier. This hilly land was fit for little but ranching. Its winter coat ran from tan to faded gray-green broken only by dark lines of trees along the creeks and down in the riverbed.

Finally the Kilgore ranch house appeared in the distance, a limestone-pillared three-story that stood out like a timeless fortress. Smoke curled from tall chimneys at either end of a steep-pitched red tile roof. A small collection of low stone buildings huddled behind.

Justin had converted his family's historic ranch house into

communal living quarters and offices for the Light at Five Points. Frankie was astonished at the changes in the place.

The undocumented aliens that took shelter there had restored most of the stonework, cleared a tremendous amount of cedar and erected sturdy modern fencing in place of the crumbling split rail. Her sister Markie had started teaching English classes right after Christmas. The place already felt settled, productive, and Frankie was impressed.

Yolonda, however, was not. She folded her skinny arms across her chest and glared at the back of Luke's head.

Luke ignored her, braked the truck and said, *"Vamos."*

They got out and the smell of cedar smoke hanging in the cold air made Frankie nostalgic. Nothing was quite as magical as a clear Hill Country morning out on a ranch.

Markie stepped out onto the porch, looking stylish at eight in the morning as only Markie could, wearing tall boots, snug jeans, a black turtleneck and a red boiled-wool vest. The sisters shared a similar brunette prettiness, but Markie wore her shiny dark hair in a more casual style than Frankie's classic pageboy.

Frankie could see that marriage agreed with her little sister. Her alabaster complexion was glowing and her smile was huge. A young Hispanic woman—very pregnant, Frankie noted with a familiar pang of envy—accompanied her.

They mounted the steps, where the sisters exchanged a quick hug and Frankie did the introductions.

"What brings you here, Mr. Driscoll?" Markie eyed Luke. She sneaked Frankie a sly little glance that said, *Wow.*

Luke *was* impressive, Frankie thought. And married.

She felt her cheeks heating again and wished Markie would mind her own beeswax. But that was not the McBride sisters' way.

"I've come back to continue my investigation." Driscoll cleared his throat and looked at Yolonda, who was starting to fidget nervously. "And I wonder if you've heard anything from Juan and Julio Morales."

The pregnant girl gasped and covered her lips with shaky fingers.

"No. Nothing. But we'd sure like to. Julio is the father of Aurelia's baby." Markie then spoke in Spanish to the pregnant girl, who tried to spirit the new girl off into the house like a hen taking a chick under wing.

But Yolonda balked. She carefully removed the denim jacket, with its warm sheepskin lining, and gave it up to its owner. *"Gracias,"* she said with sad eyes.

"No hay de qué," Luke said quietly.

"She's going to be a handful," Luke explained when the girls were gone. "Doesn't want to be here. But I need her kept safe."

Markie smiled. "We're used to handling scared teenagers. There's always a lot of mistrust at first. Aurelia will help her adjust."

"She's more scared than most. She witnessed the thing with the Morales' sister."

Markie's bright smile vanished. "We heard about that. You think that's related to your investigation then?"

"Absolutely."

Frankie felt a mild irritation that her sister knew more

than she did, and that Driscoll seemed more forthcoming with Markie.

Markie shook her head. "Danny's murder. Whatever my father-in-law is covering up. The Morales brothers. Now this trouble on the border. What a mess."

"Yes, ma'am. A mess that needs addressing." Then to Frankie's surprise, the laconic Driscoll launched into a kind of speech.

"This sort of thing is bad for relations. I've been deep into Mexico, even on down into Central America, and it's my opinion that we'd better learn to get along with these people. We could easily take U.S. prosperity all the way into Honduras. And if we don't let them work for us and improve themselves, everything will end up being made in China."

"You sound like my husband." Markie's smile returned, broader and brighter. "Justin said he liked you. Y'all want to come inside? Aurelia just made fresh coffee."

Frankie was tempted to sit by the big window in the cool stone kitchen and sip Markie's rich ranch house coffee while the sun rose higher over the hills.

But once again, Driscoll proved focused. He turned to Frankie. "We'd better get going."

"To the caves?" Nosy Markie.

"Yes." Frankie wished she hadn't told Markie that part. She turned to go, hoping to avoid this topic. She knew her youngest sister had suspicions about that area ever since Congressman Kilgore had pulled a gun on her son inside one of the caverns. Old man Kilgore had claimed he mistook the boy for a trespasser, and the local law bought it, but Frankie sensed there was something bad, something unfinished, about the whole affair.

Markie grabbed Frankie's arm. "What do you all expect to find in the *caves?*"

"Won't know until we look." Driscoll took command of Frankie's arm and touched the brim of his Stetson, steering her out and dismissing Markie.

When the truck lurched to a halt under the rusting wrought-iron Kilgore ranch gates, Luke said, "Which way?"

Frankie looked up and down the narrow gravel road. "You want the scenic route?"

Driscoll inclined his head, and even with the brim of the Stetson and the reflective sunglasses shielding his eyes, Frankie could tell he was favoring her with a patient look. "I prefer the *fast* route," he drawled.

"Left," she said with a teensy nudge of disappointment. After years with a dour husband, Frankie was in no mood for a guy with no sense of humor. Luke Driscoll might be handsome as hell, but Frankie had a feeling he wasn't exactly going to be bunches of fun.

CHAPTER THREE

As Luke Driscoll's pickup bounced past her sister's unoccupied farmhouse, up a winding gravel trail to the top of a hill, Frankie took the measure of the man driving. He had a sturdy build. Meaty forearms, a broad back. He sat squarely in the seat on muscular shanks, with his long legs canted wide.

She couldn't help making an unkind comparison to her slight-bodied husband. Kyle was forever slumped—in the seat of his Mercedes, in front of his computer, on the soft leather sectional that dominated their den.

Mentally waving away thoughts of the pusillanimous Kyle, she wondered how old Luke Driscoll was. Forty? Forty-five? Again, her eyes were drawn to the gold band that appeared to have hugged that finger for many a year. *Stop salivating over him, Ms. Separated-and-Rejected-Middle-Aged-Wife. This man, this very sexy man sitting next to you is obviously* married. Why did she have to keep reminding herself?

She turned her face to the window, determined to think about something else. But it was no good. The man was an absolute eye magnet. She gave him another covert look. Immediately he said, "What?"

"Nothing," she lied.

More details of his person registered. Tan complexion. Hawkish nose. Square jaw. Threads of gray in the thick dark hair at his temples.

He had a smattering of gray, also, in the trim goatee that accented his face. It seemed incongruous, a Ranger with a goatee…and the rest growing out in a five o'clock shadow. She supposed traveling from the border all night explained his unshaven face. He didn't seem the least bit tired, though. On the contrary. He seemed alert, intent on his purpose.

"You drove all night?"

He scrubbed a hand down his face as if she'd reminded him how fatigued he was. "The illegals walk it all the time. At least we had Old Bossie, here."

His pickup was not old. Texans loved to give their trucks pet names, even if said truck had a leather interior and XM stereo.

"Why this urgency to see the caves?"

He frowned at her. "I'm under a little time pressure. Remember how I said Yolonda was a witness to a murder and a rape?"

"A rape?" Frankie's eyes widened.

The look he gave her was sympathetic. "She hid in the mesquite bushes while some very dangerous men raped and killed her friend Maria Morales."

Frankie covered her mouth. "That poor child." Then she dropped her hand. "Morales? Like the brothers who were seen out by my brother-in-law's barn?" Frankie's voice grew bright with realization. "The ones who ran away and hid—"

"—after the fire that killed your brother-in-law. That is why this has become part of my investigation."

Robbie had said this Luke Driscoll was very thorough, very sharp, when she'd contacted him for help in uncovering the truth about Danny's murder. Frankie checked him out again.

And again without looking at her, he said, "What?"

"Do you always snap at people when you imagine they're looking at you?"

"Did I imagine it?" He gave her a sidelong glance.

No, he hadn't. He had some kind of radar. Frankie felt herself blushing again so she steered back to the subject at hand. "So this girl, who was…raped," she could hardly utter the word, "by this guy—"

"Guys."

"Oh, dear," Frankie whispered. "More than one?"

"Yes. But that's not the point. It was meant to look like the motive was sexual assault, but I don't think that's the way of it."

"Lord. Why would someone rape an innocent girl to cover up something else? I mean, how could anything be worse?"

"That's what her brothers are supposed to think. The real reason that the Coyotes killed the girl was to draw her brothers out of hiding."

"Coyotes?"

"Border runners. Smugglers. They take the money of poor, desperate people in exchange for passage into the States. Besides smuggling human beings, they're often involved in other criminal activity."

"Oh," Frankie said. She'd heard of such things, but they never touched a doctor's wife in her secure world.

"I'd like to see what's in these caves before these Coyotes beat me to it. If they haven't already. Maria Morales was wearing a vest that had a special pattern woven into it. The men who killed her kept that vest. I'm thinking it's a map of sorts."

"You mean to the caves?"

He shrugged. "I expect the Morales boys could tell us. Yolonda claims it was an ancient Mayan pattern."

"What kind of pattern?"

"Something worth killing for. Do we turn off here?" Driscoll was slowing the truck.

"Yes. Then, you remember, we'll have to proceed on foot."

"I don't remember much besides getting shot at," Driscoll said as he strong-armed the truck down the rutted drive of the Tellchick farm.

Frankie's cheeks flushed again as she recalled the day they'd first met. Then she smiled slyly, thinking how her aim had been dang good. "I suppose I could have let the snake get you."

The whine of the truck engine continued for some seconds before he deadpanned, "But then…what would you be staring at now?" He kept his gaze trained out the windshield.

"Aren't you the humble one," Frankie scoffed, though her cheeks were so hot now she thought she might have to roll down the window. A grin formed above the goatee. Maybe this Luke guy wasn't so grim after all.

"Park up there," Frankie pointed to an ancient lime-stone structure squatting among cedars and low live oaks.

"Built by the original Kilgore settlers," Frankie explained as the pickup came to a stop next to the abandoned one-room dwelling. "Way back in the nineteenth century."

"I love old places like this." Driscoll jerked on the parking brake.

He got out and marched around the perimeter of the building. Not sure what else to do, Frankie followed.

"Looks like someone's been here more recently than the nineteenth century." He pointed to the charred remains of a fire ring.

"My sister had some workers staying out here for a while," Frankie explained as they walked toward the ashes.

"Mexicans?"

"Yes. Guys from the Light at Five Points, actually."

Luke sauntered to the edge of the rise and Frankie followed. "The caves are under those mounds." She pointed.

Below them a shadowed valley spread between banks of hills. The only road into the area stuck out like a winding gray ribbon. In the distance their goal—mounds of yellowish native limestone—shone like a bald pate in the gray-green landscape.

"How far is that from up here?" He nodded at the mounds.

"Half a mile by the road, but it's been closed off with barbed wire and a padlocked ranch gate."

"Trueblood's doing?"

"No. Kilgore's."

"Ah. The congressman again." Luke frowned. "I thought Trueblood owned this farm now."

"He cut some kind of deal with Kilgore and agreed to steer clear of the caves. But we can circle around and come up along the river." She pointed at the channel of the Blue River below. "When we were kids, my sisters and I came up that way a couple of times, exploring. There's a shaft that drops pretty much straight down. We were forbidden to go there, but we did. Robbie didn't allow her kids out this way, either. But she believes Danny had discovered another entrance the night he came upon the Mexicans."

"Did he tell her where it was?"

"No. He never got the chance."

They stared out at the valley for a moment, silenced by the memory of the fire and the way Danny Tellchick had died.

"You said the caves had some connection to my brother-in-law's death." Frankie's voice became sorrowful as she surveyed the countryside that spread below the little hill. "I guess you were right."

"Coyotes hired old man Mestor to set both fires. But knowing who wanted Danny Tellchick dead doesn't tell us *why* they wanted him dead. It's my job to find out *why*. Something worth killing for has got to be a pretty big why."

"Unfortunately, Danny never told my sister what he saw."

"My guess is he told somebody. And got killed for his trouble."

Frankie cocked her head at him. "This is trespassing, you know. On the land of one of the meanest men in Texas."

"Seems minor compared to murder." Luke's gaze was level.

"We should start by looking at that main shaft. We can make it on foot if we go down that slope." Frankie pointed. "But it's pretty steep."

His gaze slid to her feet. "Can you make it in those things?"

Frankie looked down at the suede ballet flats she'd worn to work that morning. Their little accent bows looked ridiculous out here in this rocky countryside. Too late, she realized she should have gone by the house for her boots. "I'll be okay."

But still he went ahead of her, blazing the way. And still he looked back, braced his feet as if to catch her should she fall, and when she almost did, slipping on some mud, he grasped her hand and anchored his other hand firmly at her waist.

"Easy," he said, as if she were a skittish horse.

"I'm fine," she said. But she let him take her hand. She entertained no prideful notions that she didn't need his help. The soles of her shoes were dance-floor slick and found little purchase on the rocky hillside. His grip felt warm and firm. Natural. Confident. *And something else* that Frankie couldn't put a word on.

When they came to a sandstone wash that snaked down toward the river, he planted a palm on her back as he guided her across teetering slabs of rock.

His touch was as gentle and solicitous as his earlier one had been, but now something more seemed to radiate through his warm palm, something decidedly possessive, even sexual. She couldn't remember Kyle's hands ever having this effect on her.

A sudden thought spoiled her mood. Today was her birthday. Here she was, turning forty, and the simple touch of a man was giving her ideas that threw her into a little tizzy. Pathetic.

"Here. Let me help you down," he said as he stepped onto

a flat rock at the river's edge. When he turned to offer his hand up, he must have seen the foolish, pesky tears that had welled up in her eyes, because his expression became concerned.

"What's wrong?" he asked as she stepped down level with him.

"Nothing." Frankie shook her head and turned her face away. "It's silly." But she was forced to swipe at a tear.

"Are you frightened or something? We can go back. Tell me."

"No. I'm fine. I just…I remembered something."

He removed his reflective sunglasses, and in his dark eyes his concern was plain to see. His were gorgeous eyes. A smooth whiskey-brown. Very compassionate. Though right now he was also looking at her with a certain wariness. Little wonder. She was acting positively unstable. "Are you still thinking about your brother-in-law?"

"I should be." Frankie sniffed, which only caused the tears to run. "But no. That's not it."

He looked around at the river foliage, up at the sky. "Look, Mrs. Hostler—"

"Frankie."

"Right. Frankie." He paused. "Just tell me what is wrong."

Frankie decided he definitely wasn't the most patient man. "If you must know," she sniffed defensively, "I was thinking about the fact that today is my birthday."

His head jutted forward and those heavenly brown eyes bugged a bit, as if he was staring at a crazy woman. "Happy birthday?"

"There's nothing *happy* about it, if you must know. I'm turning forty and my life is falling apart." She swiped at another runaway tear. "Oh, for crying out loud. This is ridiculous."

He pushed the Stetson up on his head and scratched at his hair before resetting the hat. Before he spoke again he looked around at the rocks and trees as if they held a way out. Then the expression in those brown eyes turned tender. "You wanna just tell me exactly what made you start crying?"

Boy, she so did *not* want to tell him any such thing. How would *that* sound? *The way you touched me just now reminded me of how deprived and lonely I've been. For a long time.* Lovely. And he a married man. The thought of that ring on his finger dried up her tears, but quick.

"It's nothing," she lied, dismissing the most cataclysmic event that had ever happened in her life, the signing of her divorce papers on her fortieth birthday. "I'm having some marital difficulties, that's all…and…and this particular spot on the river reminds me of my estranged husband." An even bigger lie. She and Kyle had never even been out here. He despised the farm.

"Estranged?"

"We're getting divorced," Frankie admitted quietly. "I signed the p—" Frankie bit her lip, on the verge of blubbering again. When she regained her composure, she went on. "The papers. I signed them. Yesterday."

"I see." He paused, did that thing where he canted his hat back and mussed his hair again. "Well. I've never been divorced myself." He paused again. "But I hear it's tough."

Frankie nodded tightly, couldn't bring herself to speak. And she couldn't look at him, either.

"So." He sounded uncomfortable now. "You okay. to go on, then?"

Frankie nodded again. "This way."

Determined to keep her cool, she watched her own footing from then on. Following along the riverbank would not be as much of a physical challenge as climbing down the hill, and she preferred Luke Driscoll at her back, where he couldn't read the emotions on her face.

But when she came up over the rise above the riverbank her face got plenty emotional. She whirled on Luke, flapping her hands in warning before she hit the ground.

As she crouched down in the brush he crept up behind her, peering over her shoulder. "Whoa now," he growled. "Here's a bit of luck."

In the distance where the formations gave way to the sinkhole that led into the underground caverns, three large SUVs sat parked in a triangle. Half a dozen swarthy young men, wearing leather jackets over athletic warm-ups, stood talking inside the triangle. Talking rather heatedly. As they gestured, Frankie caught glints of sun reflecting off gold chains at their necks and diamonds in their earlobes.

"Luck?" Frankie said. "Those guys look…bad."

"Izek Texcoyo is bad all right. These are not your run-of-the-mill trespassers." Luke whispered this near her ear as he dug something out of his pocket. He didn't seem all that shook up.

"Who?"

"That one." He aimed two fingers at a heavyset guy. "I've, uh, seen his picture. A border guard gave it to me."

"Is he connected to—" Frankie's throat closed on the

word "—with—the murder?" She felt compelled to whisper, too, although the Coyotes were too far away to hear.

"He is if Yolonda will talk. The others are Coyotes, too," he added.

"How do you know?" Frankie whispered.

"The clothes, haircuts, the vehicles. Expensive. Brand-new. Coyotes'll buy cars like that," he nodded his head toward the Hummer, the Expedition, "or flat out steal them and then discard them like toys."

"My God." Frankie's voice was hushed as she moved closer to his shoulder. "They make that much money?"

"A killing, you might say." His voice had a bitter edge.

She turned her head to check his profile. The little she could see of his eyes behind his sunglasses looked grim as he looked down, working at something in his hand.

To her astonishment, he had withdrawn a device that looked like a Palm Pilot, only this had an antenna. He aimed it at the men.

She looked over his shoulder at the screen as he swiveled slightly to get the vehicles and dark figures in line with a distinctive rock formation. "Nice toy," she said right by his ear. "A BlackBerry?"

"Treo. Does more." Now he was touching the screen with a tiny wand. "Okay. Sent. Let's go." He hooked a hand around her arm and tugged her backward with him. But immediately his grip tightened on her arm as he stared in the direction of the men. He raised a hand to hush her.

The men were shouting now, in Spanish—Greek to Frankie. The fat one had turned around, waving an automatic weapon.

"By God, Yolonda better connect the dots to that one," Luke vowed as he quickly snapped some more pictures. The shouting below grew more heated. "Let's go." He pocketed the Treo.

"Don't you want to wait and see what they're going to do?"

"No." He tugged on her wrist.

But as they crawled away, echoing off the rock formations came the unmistakable popping sound of gunshots.

Luke threw Frankie to the ground and covered her with his body.

Terrified, Frankie smashed her cheek against the gritty earth. Out of the corner of her eye, she could see Luke raising his head. "What happened?" She found her voice reduced to a squeak.

"Man down," he informed her in a low growl.

More shouting caused Luke's head to slam down beside Frankie's. His hat was knocked askew and his eyes looked wild behind his sunglasses. "Musta spotted my hat." His breathing was ragged next to her ear. Beyond the rise the shouting in Spanish grew closer.

Frankie's breath caught in her chest. She could barely get her words out. "Are th-they coming?"

The shouting intensified on the other side of the ridge, unmistakably closer. Luke jerked Frankie to her feet and pulled her along, hurtling down the bank to the river.

They splashed across at a narrow place and scrambled on hands and knees back up a sandstone wash with Luke hauling her along like a rag doll.

"Head for the truck." He pushed her into the cover of trees as gunfire rang out behind them. Frankie was astonished but relieved to see him pull a gun from the back of his belt and return fire.

She needed no encouragement to keep ahead of him as they ran headlong through the woods, climbing, climbing back to the top of the small rise where they'd parked Luke's pickup. Luke shoved her fanny up over the rocks, whirling around to return fire three times.

Frankie's lungs were burning by the time they got to the top and her little beaded flats were in shreds. When the truck came into view they ran headlong, as the sharp rocks cut into Frankie's unprotected feet. As she stumbled sideways, Luke jerked her up by the arm, then scooped her into his arms and ran the rest of the way carrying her.

Frankie clawed at the door handle of the truck, and when she got it open, Luke threw her onto the seat, scrambling in behind her. He moved so fast it seemed he had crawled over her, fired up the engine, slammed it into Reverse, rammed it back into Drive, and barreled away in one unbroken motion.

Three men charged into the clearing and Frankie threw herself back down on the seat when she saw the fat one raising the automatic weapon to his shoulder.

The rain of bullets spat against the chassis, sounding like the hail that had once damaged Frankie's Mercedes when she'd been trapped in a sudden storm in the Austin traffic.

"Ah, dammit!" Luke cursed as they roared down the rutted road at breakneck speed. "There goes my paint job."

Once they'd rounded the curve at the bottom and flown past Robbie's old house, Frankie raised her head and peeked over the edge of the rear window. Above the cloud of dust raised by the pickup, she could see the Coyotes up on the hill, shrinking to the size of ants as they crabbed back up. "They're leaving," she said.

"No. They're going for their vehicles to make chase." Luke sounded calm as he pressed on at full throttle.

"Those guys…" Frankie was struggling for breath, "*shot* somebody back there. Why on earth didn't you arrest them?"

"Let's see." Luke's neck craned as he looked before executing a squealing turn onto the highway. "Five of them, not counting the one down, o' course. One of me. Think a Texas Ranger's badge means anything to those hombres?" His grimace said he found her more than a little naive. "Gotta know when to fold 'em…" His pause said he regretted informing her of this next, "…or end up being the ones down."

Once they were speeding down the highway, from the seemingly endless cache of his jacket he produced a cell phone. He punched a button and started barking facts to the sheriff's dispatcher. After an amazingly detailed description of the Coyotes and their vehicles, he broke off to ask Frankie where the ranch road intersected the highway, then told the dispatcher where the sheriff would be most likely to catch up with the Coyotes. When he was done, he handed the phone to Frankie. "Call your parents."

"Are my parents in danger? Their place is over a mile away."

"I don't think it's your parents' property that interests these guys. As long as they stay inside, they should be safe. Call them."

WHEN THEY GOT BACK to town, Luke drove Frankie back to Robbie's house so she could change into dry clothes.

He, too, was soaked from crossing the river. The dampened leather of his boots squeaked as he walked her to the door. He checked his impulse to stare at her curves as she bent to work the old-fashioned key in the lock, but the fact that she was finely made registered anyway. "You sure you're okay?" he said to compensate for ogling her.

"Yes. I think so. A little shook up." Her nervous chattering on the way to town made him think it was more than a little.

"I've never been shot at before." The lock gave and the door swung open on its creaky hinges. "Would you like to wait inside?"

Robbie Tellchick's living room looked as if a bomb had gone off in it. Toys and books and discarded children's clothes were everywhere. A pile of half-folded laundry obscured the sagging couch. Frankie grabbed up an armful of bibs and onesies and blankies to clear a space so Luke could sit.

"That's okay." He stopped her with a gentle hand, glad to have any excuse to touch her again. "I'll stand." He made a futile gesture at his soaked jeans.

"Of course." She tucked a strand of bedraggled hair behind one ear. "I'll only be a sec." She dashed up the stairs.

ON THE SHORT DRIVE over to Main Street they fell quiet. The shot of adrenaline that had gotten them through the worst had dissipated, and now they both were processing their narrow escape…and each other.

He reached over and squeezed her hand. "It'll be okay," he said softly as he studied her face. "I'll get 'em."

Frankie broke her worried silence. "Will I need to go in and talk to the sheriff?"

"He'll want to interview you. But I'll be right by your side."

Before she went inside the store, Frankie turned to him with a sudden thought. "You're not going back out there?"

His eyes narrowed, as if he were concealing his intentions. "Not right away. Local law enforcement will be all over the place, looking for evidence. I'd appreciate it if you kept this incident to yourself for now. Are you okay with that?"

"Yes, but shouldn't we tell Zack?" Her future brother-in-law was not the kind to let strangers tromp all over his land without calling them down.

"That's who I intend to see first. You said he's on duty?"

"Yes. I saw him in his uniform this morning."

"Frankie…listen. This is not the right time, but I was thinking…" Luke lingered with a hand jammed in his pocket, and for the life of her, Frankie could have sworn this tough Texas Ranger had grown suddenly shy. "I was thinking of what you said, about your birthday…"

"My *birthday?*"

"Yeah. I was thinking… Do you like the food at that little restaurant across the street?"

Frankie turned her head. "The Aggie? *The Hungry Aggie?*" Having lived in Five Points all her life, Frankie had a certain native affinity for the storefront diner. But its garish fifties-era red-and-green decor, its ancient ceiling fans coated with dust, and its scarred-up high-backed booths might not hold the same charm for everyone.

But Luke was studying the place with genuine interest. "Yeah. They serve dinner?"

"Absolutely." It was hard to resist Virgil Parson's cooking, even if you'd grown up eating it all your life. Now that Five Points drew in folks from along the Hill Country travel corridor, Virgil and his chuck wagon menu had become a tourist attraction. People drove from as far away as Austin to enjoy Parson's most famous dish, the Darlin', followed by a slice of his mouthwatering Texas cream pie. "Friday is Darlin' night."

"Darlin' night?"

"Don't let the name fool you. It takes courage to face down a Darlin'."

She caught a twinkle in his eye. "Well, I've always got my gun."

She kept her expression serious. "If you chicken out, there's always the fried catfish."

Luke looked up and down the curving Main Street. "I believe I am starting to like this place. So, you want to grab a bite to eat with me?"

The image of the wedding ring flashed into her mind, though she couldn't see it with his hand jammed into the pocket of his Levi's.

"I'm getting a room in town," he explained when she didn't respond. "I hate eating alone. Besides," he continued offhandedly, "You said it was your birthday…" He paused. "And I believe you said it was not exactly a happy one. I'd love to be the one to cheer you up."

"Mr. Driscoll—"

"Luke. It's the least I can do after getting you shot at."

"Luke, I…you're married, right?"

His expression remained calm, except for a tiny frown line between his brows. He shook his head slowly, once. "I am not."

"Oh." This caught her off guard, as she had been assuming all along, much to her disappointment, she now realized, that he was. "But…you're wearing a…isn't that a wedding band?" She gave a nod toward the source of her confusion, still tucked in his pocket.

He slid his hand out and glanced at the ring as if he had forgotten it was there. His expression grew sad. "I've kept it on ever since my wife died. For reasons of my own."

"Oh. You're a widower?"

"Yes. And you said you're in the process of getting a divorce. So. Free agents, both of us. Will you have dinner with me?"

Frankie didn't really need to mull it over. For the past few weeks she had been eating spaghetti and tuna casserole and bologna sandwiches surrounded by Robbie's rowdy boys. "On one condition."

He raised that eyebrow again.

"You let me buy the pie."

He smiled. For the first time since she'd met him, Luke Driscoll gave her a full-fledged smile. And Frankie found she liked that smile. A lot. "Around seven?"

"Six. Parson gets cranky if people keep him open too late. And we'll want to get there before—"

"The pies are all picked over?" Ah-ha. Perhaps a hint of humor, after all. She was gratified when Luke Driscoll flashed her a smile one more time.

CHAPTER FOUR

Well, so much for shriveling up and becoming a boring old drudge. Doesn't look like that's going to happen. I'm suddenly too busy hiding the witness to a murder. Witnessing a shooting. Getting shot at! And as if all of that wasn't crazy enough, I've accepted a dinner date with one very handsome man.

He's the reason for all of this...for want of a better word...*excitement*. Luke Driscoll.

We're meeting at six at the Hungry Aggie. I'm waiting at the store. I couldn't see the point of having him drive over to Robbie's house. I thought about going back there to change clothes, but wouldn't that make it seem like a real date? Like I was trying too hard? Like I was really attracted to him?

Okay. I am really attracted to him. But this set-up is all wrong. I'll feel better about the whole deal if I tell myself I haven't actually accepted a date when I'm not even divorced yet.

Life is so weird.

Robbie has just left for the evening. We did get one wall papered despite all the upheaval, but I'm exhausted. I couldn't wait to get Sissy and the baby packed off so I could jot down some of my thoughts in peace. This business out at the caves is scary. Luke told me not to discuss it, so I didn't, but it was one long afternoon.

Now I'm perched up on this stool by the credenza, looking out at Main Street through the storefront window, counting down the minutes until six o'clock and wondering if I've lost my mind.

SHE SAW HIM striding up the sidewalk toward the restaurant at six sharp. He chopped a hand up in a wave when he saw her stepping out of the shop.

He stood outside the door of the restaurant while a pickup rattled past on the brick pavers. Frankie fiddled with the balky old door of the Rising Star and finally got it locked.

She smiled nervously at him as she crossed the street, pulling her leather jacket snug over her breasts. His gaze was so steady that she wasn't sure if it was the January wind giving her the chills or those eyes.

At an altitude of twenty-five hundred feet, Five Points was cool at night, even in summer. But this evening was especially dark and wintry, with the stars emerging big and bright. The warm, mouthwatering scent of Parson's grill drifted out into the cold air and the golden glow of the interior lights highlighted the profiles of diners and beckoned more in.

Luke held the door for her. Several heads turned the second she stepped inside. Frankie hadn't counted on this, how it would feel, being seen when she was with a man not her husband. She had forgotten how thoroughly paro-

chial Five Points could be. None of the regulars at the bar
smiled at her—or Luke—as his tall frame ambled past
their backs on the stools. They stared, first sidelong at the
couple, then shiftily at one another, then back down at
their platters of chicken-fried steak.

"Friendly town," Frankie mouthed at Luke as she
unwound the silk and mohair scarf from her neck and
slid her arms out of the sable-brown leather jacket that
was not typical attire in the Hungry Aggie. Her little
sister even wore *overalls* to work sometimes, for
heaven's sake.

Luke winked, grinning at her as they settled into the booth.

She was suddenly glad she hadn't been overly fashion-
conscious when she'd changed out of her wet clothes earlier.
She had been in a rush to get back downstairs so she'd
grabbed loafers, a pair of stretch corduroys and a
V-neck argyle sweater. Thank goodness it was a conservative
outfit that said, *This isn't a date.* And it certainly isn't, she
reminded herself. It's more like an act of pity…on *his* part.

But what shone in Luke's eyes now was not pity.

She avoided his gaze by smiling up at Nattie Rose Neuberger, who skated by with a tray of blue-plate specials and
big eyes at Luke.

The waitress, a buddy of Robbie's and notoriously nosy,
was back in a flash. She had big, bottle-blond hair and party-
bright makeup. Nattie Rose had been dark-haired in high
school. Frankie wondered if a woman who was really a
brunette under all that bleach still got to have more fun.

She censored herself for such catty thoughts. Was that
another warning sign of bitterness? According to rumor,

Nattie Rose had two beautiful daughters and a husband who was loyal as an old hound dog. Frankie had neither. Her sister Robbie liked Nattie Rose, and had found the woman a faithful ally during her recent trials. Frankie planned a big tip as penance for her petty thoughts.

"Well, hi, Frankie," Nattie Rose chirped. "How's things going over at the new store? I haven't seen Robbie in a while."

"Things are coming along really well, thanks."

"You all have about got everything all cleaned up from the fire, then?" Nattie Rose snapped open menus and placed them in their hands. "That Robbie doesn't let anything get her down, does she?" The waitress filled Frankie's water glass from a sweating metal pitcher. "Did Robbie and Zack set the wedding date yet?"

"No, but it'll be very quiet, as soon as the bluebonnets bloom."

"Oh, I can understand that. There's been enough gossip about those two already. Just family then?"

"I'm not sure how Robbie is going to do it. Uh…let's see." Frankie pretended to read the menu, not sure if her sister was going to invite Nattie Rose or not.

"The Darlin's *dee*-licious tonight, o' course." Nattie Rose turned a hundred-watt smile on Luke as she poured water in his glass. "How do I know you, mister?"

"This is Luke Driscoll. Luke, this is Nattie Rose Neuberger. A friend of my sister's." Frankie offered belated intros, but was not going to play Nattie Rose's game. If you engaged her, she'd take any scrap of information and weave a whole tapestry out of it.

"Nattie Rose Kline, actually. Frankie hasn't seen much of me since I got married. You the Texas Ranger?" Nattie Rose's mascara-caked eyes studied him avidly.

Luke's eyes crinkled with a hidden smile when he caught Frankie rolling hers. "Yes, ma'am."

"Heard about the shoot-out over there at Zack's place."

Frankie couldn't imagine why they even bothered to print their pitiful little newspaper in Five Points. Here was Nattie Rose Live, ready to report. "Nattie Rose, could we have a couple of Oceans while we make up our minds?"

"Oceans?" Luke's eyebrows raised in question.

Frankie grinned. "Iced teas big enough to drown your troubles."

Luke shrugged. "When in Rome." After Nattie Rose shot off he said, "She seems pleasant enough."

"The town tattletale."

Luke studied the waitress's back at the tea station. "That might come in handy actually."

Frankie thought it interesting, and admirable, the way he stayed focused on his job above all else.

"Just don't channel anything to her that you don't want the entire Hill Country to know." Frankie kept her voice low.

His glance ticked sideways. "Incoming."

Nattie Rose swooped back to the booth with two monster glasses of iced tea with lemon slices already squeezed in.

"Thank you, honey," Frankie said, her inflection intentionally west-Texan. "I'd like the fried catfish. And this brave gentleman wants to try the Darlin'." She handed over the menus.

But Nattie Rose didn't take them just yet. She crossed her arms under her broad bosom and said, "This town has gone straight to hell, you know?" She shook her head sadly. "First it's a couple of arsons and now it's shoot-'em-ups out in the hills. Is there any rhyme or reason to this crime wave?"

Luke's eyes got that squint again. Frankie was getting used to it. Starting to like it, in fact.

"Can't say, ma'am."

Frankie liked the way he could speak the truth yet reveal absolutely nothing.

"But that's why you're here, isn't it? To figure out why those Mexicans wanted Danny Tellchick dead. I hear you work over in Austin, specializing in nasty crimes." Nattie Rose's curious gaze traveled over to Frankie. "Or are you in town for other reasons?"

"Right now he's here to eat." Frankie shot her a bright smile that said, *Off with you now, sweetie.*

Nattie Rose reverted to being the congenial waitress. "You're gonna want some of Parson's Texas cream pie for later."

"When in Rome." Luke really did have a very charming smile.

"I'll save you a big old slice." Finally, Nattie Rose snatched up the menus and left.

Frankie wasted no time in starting her questions. "Did the sheriff apprehend those men?"

"Three of them. They're down the street in the jail."

"But the fat one?"

"No. Texcoyo's on the loose."

She released a disappointed breath.

Luke reached across the table and, very naturally, covered her hand with his big warm one.

Frankie automatically curled her fingers through his. She needed the contact. For all kinds of reasons.

"You can bet the farm on this." He squeezed her fingers. "I will get that one."

She nodded and leaned forward. Next question. "Any idea who it was they shot out there?"

"No. And the body's gone."

Frankie released his hand. *"Gone?"*

"The Coyotes probably moved it when they went to their vehicles."

"Well for heaven's sake, did the sheriff's deputies look in the *caves?*" Frankie could not believe she'd gotten herself mixed up in such a mess. And she couldn't believe that she wouldn't back out now for the world. Because of *him,* she was sure. The man was just too fascinating.

He removed his Stetson and tossed it on the seat beside him, as if settling in for a long talk. He swept his dark, salt-and-pepper-tinged hair back. His forehead was high, a receding hairline, which did absolutely nothing to detract from his attractiveness.

"They found plenty of blood on the rocks," he explained, "but no trail leading into the caves. I suppose it's plausible that the guys who got away could have loaded him into one of the vehicles. The deputies took lights and looked in as far as they could. But it will take experienced spelunkers to get down that shaft. Caves are tricky. You could hit a streamway—a hole with another vertical shaft that drops to underground water—and fall hundreds of feet before you finally hit water and drown."

Frankie nodded. These were the same dire warnings her parents had always given about the caves.

"But my guess is it's going to take some doing to get this local sheriff off the dime and authorize hiring cavers."

"Why, for heaven's sake? A crime has been committed!"

Luke calmed her with a raised palm. "He's going to act like it's useless to pursue the activities of Coyotes," he said quietly.

"Is this what you meant by local law enforcement dropping the ball? What is this thing you do in Austin, this special unit?"

"It's called the Unsolved Crimes Investigation Team."

"Unsolved crimes?"

"Murders, mostly."

"Like the girl on the border?"

"The list seems to be growing around here."

The image of the man being shot flashed into Frankie's mind and she closed her eyes to shut out the horror. "I have witnessed a murder." Her voice was barely a whisper. She gulped her tea.

"Listen, Frankie." He leaned across the table, his hand almost touching hers again. "I'm placing you and your family under my protection. I don't know what the connection is yet, but too many leads come back to the McBrides, or to that land out there, for me to ignore it."

"Surely you don't think my family is mixed up in any of this?"

"No. I've checked you out. Your father's side has been

farming in this area since the pioneer days. Your mother was a Hess, German immigrant stock." He continued a litany of facts.

"You and your two sisters were raised like boys on that farm out there, singing in the church choir and babysitting for the neighbors. You, the oldest sister, married a doctor right out of nursing school."

Frankie rolled her eyes at that one. Would that she hadn't.

"Your middle sister, Robbie, who was widowed when her husband died in a barn fire last spring, has three boys and a new baby. Your youngest sister, Markie, gave a child up for adoption when she was seventeen, and went on to become a wildcat political consultant. Now the story gets interesting. She recently married congressman Kurt Kilgore's son Justin, right after the two of them were reunited with their full-grown son. They've set up house, running that place out there." He jerked his head in the general direction of the Light at Five Points. "And ever since they've had a little bad blood with Congressman Kilgore."

"He doesn't approve of Justin's work," Frankie confirmed. "He didn't even come to their wedding."

"Funny how the *congressman* keeps cropping up in this deal."

"He's not one to be messed with." Frankie's voice grew quiet.

"Neither am I." Luke's was quieter.

Frankie's eyes widened. Was this guy really willing to go after Kurt Kilgore? The congressman had a reputation. A mean one.

"I like to get to the bottom of things." Luke was still looking at her levelly. "There's a little more about *you*."

"Me?" Frankie quailed at the idea that this investigator had looked into her background. Although there was nothing to hide, unless you counted Kyle's indiscretions, damn him.

Kyle was no longer her problem, she reminded herself. And because he'd broken their covenant, she felt free to be with the man sitting before her. A Texas Ranger. One who'd checked her out. She should have known.

Somehow she'd imagined they'd get acquainted in the normal way. That is, a little at a time, with each of them conveniently hiding the parts of their lives that were less than flattering.

"I assume you and the successful surgeon are splitting up on account of he's a sneaky creep who's been boinking his little nurse."

"Oh. That."

"Yes. And a few other useless details. You happen to be a nurse, too, but you haven't practiced in a clinical setting in years now. You buy a new Mercedes every three years. You spend more money on your poodle than most people do on their kids."

Frankie's cheeks, inexplicably, burned. Maybe it was the way he'd just thrown out Kyle's affair so casually. Or maybe it was the implication that she lived the life of a spoiled rich woman. What business was it of his how much money she spent on her pet? But she supposed it would sound really lame to explain that little Charm had health issues, that the steroids to treat the poodle's grass allergy alone cost a fortune. What was she supposed to do? Let the poor little thing scratch her hide off? "Do go on," Frankie allowed herself a haughty tone. Or was it defensive?

"You hire an illegal alien as a housekeeper, another to cook, another as a gardener. And you always pay them in cash."

Now Frankie's cheeks really burned. "How did you find out such a thing?" She hoped her tone still sounded haughty. Surely he couldn't have delved into her medical records, the miscarriages, the counseling.

"I can find out where you go to church, the name of your country club, where—and when—you drop your dry cleaning, how many long-distance calls you make, and how you spend your nights. But relax. You are boring, lady. Nothing in your background is germane to this case."

"Well, that's a disappointment." Now Frankie's tone was sarcastic.

He grinned. "But you're only boring on paper. I have to admit that in person you fascinate me. You're—" He halted because Nattie Rose had swooped up, carrying two platters.

"Your catfish, milady." She placed one platter in front of Frankie.

"And for you, sir…" A huge platter touched down in front of Luke.

"The Darlin'." Frankie leaned forward confidentially. "Otherwise known as Heart Attack on a Platter."

Luke smiled down at the meal. "Well, she's a pretty little thing," he drawled.

A mound of macaroni, smothered in chili and cheese, was topped with two strategically placed sunnyside-up eggs.

Nattie Rose had placed a small empty plate at Luke's

elbow. "For draining the grease," she informed him with a kindly smile.

"Remind me to give you a big old tip," Luke said sarcastically.

Nattie Rose batted her stiff eyelashes. "Like what? 'Don't go snooping around the Kilgore caves unless you're packin' a gun'?"

This time Frankie just said it outright. "Off you go now, sweetie."

Nattie Rose sashayed away.

They smiled at each other as they lifted their forks. Luke shoveled in the greasy fare with the grim determination of a soldier downing K-rations on a battlefield. Efficient. Relentless. He only stopped long enough to wash it down with giant draughts of the sweet tea.

Frankie eyed him. *Oh well,* she thought as she sawed her crispy catfish into precise bite-sized pieces and observed his feral eating habits. *Nobody is perfect.* Certainly he'd discovered that about *her* already. She got the feeling that this relationship—if there was in fact to be a relationship—was going to be completely devoid of pretense. But somehow that wouldn't diminish the fireworks between them one bit.

He shoved away his platter.

"Amateur," she chided when she saw that he'd barely dented the grease-laden rations.

He jerked a thumb at the Darlin'. "I can feel my arteries clogging up already."

She grinned. "You want some of this?"

He reached across, plucked up a crispy bite of catfish

and popped it in his mouth. "Wow," he said when he swallowed. "Now *that's* good."

"Seriously. You want to split this?" The platter of catfish, fries and coleslaw was ample.

"No. But you go ahead and do some damage to mine." He pointed at the Darlin'.

Frankie grinned, fork poised.

"Go on. You know you want to."

"I just didn't want to humiliate myself by actually ordering it." Before she dug in, she asked him one of those questions designed to keep him talking. "So, what do you think those Coyotes were up to out there?" She lifted a fork laden with pasta and chili and cheese. *Heaven.*

Nattie Rose swooped up again. "More tea?" It seemed to Frankie the waitress was hovering a bit too close. Frankie wondered how much she was hearing, or straining to hear, rather. When she was gone, Luke kept his voice so low that Frankie had to lean forward to hear.

"I don't want to get anyone else from Five Points involved until I have a chance to figure out who's in bed with who."

"You really think somebody in Five Points is behind all of this…what is it?"

"Murder, Mrs. Hostler, pure and simple. The motives behind that are secondary."

Frankie swallowed hard and stopped eating.

The minute Frankie set her fork down, Nattie Rose trotted up again. "All done?"

They both nodded, signaling collusion with their eyes.

"Ready for the pie?" Nattie Rose gave her brows a Groucho-style wiggle.

"Oh, please." Frankie palmed her stomach.

"Now who's the amateur?" Luke smiled at her when Nattie Rose left. "I have a reputation to establish around here." His gaze swept toward the farmers' broad backs at the bar.

"Mine's probably shot, thanks to my soon-to-be-ex-husband, that cheating pinhead." Frankie said this cheerfully. But then she grew solemn. "It's actually a lot more complicated than that."

"Cheating seems complicated enough to me." His gaze, which at times had been so inscrutable, softened with understanding now.

Frankie was heartened to hear him say that. Some men might think adultery could be justified, that a wife somehow caused her husband to stray. But thanks to her sisters' clear-headed counsel Frankie harbored no such confusion. "It's never all one-sided. There were many problems. I consider myself well rid of him, believe me."

"So this divorce is your idea?"

"Yes." Frankie looked down at the table. She only wished it weren't so recent, now that she'd met Luke. He had a right to ask certain questions, of course, and so did she. "What about you? How long have you been...alone?"

"Six years."

"How did your wife...?" Frankie found herself wanting to be delicate. The look on his face grew closed as he squinted into the distance. "I mean, what happened?"

"Some other time."

Frankie angled her head to focus where his gaze had fixed, just past her shoulder. Nattie Rose came maneuvering through the tables with the pie, complete with whipped cream and chocolate shavings…and a lit candle stuck in the center. Pointedly, the waitress put the pie in front of Frankie and crossed two forks on a fresh napkin.

"Go on then," Luke drawled. "Make a little wish."

Frankie made a big one. On some level she already knew what she wanted. Looking straight into Luke's eyes, she blew out the candle.

After Nattie Rose poured them each a cup of coffee and went on her way, Frankie said, "Thanks for the candle."

"I splurged," Luke said dryly and sipped the hot coffee as if it were a tonic.

"You drove most of the night. You must be exhausted."

He just sipped more coffee.

"I don't see how you're still functioning. I didn't know what sleep deprivation was until lately. I've been taking turns getting up with the baby in the night. I never knew having a baby could be so…24/7."

"It's a great time, when they're newborn." For an instant Luke had a faraway look that he quickly masked. "You never had children?"

"No." She guessed he hadn't seen her medical records after all.

"You?"

He got that distant look on his face again. "It's a long story. Now I've got my old uncle. Beecher Driscoll's more trouble than any kid."

Frankie smiled. "Does he live near you?"

"Near me? He's holding down the fort while I run around chasing bad guys. Takes care of my dog. Kills my plants. He hates the city. He was a patrol cop, always promised himself he'd retire in the country."

"Why didn't he?"

"When his wife died I worried about him. Had him over at the house with us a lot. Then when my wife…there we were. Me and Beecher. Truth is, I doubt I would have made it without the old guy."

He seemed suddenly uncomfortable under Frankie's sympathetic gaze. He set his mug aside and frowned, making a business of studying the undisturbed pie from all angles, an investigator examining evidence he was loath to touch. "This thing's scary."

Frankie smiled. "Don't worry, it won't hurt you…much." She plucked the candle from it and handed him a fork. "One should never eat a piece of this stuff alone."

"Or at least not without a designated driver?"

She laughed as they lifted two huge bites.

"Mmm."

"Mmm-*hmm*."

They rolled their eyes in bliss as they scooped up bite after bite.

"How do you eat like this and stay so slim?" He gave her figure an appreciative once-over.

"Three boys, two dogs and a baby. Make that three dogs."

"The poodle?"

"Charm." She gave him a wry grin to indicate it was a misnomer.

They stuck to the this line of small talk until Frankie said, "So, what happens now?"

"Well…" Luke swallowed. "I reckon we'll go out on a

few more dates and I'll try to restrain myself while you finish getting that divorce." His eyes twinkled. "Then we'll get married, squeeze out a couple of cute kids, raise 'em, retire and die."

He did have a sense of humor, after all. Still, the mention of kids had set off a familiar ache in the region of Frankie's heart. Was it too late for her? And was he joking all that much?

He was watching her with a thoughtful expression that said maybe not. Despite the feelings he had stirred up, she managed another wry smile and blinked as if her patience had been severely tried. "I meant next on this case."

"Oh. That."

"Yes. *That.* A little problem called murder?"

"I'm going with you." He shoved the scraped-clean pie plate aside and stuffed two twenties under the edge of it.

"Very generous. You're going with me? Where?"

"To the sheriff's office."

CHAPTER FIVE

THE KILGORE COUNTY courthouse and the adjacent jail sat smack at the heart of downtown Five Points, facing a small grassy park that had originally been the town square.

So Frankie and Luke had simply to stroll across the park to arrive at her interview with the sheriff. Frankie was quiet, withdrawn, as they passed under the low live oak branches with their leathery winter-toughened leaves rustling in the gusting wind. She was terrified. She had never been questioned in a murder case.

"You knew he was going to question me tonight. Is that why you took me to dinner?"

"No, ma'am, it is not. I took you to dinner because you are a pretty woman who shouldn't be having a less-than-happy birthday." Luke put a reassuring palm to her back and guided her around a turn in the sidewalk. "So, what was it like to grow up around here?"

Frankie wondered if he could feel her nervousness right through her leather jacket. "Nice. Dull sometimes."

The winter moon, high and bright, cast bluish shadows across his face as she glanced up at him. He exuded a physical dominance that made her feel even more delicate and feminine than she was. In spite of her apprehensions about facing the sheriff, she caught herself having stray thoughts regarding what Luke Driscoll might be like in bed.

"I noticed 1898 carved on the cornerstone of the courthouse today. Is that when the town was established?" He was obviously trying to engage her in distracting conversation.

"This was the county seat from the start." She made herself focus on his question. "But it wasn't called Five Points until the highway was built that made it a crossroads."

"And before that?"

"Idaville."

The corners of his mouth teased into a grin. "*Idaville.* Bet you were glad you didn't have to claim that was your hometown in college."

Frankie smiled. "It wouldn't have mattered. I went to a community college in Austin. Had to hold down a job while I got my associate's degree so I didn't get to know many people. Anyway, Ida was the wife of an early Kilgore. The name fit when this was a sleepy place with only the courthouse, a school, a couple of churches and a few tiny Sunday houses."

"Oh, the Sunday houses." His interest perked up. "I've always been fascinated by them. I imagine myself holed up in one. Frying bacon. Petting Philo."

"Philo?"

"My German shepherd. He could swallow that poodle of yours in one gulp. But he wouldn't. Philo is a gentleman."

"Like his master?"

"We'll see."

Frankie felt her pulse trill at the subtle warning, but she hoped it didn't show. "Back to Idaville. It was pretty isolated until a new road brought westward traffic across the Edwards plateau. Then the town got to thinking of itself as a real town with a general store, a blacksmith, a hotel and some saloons. Some of those old structures are still in use."

Frankie fanned a hand toward the vintage stone buildings lining the curving Main Street as it flowed around the park like a river made of brick. "Like this old courthouse."

The craggy face of the place loomed ahead, a pale otherworldly cast of grey in the moonlight. Her education had taught Frankie that the building was an excellent example of Romanesque revival architecture with deep-set tall windows and gentle stone archways over the doors. Frankie had always thought of the building as charming, sleepy. A place where aging lawyers in rumpled business suits spouted law in Texas accents. But now it held a different connotation. An evil one. Now it held men who had shot another human being. Men who might recognize Frankie.

"I've always liked the Hill Country," Luke said lightly, as if they really were a couple on a date, out for a casual stroll across the park beneath a winter moon. "Especially this area out west."

They'd come under the courthouse portico where a weak light shone through the stenciled glass. "So, is this where we're gonna get married someday?" Luke joked as they climbed the steps. But he stopped her just short of going in. "Before we go in…how well do you know this sheriff?"

Frankie swallowed. "I actually dated the man, briefly, in high school." How she hated admitting *that* to such an incredibly attractive man. Joe Pultie was a troll who had not aged well. The glimpses she'd caught of him around town since she'd been back hadn't been pleasant.

Even in the dark she could see Luke's eyebrows go up. "Bet that was fun."

"No. Actually it wasn't. Joe's a bit of a brute."

"Well, when we get in there, the brute is going to ask you a lot of questions. Only answer to exactly what he asks. Don't volunteer anything."

Frankie frowned, not understanding the reason for these guarded instructions.

"You'll get confused if you say too much. The sheriff thinks I'm in town looking into some land issues and that you stumbled on the Coyotes and I rescued you when the shooting started."

"Oh." The complexity of this lie worried her. But if she had to trust either Luke Driscoll or Joe Pultie, her gut told her to choose Luke.

"My authority in this case exceeds theirs. I told them I'd question you first, then I'd be bringing you in. 'Course, there was no actual need to question you. We were both there, enjoying the whole thing together."

"Yeah. It was fun." Frankie's tone was deadpan.

Luke smiled. Then the smile faded and he leaned close, speaking confidentially near her ear. "Remember what I told you? About my agency? What we do?"

The Unsolved Crimes Investigation Team. Hadn't he said they sometimes stepped in when local law enforcement dropped the ball...or worse?

Frankie nodded. "You're talking about when local law enforcement is corrupt or something?"

He nodded, meeting her gaze meaningfully in the eerie light of the January moon. "But the brute," he jerked his head toward the building, "has to believe I'm in town for other reasons. Right now I'm going to maneuver him into a little game of good cop, bad cop. Just follow my lead." He opened the door for her.

As soon as she crossed the threshold, any illusion Frankie had had of being on a date was over.

The stone walls and concrete floors made the dimly lit entry and cross corridors feel like abandoned dungeons. The place smelled dank, musty. Metallic sounds and faint whistling echoed from down one weakly lit corridor. Old Ned Spitzer was doing his janitorial work.

In all her years growing up in Five Points, Frankie had never had reason to step inside the courthouse and she wished she didn't have to be here now. The place felt abandoned, creepy.

Luke guided her down a dim corridor, away from the clanging sounds. They came to a square of bluish light pouring through a frosted glass door. Luke rapped on the glass with two knuckles.

A disembodied voice, Joe Pultie's gravelly drawl, barked, "Enter."

Luke reached in front of Frankie and the nearness of his broad shoulder briefly reassured her. He opened the door.

Pultie sat inside, alone, with one hip propped on his desk. The harsh fluorescent lighting made his pock-marked skin look even pastier and the absence of his cowboy hat did nothing to flatter his brow line. On the hiked leg, a patch of fish-belly-white skin showed between the top of his boot and the cuff of his khaki pants. His tummy oozed out over his belt like a soggy sandbag. Frankie had the sudden urge to barf in the little trash can beside his desk.

"Driscoll." He gave Luke a nod, then stood. "Thanks for bringing her in."

Her, Frankie supposed, referred to herself. This had always been Joe's way. Talk to the dominant male. Ignore the female altogether.

But then he touched her elbow and said, "Come in, Frankie. Can I take your jacket?"

"No. I'm fine." She clutched her arms across the warm leather.

"Okay. Have a seat." The metal legs of the institutional chairs scraped against the concrete floor as Pultie pulled two out.

As they seated themselves, Frankie noticed Luke did not help with her chair. When he crossed the room and leaned into a corner with his arms tightly folded across his chest, she understood that he was already playing bad cop.

"Now, Frankie." Joe Pultie laced his fat fingers on the tabletop. "Ranger Driscoll here has already told us what took place out there. We just need your perspective, in your own words."

Frankie nodded as if anxious to cooperate.

Pultie hit the button on a small digital recorder at his elbow. "Interview of Frankie Hostler, witness to the alleged shooting incident near the Trueblood land, January third."

"Did you get a good look at the men?" Pultie said.

"From a distance, yes." Answer the question only, Luke had said.

"How many did you see?"

"Six, I think."

"Describe them."

She nodded as if warming to the sheriff. "Uh…dark complexions, short dark hair. Young."

"How young?"

"Late teens. Early twenties."

"What were they wearing?"

"Black leather jackets. T-shirts. And those sort of loose pants that basketball players wear. You know, with the stripe down the leg."

"Warm-up pants."

"Yes."

"Any distinguishing physical characteristics?"

"One was very, uh, noticeably heavyset." She bit her lip, regretting that she had glanced at Pultie's gut.

But Pultie seemed not to notice, his expression remaining focused and over-kind. "And you saw three vehicles?"

"Yes. I'm not very good at that sort of thing. Identifying cars. They were larger sport utility vehicles." She could see Luke scowling.

"Well, what color were they?"

"Black."

"All black?"

"No. The Hummer might have been dark green." She bit her lip, *volunteering information.*

Very gently, very patiently, Pultie said, "Now can you

tell me what you were doing out at those caves, Frankie? On foot?"

"Pardon?" The abrupt switch from describing the suspects threw her. That and the fact that this question had a faintly accusatory tone. Suddenly Frankie had lost her bearings. She wasn't sure how Luke wanted her to answer. She stalled by licking her lips, which Pultie observed with undisguised fascination.

She recovered quickly. "I've gotten in the habit of taking long walks in the country on my parents' land lately. I crossed that corner of my sister's farm, made my way up by the river." She paused to lick her lips again, wondering, *Did I say too much?*

"Didn't your sister Robbie hire some Mexicans out there?" This was Luke. He had been so silent until now, that his voice materializing from the corner actually startled Frankie.

She looked at him as if he were a traitor, then realized that this was the reaction he wanted. She hoped she was a good actress, then realized she didn't need to act at all. She truly was stunned, offended. "Why on earth would that matter?"

"We still haven't gotten to the bottom of your brother-in-law's death. Is there something going on out there that the McBride sisters haven't told us?" Luke demanded, suddenly pressuring her. "Things you haven't told the sheriff here?"

He moved to the table and pulled out a chair. The scraping sound made Frankie tense. He sat, sprawled back with legs wide and shoulders slanted, arms crossed over his chest.

"I don't know what he's talking about." She turned an imploring gaze on Pultie, who was leaning forward in a caring posture that was the opposite of Luke's. "That used to be my sister's land, where the caves are, but she never went anywhere near them. She didn't know Danny ever did, either, until the night before he died. We have no idea why those men paid Arlen Mestor to set that barn fire. I would think my sister would be free to go on with her life now that her husband's name has been cleared of arson. She's overwhelmed with a new baby, with starting a new business. Joe, you've known my family for a long time." She folded her hands in front of her on the table, a gesture of self-control. "You can't believe we have any connection to these…desperadoes that did this shooting today."

"I *have* known you a long time, Frankie." She was appalled when Pultie reached across the table and covered her compressed hands with his large beefy one.

Luke maintained his detached pose, but his eyes squinted briefly at the stacked hands.

"But I have to tell you," Pultie went on as she slid her fingers free of his. "Ranger Driscoll here is still looking into the fact that your brother-in-law reportedly saw some tres-passers the night before he died in the barn fire. You should be aware that his connection to those men is still unclear." Pultie enunciated all of this so carefully that Frankie realized he was talking for the benefit of the tape.

She nodded.

"Answer aloud for the tape." Luke's tone was sharp.

"Yes," Frankie blurted.

"Do you or your sister have any idea why Tellchick was out poking around in those caves?"

"My sister thought it was because he'd seen evidence of trespassing. Tire tracks and stuff. They—Robbie and

Danny—normally avoided that sinkhole and the caves. That area was way over on the border of Kilgore land, rocky land. Useless to a farmer. And dangerous."

"Mrs. Hostler, we can bring your sister in for questioning," Luke said. "These are the same men who hired Arlen Mestor to set the fire that killed your brother-in-law."

Pultie nodded, seeming to wait for Frankie to say something.

"I don't think my sister knows anything. She's had a very hard time." Thinking of Luke's instructions, Frankie stopped herself.

Pultie frowned at her abrupt silence. He waited, then said, "Before you go, would you be willing to take a look at the suspects? To point out the one that shot that man out near the caves?"

"I'll try. But I didn't see the actual shooting take place. I only heard shots. Luke was—officer Driscoll had me pinned to the ground...underneath him," she trailed off quietly. She really was saying too much, she was sure.

"You're lucky he was already on a stakeout, Frankie. Unfortunately, you came along just in time to blow it for him."

"Sorry," Frankie said meekly to Luke. This was so weird.

"But you can make it up to us by helping us identify these guys."

"Identify them?"

"Just look at 'em through a one-way glass. We're trying to verify that we rounded up the right hombres."

Luke gave her no reassurance.

"Okay. That's the least I can do, I suppose."

It was harder than she thought. After he made a call, Pultie led them down the dimly lit corridor where Ned Spitzer was still swabbing away with his mop. The sheriff used the massive key chain at his belt to open a series of doors.

Then they were in a brightly lit, sparsely furnished room with a large plate-glass window. The three suspects, hand-cuffed, were on the other side of the glass, standing against a wall under the watch of a hard-looking deputy sheriff.

Frankie could have fingered the fat Coyote in one glance. But these three were more of a challenge. They all looked disturbingly alike to her. Her mind searched for details that matched up with these men, but found none.

"I...they were so far away." She studied the cruel young faces that seemed to be glaring at her through the glass. All about the same coloring, age, height, build.

Luke said, "They can't see you."

"Not at all." Pultie put a hand on her shoulder, which Frankie immediately wished was Luke's.

"I'm sorry," she said as she moved away from Pultie's touch, "I couldn't single out any one of these three."

Frankie was relieved when the guard took the suspects away and the two men escorted her back to the sheriff's office.

Pultie got her a paper cup of water from a cooler in the corner. "Here," he said solicitously as he handed it to Frankie. "You just sip this now. I need to talk a little business with Ranger Driscoll."

WHEN THE MEN had stepped out into the hall, Pultie shook his head ruefully. "I was hoping she'd make a more credible witness. Seems to me she was withholding on us."

"She was wound up a little tight," Luke agreed, thinking, *Good girl, Frankie.*

"You might be on to something here, Driscoll. With these Mexicans and all. I thought the case was closed when we put Mestor away, but could be the McBrides are still hiding something. That family is all mixed up with the Mexicans. The other sister is married to the dude that runs that La Luz place."

"I'm aware," Luke said coolly. "I'll see Mrs. Hostler home, where maybe I can get something more out of the sister. Don't suppose you guys found a body yet?"

"Nope. Blood on the rocks. No drag marks. The five of them picked up and dropped the body down that sinkhole, I imagine."

"It's gonna be tough to make any charges stick without a body."

"Right. As it is, I haven't got enough evidence to press any charges. Most I can do is pack them off to Mexico. And good riddance. I'm betting they speak English, but they're playing it like poor dumb crossers. We even had to read 'em their rights in Spanish."

"Those were sure bilingual bullets they shot at us."

Pultie grinned. "I hear ya, man. And I believe ya. But these three are all claiming they didn't do any shooting. They didn't have any guns on them when we pulled them over. My hands are tied."

"Do you mind if I go ahead and bring in some guys from Austin to have a look down that hole?"

"Drop some spelunkers down there? Well…" Pultie hesitated a heartbeat too long, Luke thought. "Sure.

Anything you can do to further the investigation. But I've got to tell you, if they dropped the body down that hole, it'll never be found. That's a vertical cavern that drops deeper than a football field. And o' course, you'll need a warrant before you send a bunch of cave crawlers down under private land."

"A warrant? Why not simply get the owner's permission?"

"You mean contact Congressman Kilgore? Well, sure." Pultie shifted his considerable weight. "He's totally accessible to me. I'll take care of it."

Luke doubted that. "Good." He offered his hand. "Just let me know when everything's a go."

ON HIS WAY BACK to fetch Frankie he dreaded facing her ire once they were alone.

He could feel her stewing, but they were halfway across the little park in front of the courthouse before she spoke.

"Was it really necessary to cast suspicion on my dead brother-in-law?"

Luke was glad she didn't see the long-suffering look he cast her way. But he couldn't really fault her for being naive. He hadn't shared most of the facts of this case with her. "If I'd told you what I was doing before we went in, you wouldn't have acted so clueless. You know, like a victim. You did great, by the way, came across real sweet and innocent-like."

"Stop it." Her breath clouded out into the frigid air and she turned on him. "What about my sister? Now the sheriff's going to be bothering her again."

"No, he's not."

"Whatever are you talking about? You as much as accused us of keeping some kind of secrets about the caves."

It was starting to drizzle, so Luke took her arm and urged her along as he explained.

"Whoever is really up to something in those caves is already well aware that your sister has nothing to do with it, okay? And my guess is the sheriff knows that, too. For now, he's content to let me be the one to question your sister. All he cares about is having me chase my tail. And I'm content, for now, to let him think I am."

Frankie frowned. "This is all a little too convoluted for me."

"You have no idea how convoluted this deal really is."

CHAPTER SIX

BY THE TIME they pulled up to the curb at Robbie Tellchick's Victorian two-story, it was nearly nine o'clock and the drizzle had turned to a spitting snow. Luke switched on the windshield wipers to knock the gathering wet flakes aside. He pulled on the parking brake while only the rumble of the truck's engine and the rhythmic slap–squeak of the wipers filled the cab.

"Oh no," Frankie said before he could ask her the question on his mind. "Zack's here," Frankie pointed at a shiny red pickup in the drive, then at another older pickup across the street, "and so are mother and daddy. And that's my sister Markie's Jeep."

Three young boys came tumbling down the porch steps. "Aunt Frankie!" they yelled, wildly waving their arms, clad only in short-sleeved T-shirts. "It's snowing!"

Even in her preoccupied state, the sight of the boys running toward her so uninhibitedly melted Frankie's heart. Three months ago the boys had silently slunk around her in a wide swath. But lately, it seemed, she had won their trust. She could never have predicted the joy that would come from feeling like part of her family again. Somehow the life Kyle insisted on had alienated her from everything she loved.

She opened the door of Luke's truck and climbed out to welcome the youngest Tellchick son, Rob, into a hearty hug as he flew at her middle. She rested her cheek on his hair. "You're going to catch cold out here with no hat or coat."

"Cut it out, Aunt Frankie!" But Rob didn't squirm away nearly as fast as he used to. "Us guys are tough!"

"We're going in the backyard to try and scrape together some snow balls!" Frank, the one named after her, announced this gleefully as he came up alongside.

Frankie laughed. "Better hurry and catch 'em while they're falling!" In the Hill Country the light dusting of flakes would not last long past sun-up. "But first, go back inside and put on your coats." The younger two did a pivot and ran back up the steps.

The oldest one, Mark, stopped short at the junction of the sidewalk. He was red-headed, freckle-faced, handsome. All of twelve, going on twenty. "Who's the guy?" he questioned his aunt when she stepped up to give him a quick hug.

"He's a Texas Ranger, Mark. He's in town investigating something. He's trying to solve the…motive behind your father's…death." She really could not bring herself to call it a *murder* around the boys. "He needs to talk to your mother."

"Does it have something to do with that shooting today?"

"Possibly." She wondered how much they'd all heard by now. Of course, she'd made that warning call to mother and daddy. She hadn't expected Marynell just to let something like that drop, had she? And Zack. Would the sheriff have notified him, as the landowner, that there were trespassers? And of course Markie and Justin were involved because of Yolonda and the other immigrants at the Light at Five Points.

Suddenly Frankie felt very tired. In her contained little world back in Austin, she never had to deal with the messiness or intrusion of extended family. Kyle kept his people at arm's length and had made sure Frankie's felt wholly unwelcome. It had taken some adjusting to get used to the way her kin stuck their noses into every little thing. *Every little thing?* She'd been shot at, for Pete's sake. And worse, now she was bringing a Texas Ranger to her sister's door.

Luke had turned off the truck, climbed out and walked around the tailgate.

"Hello." He touched the brim of his hat in salute.

"Uh. Hi." Mark seemed suddenly shy.

"Luke, this is my nephew Mark. Mark, this is Luke Driscoll, Texas Ranger."

Mark shook Luke's hand like a man. Frankie was amazed at how quickly Robbie's boys had caught on to Zack Trueblood's manners.

"Uh. Well, Aunt Frankie, everybody's waiting on you." The boy turned and led the way, shoulders stiff, back hunched.

Luke gave Frankie an understanding glance. She hoped it meant he understood how much these children had been through in recent months.

As soon as Mark opened the front door, Angus and Awgie, Robbie's farm dogs, came out onto the porch, barking at Luke like vicious guard hounds.

"Quiet!" Frankie snapped. Those dogs got on her nerves. Her poor little poodle, Charm, spent every minute in their presence cowering on the back of Robbie's couch.

The dogs kept up the racket until Luke put the back of his hand out for them. Once they sniffed him, they quieted. Mark trotted back, collared them and hauled them into the house.

Inside, Robbie's entry hall felt too close and too warm from the old floor furnace that cranked heat into the narrow corridor and stairwell yet left cold pockets in the less-insulated areas of the house. Through the double doors to the living room that opened off the entry hall, she could see a bevy of expectant faces.

Mark dragged the dogs back to the kitchen, then bounded up the stairs two at a time, beating a retreat.

"Everybody," Frankie stepped through the double doors, "this is Luke Driscoll, the Texas Ranger who saved my hide this morning." Only in town a couple of months, she mused, and already she was starting to talk like the locals. Especially around her family.

Luke's frame filled the doorway beside her, towering above everyone except Zack Trueblood.

"Luke, this is my mom and dad, Marynell and P.J., and my sister Robbie," Frankie's voice rose musically as if these were introductions at a Bible study, "and her fiancé Zack Trueblood. You met my sister Markie, of course, this morning and—"

"He *did?*" This shrill interruption came from Marynell, who absolutely hated being the last to know about anything.

"Yes, Mother, we'll explain all that later."

"We've already met," Zack said as he stepped forward and shook the ranger's hand. Zack was good at scotching Marynell's testiness. Frankie was disoriented to see the fire-fighter still wearing his navy-blue day uniform. Had she seen him in it only that morning? That pacific morning scene on Main Street, Five Points seemed long ago and far away.

"We've met." Justin Kilgore stepped up to shake Luke's hand as well. "The last time you were in town."

"Oh, right." Frankie chided herself for blushing. Her introductions must have sounded like *Meet the Family*.

"I want to know why a Texas Ranger has to visit the Light at Five Points. Frankie, when you said there were suspicious trespassers out by the caves, you failed to mention they'd been shooting at *you*." Leave it to Marynell to open with an accusation. Frankie felt a vague but familiar sense of disappointment. Mother hadn't even asked her if she was okay.

"To think I had to hear it secondhand from Ardella," Marynell badgered on, "who heard it from Nattie Rose Neuberger." And leave it to Mother, Frankie thought sadly, to make any incident into a personal slight.

"I'm fine now, Mother." Frankie stepped over and gave Marynell a hug that was neither comforting nor compliant. Unlike her sisters, she felt she had always known how to handle their prickly mother. Maintaining a polite distance was the key.

But a cool hug was not enough to mollify Marynell this time. "I think you'd best explain this situation to your family *right now*." Marynell reared away and gave Luke a scathing look as if "this situation" were entirely his fault. "We were scared to death, waiting here at Robbie's while you were off at the jail. And for the love of deuce! You couldn't even bother to tell any of us where you were or what you were doing. On your birthday, no less."

It was then that Frankie noticed the cake on Robbie's battered sideboard. Pink, overdone, it looked like a Nattie Rose creation. Pink paper cups, plates and a pitcher of lemonade sat alongside. *Oh, dear.* She'd assumed they were all gathered here because of the shooting.

"I'm sorry, Mother, but my birthday is not important now. We had a scare but I'm okay," Frankie added, though Marynell still hadn't asked. "And Luke was with me the whole time I was at the jail. He's going to explain everything and then he needs to ask all of you a few questions. Hi, Daddy." Belatedly, Frankie hugged her father. This hug was real.

"Sorry your birthday got ruined, sugar," P.J. said quietly.

"Well, somebody better do some explaining around here," Marynell huffed.

"Mother, please." This was Robbie, asserting her role as the woman of the house.

Marynell snapped her lips shut tighter than a change purse and glared at Robbie.

With Marynell temporarily silenced, Robbie fanned a hand toward her shabby furniture. "Let's all sit down."

Frankie sank gratefully onto Robbie's saggy old couch. Charm jumped down from a back cushion into her lap. Frankie petted her like a baby and Luke winked at her over that. Everyone else found places to sit too, except Justin, Zack and Luke, who stood at the edge of the room because there weren't enough chairs.

Luke had a raft of questions for the family but it turned out they had a few for him, too. Throughout a carefully polite back-and-forth, during which Luke actually revealed very little about the two most recent murders, Frankie became acutely aware that his intense gaze kept flicking to her. And did the family notice this? And did Frankie care?

Luke tried to keep the atmosphere calm, but even so, after an hour of talk about trespassers and dangerous illegal aliens, everyone in the room was tense.

Frankie, because she was dreading explaining her presence at the caves to her mother and she hated to see her father upset over this trouble.

Robbie and Zack, because the trouble was on *their* land.

Justin and Markie, because their long-lost birth son had been threatened at gun point in the very caves in question. By his own grandfather, no less. Luke focused quite a few questions on them and that incident with the congressman. He finally asked if there was any way for him to contact the boy.

"I don't think his adoptive parents would like that very much." Markie was clearly uncomfortable.

"They don't want him having contact with people in Five Points? With you?"

"No." Justin interjected and clutched Markie's hand. "We're all on good terms. But they're very conservative people, very protective of their children. His father is a minister." Markie jerked Justin's hand. "We agree with the parents and want to protect our son as well, to protect his identity. As far as Br—the boy is concerned, the congressman is not his grandfather."

"Nevertheless, he may have observed things that are germane to the case. He did find a way into the caves, other than the sinkhole."

"It was the same way we went in. Following the glow of the congressman's flashlight shining from inside."

"Do you think you could show me that entrance again?" Luke addressed this to Justin.

Justin looked to Markie. "I suppose I could try. But the rock formations out there are very convoluted. It was a very small crawl space, as I recall. And it was dark that night. Our concern was getting Br—the boy to a safe place. The congressman has now made it clear the area is off limits. We have made up our minds to stay out of the congressman's business, and leave our son to continue his life in peace." For some reason, Justin glanced uncomfortably at Marynell this time.

Frankie knew her brand-new brother-in-law had an uneasy relationship with his new mother-in-law. Zack Trueblood was finding Marynell difficult to accommodate, as well. Was this to be her mother's pattern now? Frankie wondered. Marynell McBride had always favored Danny Tellchick in the son-in-law department. With Frankie's husband Kyle, the old girl had always been disgustingly obsequious, though Frankie doubted Marynell liked Kyle all that much. And she suspected the feeling—or lack thereof—was mutual.

As if she sensed the attention, Marynell spoke up. "Those caves are absolutely treacherous! That boy should *never* have been out there. And no one else should be going out there now." Marynell, Frankie noticed, was fairly bristling with hostility now. "What good will it do you to go poking around out there?"

"Ma'am, we can't pretend this isn't happening," Luke

said calmly. "The men causing the trouble keep coming back to those caves for some reason. They didn't just disappear after they hired Arlen Mestor to torch your son-in-law's barn." He was sensitive enough not to say, *with your son-in-law lying unconscious in it,* but the whole room was thinking that anyway.

"I'm sorry to have to put an end to this," Robbie interjected. Her voice was high; so was her color. "But it's late and I need to get the kids to bed soon." Frankie studied her sister warily. Of all of them, this latest trouble was upsetting her the most. It was, after all, Robbie's husband's death that had opened this Pandora's box. "Anybody want cake?" She turned abruptly to the sideboard.

"None for me, ma'am." Luke put on his hat. "I'll be heading back to Austin in a few days, but I will keep you all posted about any developments in this case, through Frankie here, if she doesn't mind taking on the role of conduit."

"I don't mind. I'll see you out."

She walked him out onto the freezing, darkened front porch. Frankie looked back at the dull glow coming through Robbie's living room sheers. "The porch light keeps burning out. Zack said he'd put in a new fixture, but Robbie wouldn't hear of it because she'll be moving as soon as they get married."

"Right."

"Old houses are a pain."

"Yeah, but I love 'em."

"Me, too." Frankie had only recently rediscovered her love of all things antique. Was it because antiques presented such a grand departure from Kyle's honed sterility?

"Well, I'll be in touch." Luke turned to leave.

"What a day, huh?" Frankie stepped toward him. She didn't want him to go, not just yet. It was as if there was something unfinished between them.

He stopped one step down and turned to face her.

"I'm sure glad you weren't hurt," he said softly as he looked up at her. Something about his stance—one boot propped up on the step near her leg—made her heart drum a little faster.

The snow was still coming down with soft ticks, quieting the earth a bit with each calm landing. Frankie was sheltered under the porch eaves, but Luke was standing out in the snow, exposed.

He seemed not to notice.

His face tilted up at her, shadowed from the winter moon by the brim of his hat, but she could tell he was studying her intently.

"Frankie…" He looked down and all she could see was the top of his Stetson, pale under the winter moon, and his broad shoulders in the denim jacket, getting dusted with snow.

"Yes?" Why on earth was her heart pounding?

"I'll have to work on the case from dawn to dusk tomorrow, but I was hoping I could see you again later on, maybe for dinner or something. No pressure or anything. I just…I really enjoy your company."

She smiled down at the moonlit steps of the porch, at his dark boot getting flecked with snow. "I'd like that."

He looked up into her face. "I'm probably rushing things here, but I want you to know that I think you're extremely beautiful. I thought so the very first time I saw you, when you tried to shoot me."

Her smile became a chuckle. "And, dang, I hit the snake instead."

His smile shone white in the moonlight, then, even in the darkness, she could see a tiny crease form between his brows. "A woman as beautiful as you shouldn't be giving her fortieth birthday a second thought."

"That's sweet." Why was she saying something so pat when her insides were trembling? She swallowed when she noticed that he kept glancing at her mouth.

He leaned in, an imperceptible move to anyone watching, but one that nonetheless made Frankie's eyes widen and her lips part with breathless anticipation.

He grasped her fingers and pulled her hand toward him. "I'll see you tomorrow then."

She nodded, stilled.

He studied her eyes in the moonlight, then leaned forward and kissed her, only lightly pressing his soft, barely open lips to hers.

While absolutely nothing else on their bodies touched, their lips tasted and their breaths mingled and a stirring flared up in Frankie that startled her. Was this because she hadn't been kissed in these many months?

He leaned away and smiled, squeezing her fingers, their only remaining point of contact. "Goodnight."

"Goodnight."

With a lingering touch of fingertips he left her and walked down the path.

WITH THE REST of the family finally gone, the sisters were free to commiserate while they dressed baby Danielle for bed upstairs in Robbie's room.

"How'd I do?" Robbie started in as she peeled off Danielle's day romper.

"Great. You were as cagey as they come, little sister." Frankie gave her a wink and a grin. "Seriously, I'm glad you figured out that I don't want Mother to know I was out traipsing around the countryside with Luke." Frankie was at the little dresser taking out a clean onesie, hooded towel, and baby washcloth.

"Think it'd be okay if we just skip her bath?" Robbie turned back to the baby. "It's been a long day for both of us. I hate it when Mother swoops into town."

"Let me bathe her real quick," Frankie said. "The water's all ready."

They settled beside the clawfoot tub onto the little bath kneelers Frankie had splurged on and lay Danielle on her support spongie. Once the baby was cooing and splashing happily, Robbie said, "I think Mother knows something is up, you know? So it's Luke already, is it?"

"Don't be a priss pot. We practically got ourselves killed together." Frankie calmly cupped warm bath water onto the crown of Danielle's downy head.

"And maybe did a few other things together, I'm guessing."

"Good grief, no!"

"You're telling me this dinner was just…dinner?"

Frankie let her shoulders wilt. "I see you have been talking to Nattie Rose."

"No. Nattie Rose has been talking to *me*. And anyone else who'll listen, probably. Better be careful, Sissy. The man touched your hand in public."

"Why, yes. Yes he did. Omigosh! I hope I didn't get knocked up or something." Frankie didn't even wait for Robbie to roll her eyes. "For heaven's sake. Will you get real? I just met the man."

Robbie squirted some baby wash on a miniature wash cloth and took her time making a lather. "Maybe you're the one who needs to get real. You said it yourself. You're not divorced yet and that husband of yours is not exactly known for his soft heart. He might come at you if he knew you were seeing another man around town. It would be like Kyle to see that you couldn't get a penny in the settlement. Better watch out. That Ranger is one handsome man."

"I don't really want any of Kyle's pennies!" Frankie sidestepped the topic of Luke's attractiveness.

"You say that now, but you won't like being broke. I know. I've been there. Have you thought about how you'll support yourself if Kyle gets nasty?"

"The store!" Frankie said, as if it were obvious. "I figure it will take two of us to run it."

"Oh, Sissy!" Robbie took her eyes off washing Danielle long enough to give her sister a grateful look. "Does that mean you're staying for good?"

"Of course. How could I leave you guys now? You've got a wedding coming up and then there'll be the move back out to the farm. Busy times, sweetie."

Robbie shook her head. "Well, I won't try to talk you out of it. I could sure use the help." Danielle cooed at the sisters and they smiled at her and then at each other. After a moment Robbie said, "I'll be. I sure never thought you and I would end up being so close. I know this is a hard time for you, but I am so grateful to have you here with me."

"I'm the one who's grateful. You've given me a place to stay and a reason to get up every morning."

"Big whoop. Getting oatmeal fixed for a pack of rowdy urchins."

"Aunt Fwankie wuuvs fixing oatmeal!" Frankie made big eyes at the baby and chucked her under her double chin.

The baby cooed at her aunt with an adorable toothless grin.

The sisters laughed.

Then Robbie grew serious. "But what if the store falls flat?"

"It won't. Ardella said the tourist trade is doubling every year."

"There are some in town who oppose that kind of growth, considering what's happened to other Hill Country towns. The traffic. The burden on our infrastructure."

Robbie was starting to sound like Zack. Not surprising. They were an excellent match. "Who's opposed to it?"

"Congressman Kilgore, for one. Nattie Rose says the word is, he wants to keep this part of the Hill Country *pristine*."

"I thought he was just opposed to Markie and Justin setting up a shelter for undocumented aliens, not to tourism in town."

"He's opposed to anything he doesn't have control over, I hear tell."

Frankie flipped a hand as if waving away the congressman's impact. "Markie and Justin don't have to worry about that old fart anyway. He's off in Washington all the time."

"Speaking of long distance, this Luke fella lives in Austin, right?"

"Yeah." Frankie didn't want to get off on this topic. She took over with the baby, rinsing every chubby little fold carefully.

"So, how's that gonna work?"

"What do you mean?"

"Well, does that mean you'll eventually change your mind about going back there? If you guys start seeing each other, I mean."

"Seeing each other? Let's don't get ahead of ourselves, little sister." Frankie lifted the baby out of the water and folded a hooded towel around her squirming body.

Robbie gave her an arch-browed look. "The chemistry between you two is plain as the nose on your lovestruck face. He *is* a very compelling man."

"I am not *lovestruck*. Okay, maybe I'm a little…lust-struck or something, but that's as far as it goes."

"Ah. *Lust!* I was beginning to think you weren't familiar with the concept."

Frankie shot Robbie the kind of mean look one could give a sister. "My marriage wasn't barren in every respect."

Robbie pulled a face. "Oh, right. That Kyle's a real hottie."

When Frankie looked genuinely hurt, Robbie amended. "Sorry. I only meant… Come on, Sissy. I didn't mean…I wasn't saying you were cold or anything like that."

Frankie carried the baby in to the changing table in the little alcove off Robbie's bedroom. Robbie followed.

"Sissy. Really. I was only kidding. I know you and Kyle must have had plenty of good times."

"The truth is, we didn't. And maybe it's left me a little…guarded." Frankie started drying the baby, who looked up at her aunt with a bright expression.

"I don't know. I just…" Frankie stopped with a catch in her throat. She cupped her hand gently over Danielle's damp curls and forced a smile at the baby's sweet face. "It's like a part of me closed down every time I lost a baby, you know?"

"Oh, Sissy." Robbie curled her fingers over Frankie's wrist. "I know that's killing you. But one thing you can never do is change the past. I've had a hard time accepting that fact myself."

"I know you have." Frankie felt tears building. Danielle was giving her a confused little baby frown. "It's just… Oh, nobody could know what it's like."

"But I can imagine! You think I didn't worry myself sick about you every time you lost a baby? Frankie, honey, that's a lot of dashed dreams. You'd get to your fourth month and I'd start dreading it every time the phone rang."

Frankie nodded, but couldn't speak. She swiped at a tear.

Robbie shook out a little pink sleeper and took over with the baby. "And on top of it all, now you have Kyle's betrayal. It's all so…freaking *bleak*. And now you're turning forty—" Robbie's gaze trailed up. "I'm sorry I didn't give you a better party."

"You've got your hands full, Sissy." Frankie dried her eyes. "It was sweet of you to do anything at all."

"I'm never too busy to care about you. You've got to save yourself, Frankie." She squeezed Frankie's arm.

"You've got to let yourself start over. I mean it," Robbie said with a vehemence that was most un-Robbie-like. "If this man, this Luke guy, is the way," she went on more calmly as she worked little arms and legs into the soft fabric, "if he's the way for you to find yourself again, then so be it. I mean it. Give this a chance, at least. Even if it doesn't last forever, at least this guy has put the color back in your cheeks. And that's a good thing. Don't go discounting good old lust, sister. It's not everything in a relationship, but it sure doesn't hurt, either."

Frankie had to smile despite her tears. Her sister Robbie had fallen so deeply in love, and with such a good man. Could she dare to hope that the same thing might ever happen to her?

CHAPTER SEVEN

Luke Driscoll. Just writing out his name makes him more real to me somehow. I'm a woman who's just turned forty, over the hill sexually, maybe, and now I'm getting this…buzz every time I'm around the man.

The first time he kissed me, I actually went weak in the knees. I always thought that was just an expression.

Tonight we ate dinner at the Aggie again, took another stroll in the park—so simple! With Kyle it was always some big Dallas weekend, taking a plane to the mountains to ski or something.

But when Luke took my hand, when he pulled my collar up around my chin and slowly brought his head down, touching his hot lips to mine again, taking his time, letting me taste him…I wouldn't have traded it for all the fancy dates in the world. The full moon smiled down on us from the frigid winter sky, and I wondered where this man had been all my life.

I don't have a clue what to do with these feelings. And I don't know whether Luke feels the same way at all, or if I'm just another woman to play around with while he's in town. He has been widowed several years now. Maybe he doesn't want a serious relationship.

But me, I'm getting hung up already. Is this just
some kind of backlash from being rejected by Kyle?

THE NEXT DAY a blue Norther howled down off the
Edwards plateau and coated the Hill Country in a layer
of ice tighter than a sheet of shrink wrap. Everything
was covered. Roads, bridges, barns and houses. Tree
limbs snapped and fell to the ground under the weight of
it. Cars skidded off the narrow roads into ditches. School
was canceled.

"I am not risking my neck to trudge downtown in this
mess and open up that store," Robbie pronounced.

"I agree." Frankie felt almost gleeful as she looked
outside at the frozen landscape, sparkling in a pink dawn.
She never dreamed she'd be so pleased over finding herself
trapped in a creaky old house full of children in an ice storm.

But for her, this was bliss. All weathered-up in a cozy
old house. Nothing to do but cook soup, scribble in her
journal and play with the baby. She had always longed to
have a day exactly like this.

The women were still in their robes when Zack came
by right after his shift ended. He kissed Robbie and cuddled
the baby before going to his own house to crash. Though
Zack had done a lot of work repairing Robbie's house,
Robbie would not let them co-mingle their living arrangements, Frankie had noticed. Probably because she did not
want to confuse her children. Until the wedding, Robbie
had her house, Zack had his.

When the boys got up Frankie made pancakes. Then she
helped Robbie catch up on laundry.

Right before noon Luke showed up.

He was stomping the slush off his boots on the porch and gave Frankie a sheepish grin as she opened the door. "Pizza." He held a large box forth.

Frankie grinned. "You shouldn't have." She opened the door so he could come in.

"Told you, I don't like to eat alone," he said in a low voice as he went by.

"Oh, hi, Luke." Robbie smiled as she descended the stairs with the baby on her shoulder. "'Scuse the way I look. Snow day, you know." Robbie looked like a holdover from Halloween in a baggy faded orange Longhorns sweatshirt and stretched out black yoga pants with her carrot-red hair clipped up high on her head. Zack had actually said she looked "cuddly" when he was there earlier. Which confirmed for Frankie that he truly must love her sister.

For her part, Frankie was glad she had showered and made up, as was her compulsion. Her creamy cable-knit turtleneck accented her dark hair, and a pair of trim-fit fine-wale baby-blue cords hugged her curves perfectly. Her clothes were sleek except for a pair of Robbie's thick, loudly striped winter socks. Luke smiled at these.

The boys came whooping up when they caught the aroma of pizza and Robbie let them take it in front of the TV while the adults took the baby off to the kitchen.

Frankie couldn't stop smiling, couldn't take her eyes off Luke, as they sat by the bow window at Robbie's little spindle-legged table eating stew, drinking tea, enjoying the glacial winter scene outside. Was she dreaming? Was this real? It seemed as far from the life she'd left in Austin as a life could get. But Robbie broke the spell by asking about Luke's investigation.

"Have you figured out who killed Maria Morales yet?" Robbie had never been this blunt before Danny's death.

"No, ma'am, not yet."

"That girl hasn't told you any more?"

"Yolonda? Doubt she knows much."

"She knows those brothers! She came up here to be with one of them, I heard." Robbie's messy hair bobbed as her speech grew agitated. "Those varmints were sneaking around the caves the day before Danny died. It's all connected. And who better to connect the dots than a Texas Ranger?"

Frankie bit her lip. Sometimes she marveled at how her sister had gone straight from milquetoast to militant.

But Luke was regarding Robbie seriously. "Did you tell me your husband knew Kurt Kilgore?"

The name echoed in the tiny kitchen like the crack of a whip.

"Nobody knows Kurt Kilgore." Robbie fidgeted with a stray curl, then hopped up and started fussing with the baby. "Would you look at this messy little face."

Frankie studied Robbie's back. *Was* her sister hiding something?

"Can I take you to dinner again tonight?" Luke asked when Frankie walked him out onto the porch later.

Frankie shivered in the cold wind and he stepped right up to wrap his arms around her.

A rattletrap old pickup inched by on the icy street, the high-noon winter sun glinting off the heavy chrome work. It was old Sam Landsaw, straining his neck to get a good look at them as they hugged on the porch. But Frankie didn't care. She smiled at Luke. "Sure. The usual place?"

"Haven't tried everything on the menu yet. I'll pick you up about six."

"Okay. But won't these streets be pretty bad once the sun goes down?"

"I'm close by. Over at the old Downtowner." That was an ancient hotel facing the courthouse, and of the same vintage. "It's only a few blocks from here and then a few back to the Aggie. And," he said, winking, "Old Bossie's a four-by-four."

They ended up going to the Aggie every night that week, frozen landscape or no frozen landscape. The food at the Aggie didn't seem boring to Frankie in the least. She had never been so excited to be in a man's company. He made great conversation. His wit was quick. His eyes, beautiful. His body, sexy.

They had a comfortable after-dinner ritual of walking in the small park at the center of town, which all that week remained a fairyland of icicles and frosted foliage. Tonight, Luke wrapped an arm around her shoulders to keep her warm.

"This weather is incredible, huh?"

"I've never seen anything like it in the Hill Country. My dad says all this moisture means we'll have an early spring. And that'll be good for my sister and Zack. They're going to have their wedding as soon as the bluebonnets bloom. They're ready to be a family."

"I imagine so. What will you do when they move back to the farm?"

Frankie shrugged and felt the comfortable weight of his arm. She sighed. "My life's such a mess."

He leaned in and kissed her temple. Just the light touch of his warm lips made Frankie feel better, giving her that melting feeling in her middle again. "Your life's not a mess," he said with a smile in his voice.

"How did you find your bearings again, after...everything?"

She felt him withdrawing from her slightly.

"I wouldn't say I ever got my bearings. I live day by day."

After all this time? Frankie wondered why his wife's death haunted him so. "How did she die?"

"I'll tell you some other time."

"Don't you ever feel cheated? Especially since you didn't have kids?" That was the one thing in all of this, Frankie was sure, that she would look back upon with regret.

His mood grew suddenly dark, and his withdrawal from her became more obvious. "I'm getting a little long in the tooth to worry about having kids. I don't think I'd make a great father anymore."

"Why would you say that?" Frankie had already found herself having fantasies in that department. Luke was so warm and manly and down-to-earth and just plain decent. Who better to be a daddy?

"I'm always gone from home. Always obsessed with some case or other. Even my dog gets to feeling neglected."

"You haven't said much about your family."

"Well, there's Uncle Beecher."

"Nobody else?"

"My parents. They live in California now. I don't see them much. They blame me." He stopped abruptly, looking down.

"For what?"

His breath beat out in two frozen puffs before he said, "The death of their granddaughter."

Frankie came up short. "Their grand—you mean you had a *child?*"

"Yes. A little girl."

Frankie stared at him, mouth agape. He'd had a child…a child who had died? "And she died? How? When?"

His mood shifted again suddenly, becoming tender. "Really, sweetheart. Not tonight, okay?" He reached up and stroked a stray strand of hair from her cheek and adroitly focused back on Frankie's concerns. "Sometimes living day to day is the best you can do. And sometimes good comes out of bad. Just think, if you hadn't been staying out at your parents' back then, we would never have met." He leaned in closer. This time for a real kiss.

When it became prolonged, more demanding and sexual, almost desperate, she shivered.

He stopped. "Are you getting cold?"

"No. I'm fine." She was thinking about that little girl, his daughter. It was the hardest thing she'd ever done, respecting his wish not to talk about it. Not tonight, at least. But eventually Frankie wanted to know. Was that why he had given up on being a father?

He pulled her closer. "Come on. Let's go back to my truck. I'll warm you up. And I want to show you something."

They climbed in the cab and as he goosed the engine to generate heat, he generated some of his own by leaning over and kissing her again. He had snatched a candy on the way out of the café and his mouth tasted like peppermint.

Frankie drank in the taste of it and the compelling masculine scent of him. When he stopped, he opened his eyes inches from her face and smiled.

"I have a surprise for you."

He put the truck in gear and even with the four-wheel drive, his progress around the few short blocks was slow and deliberate. He parked the truck on a street that featured a neat row of historic "Sunday houses." The narrow two-story structures, so small that the stairway was often attached to the outside, had originally been built by nineteenth-century farmers and ranchers who stayed in them when they made the long trip to town for market day and to attend church. Sunday houses were cozy retreats and Frankie had always loved them.

"What do you think?" He nodded toward a tiny rock-faced one.

It was dark, the house was shrouded in giant ice-laden trees. She peered out the window. "I can't make out much. What am I supposed to be looking at?"

He reached in front of her and fished around his glove box, producing a flashlight. "Come on." He climbed out of the truck, came around and opened her door, helped her down, and led her by her gloved hand as their boots crunched on the frozen moonlit grass. She was surprised that he had a key.

The heavy door creaked open.

"What are we doing?" Frankie whispered as he took her by the hand again and led her inside, thinking this was police work.

The space was totally empty, not even any coverings on

the high casement-style windows. It smelled of old wood, closed up and dry.

"Looking at my house."

She stared at him, then around the tiny, musty living room, illuminated eerily by his flashlight. "*Your* house?"

"That downtown hotel is getting old quick. I may be here for a while. I've always wanted a vacation home in the Hill Country. Or maybe…" He looked at her, seeming to be checking her expression for something. "Maybe it's time I got a more permanent residence."

When she gave him a curious look, he veered off in another direction. "Old man Mestor owned this old cracker box, so it's not in very good shape, but before long I'll give it the Driscoll touch."

"Mestor sold off Robbie's rent house, too," Frankie observed, pretending to be engaged, though her mind was still spinning, still struggling to process all of this man's secrets. He had lost so much. And yet he had gone on with courage and now he'd bought a house right here in Five Points. Her admiration for Luke Driscoll grew deeper every day.

"I guess he was forced to liquidate his assets to pay his lawyer. Come on," he tugged on her hand gently. "Have a look."

The thick stone walls, oak flooring and tall deep-set windows were classic. "It's charming," Frankie breathed, "but tiny."

"I already talked to Zack about bumping it out back without stressing the older structure or ruining the integrity of it from the street. The add-on will house a kitchen and great room, with plenty of windows to show off those old pecan trees." His voice warmed with excitement. "The existing kitchen is shot. I'm going to make it into an office."

He dragged her by the hand to that room, a nook that protruded from the house. "My desk will go there. The bathroom's a wreck, too," he allowed cheerfully. "I'm going to make it into a guest bath, with kind of a water-closet feel. I'll install a large master bath upstairs, of course. There's a lot to do, but the majority is cosmetic. The core structure is fantastic." His eyes were shining as he turned to face her. "Even the wood floors can be salvaged. It's all quality stuff. Those old German settlers knew what they were doing."

Frankie was flabbergasted. This was a side of him she would never have imagined. He was actually excited about renovating a historic house. And he was…investing in it. And in this town? In her?

"When are you going to have time? What about the case?"

"Dragging on. The illegals have been sent back to Mexico. The state won't risk sending spelunkers down for evidence while there's ice all over the rocks. The local sheriff keeps insisting that if there was a body, the Coyotes that got away loaded it in their vehicles."

"Pultie's just lazy." Frankie shared his disgust.

"Maybe. Or maybe he's cagey."

Their gazes connected in the oblique flare of the flashlight.

"You think he's involved in this somehow?" Frankie said softly.

"Guys like the congressman keep retainers, especially in local law enforcement. I see it all the time. I'm going to have to continue my investigation quietly. Which means I'll need a plausible reason—" he glanced around "—for hanging around town."

Frankie's heart fell. There was her answer.

"Besides you, that is."

Her heart rose again and she actually felt herself blushing. Hearing this man say that felt so astonishing, and yet so right.

"Looks like," he went on, "I'm going to have to get inside those caves and look around without using spelunkers."

"I have an idea of who might know a way in. My nephew. The one from Dallas." Frankie had only met Brandon briefly at Markie and Justin's wedding. He seemed like a nice young man.

"The one who followed Kilgore to the caves? I need his name."

"Markie will kill me for getting him involved."

"I won't expose him to any danger. I'll even contact his parents."

"Brandon Smith," she said before she lost her nerve. "He's a student at the University of Texas in Austin."

She hoped she hadn't opened Pandora's box.

BY THE NEXT WEEK more freezing wind had gusted in and left fresh sheets of ice. The worst winter storms central Texas had experienced in decades, the weather channel reported.

Despite the weather, Luke and Zack started right in on the Sunday house, but had to limit themselves to repairs inside since the steep-pitched roof was frozen slick as glass.

By hanging out at the hardware store and the Aggie and the gas station, Luke started to navigate his way through the various cliques of townsfolk, beginning to get a better picture of who was in whose pocket.

Every time he encountered Joe Pultie, the sheriff made tsking noises about how the Coyote case had gone cold. How he had seldom satisfactorily solved a case where illegal aliens were involved. "Off they go to Mexico." He flipped sausage-like fingers to the south.

In the meantime, Luke kept up his quiet investigation.

A couple of the firefighters Zack had set him on to swore that there was something fishy about Danny Tellchick's death. It was obvious they loved endlessly hashing over the town's most sensational arson case. They said they didn't want to second-guess the Fire Marshal, a man of influence, a crony of Congressman Kilgore's, in fact, but there had to be more to it than the official report showed.

Luke found the times he snatched away with Frankie a blessed relief from all of this.

He didn't care what they did or where they went. All he wanted was to touch her, to look into her gorgeous eyes and hear about her day. But he figured a classy woman like Frankie was going to get weary of eating in the same old booth with the same old stodgy cop.

He was going to have to get more creative about their dates. No small feat in a town the size of Five Points in the dead of January with ice on every road out of town.

CHAPTER EIGHT

MARYNELL MCBRIDE WAS waiting inside Ardella's where she had a clear view of the Rising Star's fire-engine-red front door. Here, in the gentle curve of Main Street, Ardella's storefront angled toward Robbie's just enough for some see-but-not-be-seen spying.

That Robbie. The thought of her middle daughter gave Marynell a pang. Robbie had certainly changed since Danny's death. Moving back to town, throwing her heart into this silly little craft store, losing her head over a younger man and now getting ready to remarry. Nearly forsaking the farm. The very farm that had cost Marynell so much. Her grandson. Her pride.

Kurt Kilgore had never said it aloud all those years ago, but on that awful day when they'd made their deal, Marynell had read the accusation in his eyes as clearly as if he'd shouted it. *Your daughter is just like you, Marynell. A slut.* But she had swallowed her pride and asked anyway.

"Just give me the whole section, Kurt. Six hundred acres is nothing to a Kilgore. That land's no good to you anyway, especially the north end up by the river." Back then, they had both known what she was talking about. The limestone

formations where the caves were. Rough, rocky land.
Pocked with subterranean shafts and seeping springs.

"Danny's too lazy to do anything with it anyway. He'll
just let it go to brush. We'll be lucky if he doesn't let the
whole valley go fallow."

"Why do you want it then?" Kurt squinted at her. He
had adopted those ridiculous little wire-rimmed glasses
by then. His trademark. He had changed in countless
little ways after he'd gone off to congress. And none for
the better.

"It makes a clean section. No boundary disputes. No
Kilgore land on this side of the river."

"That's it, isn't it? Avenge your daddy, is that it?" He
sighed as if dejected. "I expect that rocky area's no good
to anybody anyway."

More than anything about that fateful conversation,
the mention of her father had sawed on Marynell's mind.
The Kilgores had cheated her daddy of the land along the
river years before. And she, Marynell, had betrayed her
own father by taking up with a Kilgore son. But Kurt had
been so handsome in his day. And breathtaking in his
sexual aggression.

It hadn't occurred to her that day that Kurt had agreed
to her terms all too easily. She figured it was because he
was so upset about Markie's pregnancy. What a fool she'd
been. And it had all been for nothing, because Markie
hadn't gotten the promised abortion after all.

And that Frankie. Hiding her younger sister in a maternity home like that. Behind her mother's back.

All three girls had betrayed her, in the end. How

damned ironic! When it was for *them* that she had done all these things.

It was all so infuriating, so frustrating. So painful. She wound her thin arms across her middle and pressed her eyes so tightly closed that Ardella said, "Are you okay, hon?"

"I'm fine."

Ardella gave her a wary look and went back to work weaving a silk garland at the counter.

Their lifelong relationship had grown strained lately. Marynell could feel Ardella's allegiance pulling away from her, toward the girls, especially toward Frankie, whom Ardella clearly admired. Ardella talked, these days, of what a hard worker Frankie was, of how refined and intelligent Frankie was. Of her daughter's integrity.

Integrity, *bah*. Frankie was sneaking around town with that commoner of a cop, while her estranged husband, a hardworking surgeon, was left to his own devices in Austin. If Frankie had performed the duties of a wife well enough, Kyle would never have strayed.

Even as Marynell thought these spiteful thoughts, the object of her disdain approached.

"Here he is," Marynell said aloud as she stared out the display window.

"I told you. Every day at closing time." Ardella came up behind her and shook her head. "I could set my watch by the man."

He was wearing a sheepskin-lined denim jacket. That, the goatee, the Stetson and the tight-fitting jeans made him look like a Ralph Lauren ad. Marynell could practically smell the aftershave.

"What is *my* daughter doing, taking up with such a man as that?" She had spoken aloud again, although she was not especially predisposed to share her misgivings, even with her lifelong friend.

From behind her, she caught a small, strangled sound, as if Ardella had choked back a comment. She could only imagine. The two of them had been mere seniors in high school when Marynell had taken up with *a man such as that,* by the name of Kurt Kilgore.

And hadn't Marynell gotten her skinny little heart good and broken for her trouble? Frankie was heading for a similar train wreck, but the hell of it was, Frankie was the one who was too good for this man. And Frankie was hardly a high-school girl.

Marynell watched as her daughter opened the shop door and the man angled one broad shoulder down, scooping an arm around Frankie's back as she threw herself at his neck. Pity's sake. They couldn't even wait until the door was fully closed to start groping at each other.

THE SMELL of the little shop, the smell of *her,* was becoming addictively familiar to Luke.

The Rising Star was filled with the potpourri fragrances typical of a gift shop. Fresh spruce and old wood. Citrus and candles. That flavored coffee Frankie made.

But Frankie's scent was rich, distinctive. *She* smelled like fresh flowers and new-mown grass, heady to Luke's senses in the dead of winter. He buried his face in her hair. And she had just a hint of some fragrance he'd first encountered on an old college girlfriend. Patchouli? He'd forgotten how hypnotic it was…until Frankie.

The tall red door had hardly closed before he assailed her mouth. He had first kissed her only a few days ago, and he'd been coming back for more ever since, like some lovesick teenager. He drank her in as his lips lingered over hers.

"You taste so good," he finally murmured. "And you smell so good. I'm getting hooked on you, I think." This had been the way it was with her. He just seemed to blurt out his thoughts, base as they were.

He hoped she understood his headlong behavior. How crazy he found himself to be about her. How novel this feeling of smitten giddiness was for him, after all these years of mucking his way through blinding grief, wondering when, *if,* it would ever end. It was like coming up for air out of a murky pond.

"What is that?" He inhaled deeply. "That fragrance?"

"Wallpaper paste?" Her moist, pink-tinged lips teased into a grin. She was so cute, so very kissable.

He did so again.

This time Frankie got into it and moaned. He sensed that she always tried to start out so cool. Tried to keep control. And when she failed, he exulted. She always ended up making some involuntary sound in the back of her throat that made him want to press on until he had her screaming in bed. With any other woman, it probably would have been a done deal already. But with her…with her he wanted to wait. With her, it was going to be right, not rushed.

"Anybody else here?" he murmured against her lips as he danced her backwards.

Frankie shook her head no, looking in his eyes with an innocence that was incredibly seductive. "All alone. So, am I safe?"

"Hardly," he growled and attacked her lips again. *So, so sweet.*

"Down boy." Breathless, she tore her mouth free from this deeper, far more aggressive kiss.

She repositioned his hands from where they'd strayed down her hips, around to her backside. "I've gotta close up now. Why don't you go on over to the Aggie and sip a nice cold Ocean?" She rocked her hips against him, and he knew this movement was partly instinctual, as were those soft unbidden sounds she made. "And I'll meet you there in a bit?"

He straightened. He held her lightly, looked in her eyes and stroked her cheek. She was going to make him crazy. He wanted to consummate this thing now, tonight. But he was leaving town tomorrow. The kid down in Austin was sharp. Luke's gut told him this was a strong lead.

He had to find a way to tell her without making it seem like he was running off, dropping what they'd barely started. Abandoning her like her sorry husband.

Immediately, she seemed to sense that he was dreading something. His wife had acted like that sometimes. Sensed his mood before he'd even spoken his mind. It was a female thing, he supposed. "Frankie, listen. I've got to leave town. They need me back in Austin to analyze some crime-scene evidence. And I've got to meet with your nephew."

Her eyes, already showing her disappointment, shifted away from his gaze. "Evidence about that poor girl on the border?"

"Yes. We've secured her personal effects finally. I've got to go. I'm sorry."

"Don't be. I...I understand." She inched away, which made him instantly reach out, aching for her. When had this *need* for this woman started? Beyond getting shot at together, they'd done little except share a few dinners at that greasy spoon across the street. A couple of moonlit strolls in the little town square. These few kisses. That was nothing.

This was nothing.

Tell that to your heart, buddy. Already, he had decided. Here was the one, the one he'd been waiting for. The one who would break him free of the bondage of pain that had held sway over him all these years.

"I promise we'll get together again. Soon." It sounded like some lame cliché that men spout when they're getting ready to chill on the relationship, but he meant it. *Soon.*

"Yes, I hope we will." She said it softly as, right before his eyes, she morphed into something like the cool, dignified doctor's wife. "Whenever you find yourself back in Five Points, don't hesitate to give me a call."

Don't hesitate? He wasn't about to *hesitate*. It was all he could do to keep from ripping her clothes off. "Whenever I find myself back in Five Points?" He shook his head, grabbed for her arm. The underside felt soft, warm. Oh, how he wanted her. All of her.

"What's being in Five Points got to do with it? You can come to Austin, can't you?"

"I don't want to come to Austin for any reason, Luke."

"You're afraid of running into him?"

"Not afraid. It's just…If Kyle knew I was seeing another guy, he'd… I don't trust him to be…fair."

"I see." He did and he didn't. Why didn't she just go on and live her life? Her ex-husband was the one who had broken their bond. The divorce had been filed. But something about the way she looked now—not scared, exactly, but definitely intimidated—made him want to help her free herself in any way he could. If that meant he had to bend a little, or even a lot, then so be it.

"Then it looks I'm gonna have to come back to Five Points. In the meantime, we'll talk every day. I'll call you as soon as I'm on the road. Several times a day. I mean it." He cupped his hands on her shoulder and turned her into him. "You'll get sick of me."

"Never. You know," she said lightly, and to his dismay, turned from his touch, "it occurs to me now that I never even asked." She tilted her head away, looking at the floor. "Are you involved with someone back in Austin?"

More downstream effects because of the bastard. But he couldn't blame Frankie for protecting herself. It would undoubtedly take her a while to recover from the damage that jerk had caused. He'd just have to show her. He'd found that was universal with people. Whether it was with do-wrongs or the ladies, talking didn't count. You had to show them. Even so, he couldn't help trying to reassure her right away.

"I've dated some nice women, but there's no one in particular. And Frankie?"

Finally, she looked in his eyes.

"I intend to show you that not all men are jerks."

WHEN THE SHOP DOOR opened again and Luke Driscoll emerged, Marynell was ready to pounce. She bristled anew as she watched Luke bend to give Frankie a quick kiss on the lips, then whisper something in her ear. Their leave-taking seemed tender, reluctant and prolonged, before he finally strode down the sidewalk, with her daughter watching his departure from the store's stoop like a lovesick war bride.

"I'm going, Ardella." Marynell reached behind the counter for her coat and purse. "Sorry I had to use your place to spy."

Ardella came around the counter. "It's okay, honey. I never would have thought Frankie would be one to act this way. She always seemed the most levelheaded of your girls."

"Which, apparently, isn't saying much. But that's why I needed to see with my own eyes. I can't believe she is actually getting involved with that man…in that way."

"Well, maybe you can stop her before she makes a big mistake."

"You can be certain I will do everything in my power."

"FRANKIE."

"Yipe!" Frankie jumped, banging her head on an open door of the antique hutch under which she had been storing some decorative cord covers. "Ouch." She stood to face Marynell, rubbing her head. "I didn't hear you come in, Mother."

"I am not surprised, with the way you've got that honky-tonk crap blaring in here."

A country-and-western station, a good one that Luke

had introduced her to, played from a stereo on the credenza at the back of the store.

Frankie pushed herself up from her knees and wove her way through the room to go turn it down. "What are you doing here?" she said as she made her way back to her mother.

"I needed to talk to you, in private."

"Here? In Robbie's store?"

"It's not open for business just yet, and it's after hours." Marynell reached up and turned the lock on the red door.

"Robbie isn't here?"

"No. She took the baby home hours ago." Frankie turned away, gathering up the wallpapering supplies she'd finished with earlier, hoping if she stalled long enough her mother would just go away. Marynell had always had a thing about serving P.J. his dinner on time. But it was more a point of pride with Marynell than consideration for the old farmer. "Can't this wait until I've finished cleaning up? Could you come by the house later?"

"No. I can't very well discuss a delicate subject like this with Robbie's boys within earshot."

Frankie's eyes narrowed. *A delicate subject like this?* Something about her mother's tone made her defenses go up. "What delicate subject?"

"Your foolish behavior of late."

"My *what?*"

"With that man," Marynell went on. "I know you don't want my opinion, but Frankie, this is highly inappropriate. You are not yet divorced."

"Oh, for pity's sake. In my heart I have been divorced for a long time. And now I've actually filed."

"And have you even talked to Kyle since you took that rash step? Do you have any idea what he thinks about it?"

"I don't need Kyle's permission to end this marriage. He's the one who had the affair, not me."

"There are two sides to every story, Frankie. You are running from your problems instead of facing them. Have you really given any of this any rational thought, or are you too busy making a fool of yourself over that... cowboy?"

Frankie straightened fully, understanding now what this surprise visit was about. Perhaps Marynell had even been watching them, spying on them. From over at Ardella's perhaps? This was Marynell's pattern, a pattern that went back years, at least as far back as the time she had snooped in Markie's diary and discovered Markie was pregnant.

Frankie wondered what had made her mother this way. What unhappiness, what bitter turn of events, had set the woman off on a path where she was threatened even by her own daughters' happiness? Frankie wondered if she herself was going to end up embittered this way. She wondered if Marynell had ever actually been in love. This last thought turned her attention back where it belonged, to defending Luke. "Luke isn't a cowboy, Mother. He's a Texas Ranger. A highly skilled one."

Marynell wrung her bony fingers and minced off two rigid paces in front of the high counter where the register sat. "Honestly." She looked down as her toe bumped into some objects that Robbie and Frankie had been artfully arranging—rolled rag rugs, wrought-iron fixtures, buckets of silk flowers. "This place is already looking so cluttered."

Frankie was trying to stay calm. "It's a *gift* shop, Mother. Robbie wants people to have the feeling that they've happened upon a wonderful discovery. She wants people to feel cozy and relaxed so they'll take their time shopping."

"Well, I don't think people will like it at all. Most folks prefer a sense of order."

Oh, right, Mother. When you say order, what you really mean is sterility. Frankie was able to stop herself before she voiced that mean thought. "I think this place is charming. Sometimes letting things flow has a way of…freeing people."

"Oh, you'd know all about freedom, wouldn't you? Which brings me back to *that man.* So. Are you planning to continue seeing him?"

"I don't know." Sidestepping her mother's inquisition, Frankie headed for the storeroom in back, carrying the wallpapering supplies.

"Everyone is talking about the two of you!" Marynell called after her.

When Marynell's goading didn't get any response, she added in a louder voice, "You are as guilty as Kyle is in all of this!"

That caused Frankie to stop. And turn. "Mother, you are an incredibly meddlesome woman, you know that?"

Her mother seemed unfazed by Frankie's bluntness. Her gaze remained level, as cold as the ice on the streets outside. "And you, young lady, are a married woman."

Frankie wanted to smirk and thank her mother for

calling her a *young lady* when she was now forty. But this wasn't the time for sarcasm. "Only legally. Not spiritually. Certainly not emotionally."

"You are simply justifying your behavior," Marynell plowed right along. "Even if you are too stubborn and prideful to consider reconciling with your husband—and you very well *should* consider a reconciliation because no divorced woman I ever met was actually happy—"

"Mother, that is perfectly a hideous thing to say. I know lots of happy, well-adjusted divorced women. They've chosen to act courageously and live their lives the way they see fit, instead of merely existing in a dead marriage, or worse, a sham of one."

"Courageous? Is that how you see yourself? You think it's courageous to be running around in public with this man? Kissing him right out here on Main Street?"

"Did I ask you what you think?" Frankie's voice rose.

"Don't you get ugly with me, young lady!"

If Frankie hadn't wanted to strangle her mother right then, she would have smirked this time. Being called *young lady,* now of all times, should have been music to her ears. But the truth was she wasn't so young anymore. And a forty-year-old woman was way too old to let anyone interfere in her love life.

She took a deep breath, striving for calm one more time. "Mother, I have work to do. The door up front will lock automatically when you go out."

But Marynell would not let up. "I am not leaving until you let me talk some sense into you. I am trying to help you. What you're doing isn't courageous at all. It's tacky…and sneaky."

"I thought that was the problem. That we're *not* sneaking around."

"Stop twisting my words!" Marynell's hollow cheeks turned as red as the shop door. It was far too easy to get under her skin, and suddenly Frankie felt sorry for her mother.

Markie used to enjoy goading Marynell this way. Frankie did not. She relented.

"Look, Mother," she finally managed in the calm voice she had been striving for, "please try to relax about Luke. He's leaving town tomorrow morning. After tonight we won't be embarrassing you as much, I expect."

"Oh." Marynell, with nothing to battle, seemed suddenly lost. "I see. Why?"

"He's been called back to Austin to interview…some witness."

At that information, Marynell's eyes grew unnaturally bright.

CHAPTER NINE

THE NEXT PERSON to show up at the Rising Star, bright and early the very next morning, was none other than Frankie's soon-to-be-ex-husband.

The little bell on the door tinkled and Frankie turned, hoping it was Luke, coming by for one last kiss. At the sight of Kyle she jumped, more startled even than when she'd seen her mother the night before.

"Kyle." Her face, she hoped, did not reveal her aversion. "What are you doing here?" He'd gotten the papers, no doubt. He must be angry. But his style had always been to either blow up on the spot or withdraw and pout. Or both. This time, since he hadn't called screaming into the phone, she was hoping for pouting. After all, it was his idea to communicate through their attorneys. So what was he doing here?

"We need to talk, Frankie. Would you mind going some-where private with me?"

"Private?"

Kyle, looking as sleek as a male model in gray cash-mere and black worsted wool, crossed the room to the antique coat tree by the register and lifted Frankie's jacket from a hook. His pale hair was gelled back. His surgeon's hands and manicured fingernails were immaculate. But his clean-shaven countenance looked puffy and sallow, betraying stress.

"This is nice." He rubbed the fabric between his fingers as he walked back to Frankie. The hacking jacket was made of a soft wool Yorkshire plaid. Classic shades of green and spice. Brown velvet lapels. A sucker for style, Kyle had always shown an unnatural awareness of Frankie's clothes. What flattered her. What didn't. He had picked out much of her wardrobe himself. "I haven't seen it before. Is it new?" He also recognized *expensive* and was no doubt wondering where she'd gotten the money to pay for this kind of quality.

"Markie gave it to me. For Christmas."

"Ah. Miss Markie. I heard about that mess. The congressman. The long-lost boy. The...*reunion,* I guess you'd call it."

"Where did you hear about that?" Frankie certainly hadn't told him. As birth parents, Markie and Justin were determined that nothing would disrupt their son's life at this late date, especially not a public and illegitimate connection to a praetorian politician such as Kurt Kilgore.

But what did Kyle care about this? He had washed his hands of anything to do with Markie's baby before the child was even born.

"Marynell told me."

He's been talking to Mother? That explained a lot. Something in Frankie's gut tightened.

"Marynell is hurt by everyone's reaction to what happened." Kyle shook his head. "She was only trying to protect Markie back then."

"No," Frankie corrected. "She was trying to *use*

Markie's pregnancy, it turned out. As blackmail to get her hands on the Kilgore land by the river."

"You can't blame her there. That farm used to be in her family."

"And later, she only wanted to move Robbie and Danny out there because Danny was weak and she thought she could control him."

"Poor Danny. I still can't get over it. It's hard to believe the poor guy's gone. What a horrible way to die."

Frankie doubted Kyle sincerely meant any of those sentiments. He had despised his good-old-boy brother-in-law from the get-go.

"Well, at least the farm belongs to Zack Trueblood now, free and clear. He and Robbie are happy together and, unlike Danny, he's a very strong man. When he and Robbie get married and move back out there, I guarantee you, Mother won't be controlling Zack."

Kyle frowned. "Still, I feel badly for Marynell."

Frankie doubted that, too. What was this all about?

"You girls are all angry at her. Your father is avoiding her. She seems so alone now, way out there on that god-forsaken farm."

"She brought it on herself. You can't manipulate people without consequences."

"Weren't we manipulative? Helping your little sister deceive your parents that way? There's plenty of blame to go around for the past, Frankie. But I must say, when we finally got it all out in the open, your mother was fairly decent about our role in things. She doesn't seem to be holding the past against *me,* at least."

Frankie wondered what Kyle had told Marynell about the time when they'd moved her teenaged sister to Austin and helped her give her baby up for adoption. It didn't matter. Frankie was beyond caring what anyone thought of her. Least of all her mother. Least of all this man. "You didn't do anything, Kyle. Markie and I take full responsibility for what happened."

"You're forgetting that it was I who lied and told your parents that Markie had mono, when what she had was a full-term fetus."

Frankie twisted her face away from him. Was his wording intentionally cruel? *Full-term.*

"Well, let's not get sidetracked by Markie's train wreck of a past." Kyle leaned around to peer in her face. "We have our own problems now, don't we? Come on." He held forth the jacket. "Let's talk."

She slid around behind the counter, away from him, and fished her keys and cell phone out of her purse and punched a speed dial number. "Robbie?" she said with her eyes on Kyle's calm features. "Kyle has shown up here at the shop— No, everything's fine. He says he wants to go somewhere and talk. Will it be much longer before you get in?… Okay. I'm going to lock up and go on then. I love you, too. Bye."

Frankie snatched the jacket from Kyle and slipped her cell phone into one of its flat besom pockets. "Where do you suggest?"

"Not in town. People will see us, and it sounds like you've endured enough gossip already. We'll take a drive out in the country."

It sounds like? Marynell again. Frankie was anxious to get this over with. "Whatever you say." She turned and marched to the door.

He was right on her heels and held the door open. "See?" he taunted. "I can be *nice.*" He scowled as she walked past without comment. "I hope you realize I came all the way up here to talk because I care about you," he said, but the look on his face belied his words.

Frankie felt tense and was doubly frustrated by the tricky old-fashioned key, aware of his eyes on her backside. She was going to change this lock set to a properly functioning one herself, the hell with Robbie's penchant for "authenticity" and her tight-fisted penny-pinching. Finally, the lock clicked and she dropped the shop keys into the other besom pocket as she marched toward her Mercedes.

THEIR MERCEDES were parked side by side at the curb. His black. Hers white. Frankie pressed the clicker to open hers.

"Still the boss," Kyle snarled and slid into the passenger's seat.

They were a mile out of town before either one spoke. It was Kyle. "Things never change much around here," he said as his sunglasses reflected the rolling countryside. "Don't you find that rather stifling?"

"No. It's comforting." Frankie did not take her eyes off the road. "What's on your mind, Kyle?"

"I suppose I can appreciate that—your need for security has always been so great. I suppose there is a certain serene quality in these hills." The Mercedes floated along the road for another few seconds before he said, "So, when are you coming home?" He reached up and curled his long fingers around her forearm, but Frankie shook them off and gripped the wheel tighter.

"Home? I don't have a *home* anymore."

"We have a beautiful home. And we have a twenty-year marriage to consider here. If you don't forgive me, you'll only turn bitter. It's time to put all this crap behind us now and get back to our marriage."

"Our marriage?" She gave a rueful laugh that filled the car and sounded completely nasty, even to herself. Maybe she *was* getting bitter, God help her. "We didn't have a *marriage,* Kyle, not with one of us off sleeping with somebody else."

She clutched the wheel as the sedan flew around a sharp curve and the tires squealed.

When she'd regained control of the car, Kyle looked angry. "You can't just run off to Five Points, keeping that silly shop and never looking back. Don't you think you've punished me enough? I want you home."

"*You* want me home? What about what *I* want? Oh, that's right," Frankie went on sarcastically without giving him time to respond, "We're not interested in what Frankie wants. This is all about Kyle."

When she glanced at him, Kyle's face looked briefly vulnerable, so wounded that Frankie almost felt sorry for him. "I've always tried to give you whatever you want, Frankie," he said petulantly. "You're making me the bad guy when you know we were both at fault. You can't keep being angry, blaming me for things over which I had no control."

She wanted to say, so you had no control when you

jumped into bed with that little piglet? But she wouldn't stoop. Even if Sammie Rayburn was a double-D sow drenched in cheap perfume, that girl wasn't the real problem. Frankie knew he was talking about the babies now, which he soon confirmed.

"I never denied you anything," he said quietly. "It's not my fault you miscarried repeatedly. You have to admit I did everything I could. But your obsession with having a child sapped all the fun out of sex."

She would not cry. Frankie squinted at the miles of fencing, the hard-won acres rolling to the horizon. She'd been raised in this wild country, floating down rivers on inner tubes, riding horses through the underbrush, lying out on the rocky ground in a sleeping bag, watching the stars come out. She wondered how she had ended up compromising her once-fierce independence, why she had married a cold, selfish man like Kyle right out of nursing school. Was it a reaction to an entire childhood of her mother's bizarre ways? She knew one thing for sure— what had driven her to marry Kyle sure wasn't real love. When had she figured that out, exactly? The answer wasn't *when*. It was *who*. And his name was Luke Driscoll.

"Say something." Kyle's demand broke into her reverie like a slap.

She favored him with a mean sidelong glance. He was mistaken to want to have this conversation outside of town. The land had given her strength. "Oh, I'll say something. But I seriously doubt you'll like it. You have a lot of nerve, blaming me for your betrayal. The reality is you rejected me more with each successive miscarriage, until I felt like a complete failure. You have a knack for that, you know? Making a woman feel like a failure…as a woman. With your toys and your porn and your little affairs."

"Don't pretend you didn't like our sex life. What we had was hot, and you know it."

Hot maybe, but never intimate, Frankie thought. Sexy, but sterile. Tears finally stung her eyes as she fully admitted that to herself. Meanwhile Kyle was still talking.

"I despise a phony. The kind of woman who wants a man with balls and then complains when he uses them. Besides, I'd say we're even now. Apparently, you've had yourself some kind of little fling."

Frankie blinked to clear her blurry eyes. *"What?"* The tires of the sedan made a squealing sound as she rounded one of the curves in the road too fast again.

"Goddammit!" Kyle exploded as she righted the car. "Will you stop driving like an idiot? Let me drive before you tear up my eighty-thousand-dollar car!"

"*Your* car?" They were in *her* Mercedes.

"I paid for the damned thing. Now pull over!"

She did, lurching off the road onto a rocky shoulder where she braked so hard it threw Kyle forward against the dash. Belatedly, she realized that Kyle had rattled her so much by showing up unannounced at the store that she'd left her purse behind. All she had was the contents of her pockets— the phone and the store keys. She had no business driving these treacherous roads with tears in her eyes and no license.

They got out, slammed doors, yanked opposite sides open, and switched seats. "Take me back to town," Frankie said. "We are finished."

"Hardly." Kyle revved the engine and jerked the wheel onto the road, heading away from town.

"What are you doing?"

"We are going to resolve this. May I remind you that you are still my *wife,* Frankie. And I refuse to sign off on any damned divorce, amicable or otherwise."

"When did you decide this?" When he found out another man was involved, Frankie would bet.

"I told Sammie our affair was over. I don't know what I was doing with that little trollop. We have nothing in common. And she's a complete incompetent. Made a wreck of the office schedule in less than a month. I want *you,* Frankie. And I want our life back."

When she didn't respond, he upped the ante. "And I still want a family if that's what you want. It's not too late. I've located a new fertility specialist."

Frankie's eyes got wide and her jaw dropped. "You still want to try for a baby? After all that's happened?" He might as well have thrown a punch to her gut.

"Of course." His voice was gentle now, conciliatory. "You know I want a child of my own as much as you do."

Fleetingly, but only fleetingly, Frankie wondered if she was the crazy one. Should she go back and give the well-ordered life she had built with Kyle one more try? Especially if it meant a child? That would be the grown-up thing to do, instead of getting all sidetracked by a lawman with broad shoulders and sweet lips.

But thinking of Luke undid her. It was too late. She could already see the prize on the horizon. True love. With a real man.

"What are you thinking about?" Kyle eyed her, then looked back at the road.

"Nothing." Frankie snapped herself out of her musings. "So. You've been talking to Mother?" It was a guess, but a good one.

"If you must know, yes. She called *me*, Frankie. She's very worried about you. She sees you throwing your life away, getting involved with some freak who—"

"Luke is not a freak!"

"He's not your husband, either, dammit!"

Suddenly, Kyle jerked the wheel, pulling onto a gravel ranch road.

"Where are you going?" Frankie clutched the seat.

He tensed. "Someplace quiet so we can talk rationally."

Frankie had never been down this road. As it dropped below a hill and became narrow and wooded, she felt a deep uneasiness starting to set in. As her mind froze with wariness, she was hard-pressed for an argument to stop him, but she knew she wanted to go back.

After a couple of minutes Kyle pulled the Mercedes to a bumpy stop under a dark copse of trees.

He killed the engine, angled his body toward her, and draped his arm along the back of her seat. "I mean it, Frankie. Come back and I'll give you whatever you want. A baby. Travel. Money. Think about it. A precious little baby, all your own. You could decorate a nursery to the nines. Buy it lots of cute clothes. The best schools. Everything you ever dreamed of. We can still try," he went on, seemingly oblivious to the shift in her mood. "We can be happy."

Frankie doubted that. Certainly not since the introduction of Luke Driscoll. She cast about for a way to end this.

But then, in a move that caught her off-guard, Kyle reached up and touched her hair. "I still want you, you know. Sammie meant nothing," he said, winding a strand around his finger, rubbing it with his thumb.

Frankie angled her head, turning to look at him, attempting to read his face as her uneasiness grew. "Kyle—"

"I won't hold your indiscretions against you," he said softly. "I can see why you fell into some cowboy's arms." Kyle continued talking quietly, gently, but Frankie sensed something malignant brewing under his smooth words. "Who knows? Maybe you even learned a few new tricks. But you have nothing in common with some rough-cut cop from Austin. It will be different between us now, Frankie. I promise."

"Kyle, don't." She reached up and unthreaded her hair from his fingers. "Let's just go back to town."

She twisted away from him, pushing at his chest with one hand, grasping for the door with the other, belatedly considering just getting out. But to what purpose? She had no idea where she was.

Her resistance only made him more forceful. He yanked her hips toward him with one hand and clutched the back of her hair with the other. "Frankie," he breathed against her face. "Do you know how sexy you still are?"

"Kyle!" She pushed at him. "Stop! This isn't right!"

"How so? We're man and wife. Unlike you and that *Ranger*." The way he bit out the last word sent a quake of real fear through Frankie. There was immense anger in it. What was he doing? But the answer was all too obvious as his hand traveled under the jacket, yanked at the hem of her shirt. "And I want my *wife* back." His grip grew suddenly fiercer as he slammed her slender body against his.

"Kyle!" Too late, she fought him in earnest.

They struggled in a tangle of arms and legs that erupted in the confined front seat. The feel of his touch, brutal as he manhandled her and tore at her clothes, made Frankie bite back a scream. Good Lord, was he actually going to rape her?

She wedged an elbow under his chin, pressing on his windpipe, but he grunted and shoved it aside. Then he slapped her hard, making her head snap back. She pressed a palm to her stinging cheek and they stared at each other with ragged breathing for one instant before he grabbed her wrist, twisting as he jerked her hand down.

"My little *wife,*" he spat. His features were contorted with rage, damp with sweat. He raised a hand to strike again just as the shrill ring of Frankie's cell phone split the charged atmosphere in the sedan.

By some miracle she fumbled the phone out of the tight besom pocket with her free hand and flipped it open. Luke's number was on the screen. Kyle tried to snatch the phone away but a tinny voice sounded, freezing his hand. "Frankie? Frankie?"

"Luke!" Frankie called toward the open phone.

Kyle flung her wrist away. Shakily Frankie pressed the phone to her ear as Kyle stared at her, venom shooting from his eyes.

"Hi there," Luke was saying brightly as she pressed the phone tighter. "Told you I'd call first thing and bug you. I'm barely a mile out of town and miss you already."

Frankie was breathing so hard she couldn't speak, though she swallowed dryly and tried. "Lu—" She coughed on the word.

"Frankie?" Luke's voice snapped alert. "Darlin'? Are you okay?"

"Luke," she finally choked out, fumbling for the door handle at the same time. Her wrist burned like fire. She worked the door open and fell out into sunny morning air so crisp and cold it felt like pure salvation.

"Luke." She sucked in air as she stumbled back from the car. "Could you come and get me?" Her voice, she knew, sounded high with terror. "It's Kyle. He—he tried to make me—" She found her legs and started to run. Behind her she heard the Mercedes' engine roaring to life.

"Your ex-husband?" Luke was saying. "He's with you now?"

"No." She gulped for air. "I g-got away."

"Did he hurt you?"

"No. Not really. But—" Her voice cracked as she couldn't admit out loud that he had most certainly intended to.

"Where are you?" Luke demanded, sounding suddenly alarmed, almost panic stricken. "Just tell me where you are."

"I don't *know* where I am." She was near tears and her breath was coming in hard rasps, but she fought to be rational. "We're out on some damned…gravel road I've never seen before. It went off to the right."

"Off which highway? I'm not that far out of town."

Of the five, which had they taken at the juncture? Frankie had been the one driving when they'd left town, but she had been too busy fuming to pay attention. "Forty-one." She pictured the signs in her mind. The one back to Austin. The one Luke must be on now. *Thank God.* "There's a gravel ranch road. About two miles out. Top of the hill."

"I'm coming up on a hill now. Stay with me." She could hear Luke doing a tire-squealing turn. There was the sound of accelerating, flying gravel, then he said, "What the hell happened?"

"Kyle just showed up at the…" she gasped for breath as the terrain grew steep, "at the store. I think he… Oh, I don't know, Luke. Just hu-hurry. He was acting so weird. He hit me."

"I'll be there in a minute. Stay hidden."

"Hurry." Trembling with rage and fear, she flailed her way into the brush at the top of the knoll, deeper into the trees. She could hear the Mercedes gunning in the distance, but Kyle wouldn't drive a luxury sedan into this thicket. Still, if he got out and chased her on foot she feared she couldn't outrun him.

CHAPTER TEN

LUKE HOPED he was on the right gravel road. There were no distinguishing marks, only rocks and trees and more rocks and trees. He swore out loud when he spotted the white Mercedes at the bottom of the hill, roaring toward him.

"I've located your husband," he said into the cell phone. "Hold on, sweetheart." He threw the truck into a stem turn that blocked the narrow road. He grabbed cuffs and gun and hurled himself out, snapped the gun up, legs braced wide.

The Mercedes braked in a spray of gravel, coming to a stop right in front of his knees. He aimed the gun at the windshield and yelled "Get out!" The driver, a slender man with a receding hairline and wrap-around sunglasses, slumped back in the seat.

The electric window glided down and the man tilted his head out with a cell phone raised to the ready. His graying blond hair was gelled back and his tan looked artificial. "Move that truck," he said indignantly, "Or I'm calling the law."

"I *am* the law. And I told you to *get out* of that car."

"You cannot hijack a citizen out in the middle of nowhere."

"Get out."

"What are you going to do? Shoot me?"

"Out, Hostler. You don't want resisting arrest on your rap sheet."

"Oh, for Pete's sake." Kyle slowly angled his body out and slammed the car door. He was taller than Luke, but not better built. "What is the meaning of this?" He forked his hands at the hips of his tailored pants.

"Hands up." Luke breached the gap between them in two long-legged steps and spun Kyle to face the car.

"I demand to know what you think you are doing," Kyle said while Luke frisked him. "You cannot detain me. I have patients waiting. Surgeries scheduled. This is patently ridiculous. Absolutely ludicrous." He resorted to foul curses when Luke twisted his arms behind his back, cuffed him and forced him face down onto the hood of the Mercedes.

Luke repositioned the gun on his captive. At his temple, to be precise. "Where did you leave her?"

"Are you charging me with some kind of crime? Because if not, this amounts to assault. You cannot aim a loaded weapon at a doct—"

"Where," Luke cocked the gun and pressed it deeper into Hostler's flesh, "is she?"

"If you mean my wife, I have no idea. We had an argument and she bolted from the car. While she was on the phone with you, I believe. She gets very emotional like that. Very high-strung woman."

Luke fished around with his free hand and came up with the guy's billfold. He pocketed it, then left him sprawled on the hood and went around and extracted the keys from the Mercedes.

Back in his truck he snatched up his cell phone. "Frankie?"

"Yeah."

"Do you know where you are, darlin'?"

She sighed, sounding calmer than she had before. "No. Sitting on a rock. Somewhere higher up on the hill."

"Can you find the road?"

"Boy, I don't know. Dumb, just tearing off like that, huh?"

"Not if you were truly frightened." Luke scanned the hill. The live oaks and junipers were dense. He was at the place where the road dipped down and circled the bottom of the hill. Dr. Fancy Pants couldn't have driven too far before he'd stopped him. "How far back does this road go, Frankie?"

"We went a ways. Can you come and get me? Or maybe the best thing for me to…is find…it."

"You're breaking up."

"I said," he heard her shouting into the phone, "if I keep walking down, I should…the road. I'll head towar…you."

"Can you make it?" He shouted into the phone equally loudly. "Are you okay?"

"I'm star…eeng to feel some bruised places, but…fine. Look. I'm losing my sig…"

Outside on the hood of the Mercedes, Dr. Fancy Pants was turning purple in the face, bellowing about his rights between fits of cursing.

"Let me get this dickhead locked down, then I'll come looking for you." But Frankie's signal had gone dead already.

Luke worked fast. He got back out of the truck, lowered the tailgate, jerked Kyle Hostler to his feet and forced him into the bed of the pickup. "Sit," he ordered.

Kyle sneered down at the gritty bed liner. "No thanks."

"Suit yourself," Luke said. He unlocked one handcuff and

jerked the guy's arm toward one of the eye-hook tie-downs on the side-rail, forcing Hostler into an awkward slump.

"You had better officially arrest me before you do that," Kyle threatened, fighting at Luke's tugging. "I insist you read me my rights."

"Shut the hell up." Luke practically jerked the guy's arm out of its socket, clamping the cuff into the eye-hook.

Back in the Mercedes, he fired up the engine, threw it into Reverse and backed full-speed down the narrow, twisting road.

He hadn't gone a hundred yards before Frankie popped out of the trees like a startled rabbit. He braked the car and jumped out, running to her. Their bodies collided at the center of the weedy road.

"Oh, God!" she cried as he whipped his arms around her and lifted her off her feet. "Thank God you called when you did! No telling what he would have done. He—" Her voice choked off with emotion. "He…he actually hit me. He's never been like that before. He's usually so cold and controlled."

"The guy's a chicken shit." Luke hugged her tighter to his chest. "And he's never coming near you again." How had he grown so protective, so possessive, of this woman in only a couple of weeks?

"Let me see you." He ran his hands gently over her hair and neck. The sight of missing buttons at the top of her blouse set his jaw in a clench. He reared back to inspect her cheek. "It's turning purple. Come on. I've got a cold pack in the truck."

They held hands as they walked back to the Mercedes.

Luke opened her door, practically tucked her inside. The car bumped down the rutted road and when the pickup came into view, Frankie flinched. "What's he doing?" she squinted.

"Stooping. I nailed him to the truck bed."

She smiled, and Luke was glad to see it. But immediately she winced and touched her cheek.

"I'll haul him into town," he said as he pulled up to the truck. "Can you drive the car back yourself?"

"Of course. But then what? Once we get to town?"

"Jail. I'll have a deputy book him."

"For what?"

"Kidnapping."

"Kidnapping?"

"Didn't you ask him to take you back to town?"

"Well, yeah."

"But instead he drove you down this remote road?"

"It wasn't as clear-cut as you're making it sound. But yeah." She nodded. "I guess that's basically what happened."

"Then that's kidnapping."

"Technically, I guess, but…"

"It's up to you, Frankie, but it's better to press charges if you want a judge to give you a protective order."

"A protective order? Is that really…? I mean, won't that have a negative impact on his practice?"

"What do you think would have happened if I hadn't called when I did?" Luke looked pointedly at her white shirt, jerked loose from her pants, buttons missing.

Frankie had to look squarely at the facts. Kyle *had* driven her out to this remote place. He *had* gotten physical with her despite her protests. He *had* hit her. She had so wanted to keep her divorce, already so high-profile back in the medical community in Austin, from becoming messy. Too late now.

As they walked to the truck, Luke positioned himself like a shield between Frankie and Hostler. Kyle jeered down at them as they walked past anyway. "Sucked the lawman right into your little drama, didn't you, Frankie?"

"Don't make me gag you." Luke tossed this threat over his shoulder while he helped Frankie up into the front seat of the truck.

When he got inside, he took a chemical cryotherapy pouch from the glove box.

Outside, Hostler started up the angry vocalizing about his legal rights again.

"You don't believe that crap about me, do you?" Frankie said as Luke ripped open the package and popped the pack. "You don't think I'm some kind of kook? Dragging you into my little drama?"

"Hell no. He's the one doing all the yelling." Luke reached across the crew seat and banged on the back window, which temporarily shut Hostler up.

Frankie nodded. "Good. Because he's completely distorting the truth."

"That's part of the pattern. I want you to go to the ER and get this checked."

"What pattern?"

"You sure he's never pulled anything like this before?" he said as he pressed the cold pack gently to Frankie's cheek.

"You mean hitting me?" Frankie winced.

"Yes. It's usually a pretty predictable pattern with these guys."

"He's always had a temper. He pouts a lot. But no. No hitting. I think he did this out of extreme stress."

"Which is?" Luke looked as if he weren't buying this stress theory.

"He found out I've been seeing you."

"Ahh, now that's rough." His sarcasm said it wasn't at all.

IN TOWN, Luke was far from merciful with Kyle. He drove the truck, with the slender doctor exposed and finally cowed down in the bed, straight to the courthouse on the square.

He dragged the shivering Kyle up the steps and into the sheriff's office as if he were road kill.

"Who's this?" Pultie rose to his feet behind his desk, staring Kyle up and down.

"Off with the sunglasses," Luke ordered, yanking them off the nose of the bound man. "Kyle Hostler. I'm handing him over for the attempted kidnapping of Frankie McBride. Unfortunately, he'll probably make bail, so we'll need a fast V.P.O. from the judge."

"Sheriff, I am Dr. Kyle Hostler," Kyle said belligerently through chattering teeth, "and John Wayne here," he gave Luke a scathing look from his Stetson to his boots, "has made a ridiculous mistake."

Pultie arched an eyebrow as he pressed a button on the phone, calling for a deputy. "Hostler?" he said while they waited. "You Frankie's ex, by any chance?"

"Not her *ex*. We are still married. My wife and I were attempting a reconciliation when this yahoo butted in."

Pultie looked to Luke for comment. Luke shook his head.

"Where is Frankie?" Pultie said.

"Emergency room. This asshole roughed her up. But she was still able to drive herself in."

Pultie called for another deputy to go over there and talk to Frankie.

"This is serious, Dr. Hostler." Pultie turned on the man. "We'll have to hold you for questioning. I can take over now, Luke."

He was being dismissed, which was okay, since he wanted to go to Frankie anyway. He unlocked Hostler's handcuffs.

"I'm going to the hospital. Don't forget the V.P.O.," Luke warned.

"No problem." Pultie was taking Hostler by the elbow.

IT MUST HAVE BEEN a slow day for the law in Five Points, because the deputy had arrived even before Luke. He had taken Frankie's statement, shaking his head, tsk-tsking and yes-ma'amming.

"I don't think he believes my version of things," Frankie told Luke when the guy was barely out of ear shot.

"There are still cops who don't get it." Luke stepped up beside her gurney in the Five Points Memorial Hospital emergency room. "Listen. I've decided to stay on in town for a few days."

"What about that lead in the Morales case in Austin?" Frankie raised up on one elbow, then winced. "Ouch! I'm getting sore all over."

"Lie back." He pressed a warm palm to her shoulder. "The nurse said she'll be here in a second. I'll follow up on the border case by phone. It'll keep until I'm convinced you're safe."

Frankie shook her head, distressed. "You don't have to stay in town on my account. This is getting all blown out of proportion. Kyle and I had a bad fight. It's happened before."

His head ticked to one side as he gave her a shrewd look. "I'm sure it has. But has he ever tried to rip your clothes off?" He reached up and repositioned a stray strand of hair on her forehead.

Frankie sank back fully on the pillow. She bit her lip, trying not to cry. "Thanks a lot, Mother."

"What's your mother got to do with this?"

"She's the one who told him…about us. She came to the store and confronted me after you left last night. My guess is she immediately trotted home and summoned Kyle."

A nurse stuck her head inside the curtain. "Frankie? You can go. The X-ray of your wrist looks fine. It's just a sprain. You might want to wear this brace for a few days."

The nurse, a chubby older woman with kind gray eyes, fastened the Velcro tabs of the wrist support while Luke looked on with a concerned frown.

"Thank you." Frankie swung her legs over the side of the gurney and Luke's gentle hands were on her immediately, helping her hop down.

"I see you have a helper." The nurse smiled at him and left.

"It doesn't really hurt that badly." Frankie waggled the bright-blue brace. "This was so not necessary."

"Actually, the trip to the ER will serve the purpose of making a record."

"Oh, dear."

"I'm sorry. I know this is hard." Luke jammed his hands in his jeans pockets, hesitating before he asked his next question. "Have you ever considered that your husband has a problem with abuse?"

"No. He's never hit me before. Only yelling. Cursing. Name-calling. Stuff like that."

"Only? Verbal abuse is the worst kind."

"Why do you say that? I've always been able to shrug off Kyle's outbursts."

"Just because you're a strong woman who's been able to endure a lot doesn't make his abuse okay."

Frankie looked down, struggling to absorb the fact that she had very possibly been the victim of abuse. Again she bit her lip to stem the tears, but this time it was no good. "Oh, man." She rolled her teary eyes toward the ceiling. "Sometimes I just want my life to be normal again."

Luke took her uninjured hand gently in his fingers. "Maybe it has to get worse before it can get better. Until then, take it one day at a time. Here." He helped her wiggle the brace into the sleeve of her jacket. "Listen." He placed his hands lightly on her shoulders once she had it fully on. "At least now you know what the real problem is."

"I never considered that abuse could be the reason I've been increasingly unhappy in my marriage. I kept thinking it was my fault. And then at the end, I don't know why, but I preferred to think Kyle's philandering was our real problem."

"It's often a package deal."

Frankie nodded and sighed. She was seeing it now. "Well, I suppose the whole town'll know about this by lunchtime." She reached up and dabbed away a tear from her bruised cheek.

Luke frowned. "You haven't got anything to be ashamed of, but I doubt this little ER nurse will talk."

"No. But it turns out I have the sorriest luck. Ardella was delivering some flowers when I came in here."

"I see. And you're afraid Ardella will tell your mother."

"If Kyle doesn't beat her to the punch. He and Mother have always been real tight. He'll make it all sound like my fault, of course."

"That's typical, too. Listen." Luke gave her injured jaw a stroke with one knuckle, lighter than a feather. "In my line of work I see a lot of this stuff. Guys like your husband are hard-wired. And nothing sets them off like another man in the picture. I'm sorry my presence made it worse, but maybe it's best to face this now. He's not going to change."

"I wasn't hoping for change. I told you, I'm done with him."

"Good girl. Now, can I hold you for a minute?"

They were standing out in the brightly lit green tile corridor of the tiny Five Points emergency room. "Here?" Frankie looked around.

He folded his arms around her. "Right now. Right here."

She relaxed against his solid warmth immediately.

"You'll be all right." He kissed her hair. He held her close for a long while, rocking them in place.

Frankie sighed, enjoying the comfort of pressing into his chest. "I feel better already."

"Good. Now why don't I follow you back to the store and help you explain this to your sister?"

"Thank you." She sighed deeply. "I could use some support."

"I am going to personally make sure you get plenty of that."

CHAPTER ELEVEN

Even as a teenager, Markie had Kyle pegged. An a-hole. Gosh, it really did feel good to write that. Markie and Robbie may be on to something with this journaling stuff.

Of course, Robbie has strict instructions to burn this thing if I am ever, say, mowed over by a car out in front of Ardella's or something.

And, of course, that's just one more good reason to be living in town instead of out at Mother's. Avoiding Mother's meddling. I can't imagine what she was thinking, reading Markie's diary, even if my sister was only a teenager at the time. I wonder if Mother read my diaries back then? Not that it would matter. I was straight as a string in high school, skinny as one, too. A boring dweeb who married another boring dweeb. One who quickly got full of himself.

And now, it appears he's an abusive boring dweeb.

Why couldn't I see it before? Why did I have to hang on all those years? Did I think he actually loved me? No delusions about that one anymore.

Kyle used to be handsome in a silky way. I was

looking at pictures of him when I was out on the farm. Mother has family photos marching down the wall of the stairwell with military precision, arranged chronologically—Robbie's group, Markie's group, my group. Which consists mostly of Kyle and me on various vacations. Anyway, I was looking at him, really looking at him, from our wedding day to the one of us in front of our all-white Christmas tree last year, and it seemed to me that his looks didn't stand the test of time. Then one day out of the blue he started working out at the gym and coloring his hair. Got LASIK on his eyes and actually started talking about plastic surgery for his sagging jowls! I should have known something was up. The guy's like some ridiculous middle-aged cliché.

It's funny. I don't even care. My sisters don't believe me when I say this. But it's the truth. I realize now that it hurt a lot more to lose the babies than it has to lose Kyle.

It seems the cruelest blow of fate that I couldn't have a child of my own. But now that I'm forty my chances are looking really dim. Especially since I just signed divorce papers. At least I have Danielle. I don't know what I'd do if Robbie didn't bring her to the store with her every day. My precious little angel!

"SCRIBBLING in that diary again, Sissy?" Robbie was fumbling her way into the doorway of the shop with a baby carrier in one hand and a box from the bakery

balanced on the other. Frankie was perched on a stool by
the credenza, writing in her journal again, a compulsion
these days. There were so many new feelings to sort out.
She hopped down and trotted around the store's growing
miscellany to help her sister.

"Helps, doesn't it?" Robbie grunted as Frankie took the
heavy carrier holding Danielle. When her hands were free
she offered up the pastry box like a crown. "More goodies
from Luke. June Johnson over at the bakery pulled it out
when I went in to get the scones. Apparently he said he
would stop by and see how you like it later."

Luke had been true to his word. Over the past couple of
days he had given Frankie plenty of support, moral and otherwise. The goodies, as Robbie called them, and flowers—
a single rose, a clutch of daisies. And kisses—the kind that
kept her awake long into the night.

"Gosh. I'm starting to feel like I've got a real boyfriend or something." Frankie grinned at Robbie and
opened the box.

It was a giant cookie with Luke + Frankie written in red
icing across the face of it. Such silly gestures made
Frankie smile but did nothing to quell the meddlesome
gossip about the two of them that now circulated along
Main Street.

Robbie got the baby settled, and while they were hanging strings of red twinkle lights in the store window in anticipation of their official re-opening on Valentine's Day,
the sisters analyzed the gossip. And Luke.

"He's a *brave* boyfriend." Robbie grinned down from
the ladder she was standing on as Frankie handed up

another string of lights. "When June was closing the box on that cookie, she asked me who was this Luke fella. She allowed as how that was one good-looking cowboy."

"What did you tell her?"

"That he's your boyfriend."

"Stop it." Frankie slapped Robbie's calf. "It's not funny."

"I doubt he told old June anything. She probably just drooled over him while he ordered the cookie. But I'll just bet every time Luke goes into Ardella's to buy flowers she's lookin' at him like he's the devil incarnate." Robbie had been one of Luke's biggest fans ever since he'd pulled strings to get a copy of Danny's autopsy for her.

"Yeah. I imagine by now Ardella has told everybody Mother's version of…the incident."

"I imagine lots of people have heard it. Zack even knew about it. He stopped by on his way to the fire station."

"What did Zack have to say?" Frankie respected and loved her brother-in-law-to-be more with each passing day.

"He thinks Luke is plenty hung up on you. He thinks the way Luke is fixing up that Sunday house indicates a man wanting more than a little vacation home. Hand me that sticky hook."

Frankie handed one up. "What do you mean the way he's fixing it up? I thought Zack was just making some simple repairs inside."

"Simple repairs? They've knocked out the back wall, weather or not. Luke's going to add an open Texas-style country kitchen and a screened porch. If the weather warms up, they'll pour the slab this weekend and they're sealing the poured concrete floors with tinted sealer after that.

He's installing real copper fixtures. All very first-class. You still haven't seen any of this?"

"No. He keeps saying he wants to surprise me."

"Well, you'll be surprised all right. Terra-cotta floors. Crown moldings. New glass block in the bathroom. It's costing a fortune. Doesn't that sound like a man with a plan?"

"A plan?"

"You, sweetie. *You* are the plan. Luke isn't getting that house all dolled up so it'll just sit there. A man fixes a house up like that so he can move a woman into it. He knows Zack and I are getting married and moving to the farm soon and then that run-down rental on Cypress Street will be history. Not that you couldn't keep living in it if you wanted to, of course. But I think a certain man might be thinking of a future with you."

"A future? Luke hasn't indicated anything along those lines to me. We're just…dating, for heaven sakes."

"Maybe, but it's the kind of dating that leads somewhere. And I think you should go for it, Sissy, no matter what anybody else thinks."

"Anybody else?"

Robbie sighed. "Daddy told Zack that Mother blames Luke for coming between you and Kyle."

"Which is pur-dee ridiculous. *Kyle* came between me and Kyle."

"Then set her straight."

Robbie had it right again. Frankie knew she was going to have to face her mother sooner or later, but she was dreading it. She had decided Luke shouldn't be anywhere in the vicinity when the blow-up came. Fuel to the fire, and all that.

"I'll be driving out to the farm tonight—"

"Good. I'll go with you. Zack is taking the boys to the high school basketball game, so we don't even have to worry about them. So we'll load up Danielle and—"

"Alone."

FRANKIE HAD plenty of time to think as she drove the winding country roads. The weather was chilly and threatening precipitation again. Mother's attitude would no doubt be as frigid as a sleet storm, Frankie thought. So, she was prepared when Marynell's reception was cold.

Looking thin and uptight in gray sweats and snow-white jogging shoes, the older woman stood on the porch with her arms twisted tightly across her middle as Frankie pulled up in the drive.

"Hello, Frankie." She greeted her daughter as if her presence were a big pain.

She led Frankie to the kitchen and offered coffee, bristling with hostility the whole time. When she started making the coffee, her movements were brisk, defensive.

Frankie sat down at the small dinette table and started right in. "Mother, I'm not sure if Markie and Robbie ever made this clear to you, but I feel compelled to tell you that when it comes to my life, I'd appreciate it if you'd mind your own business."

Marynell's mouth popped open, and she turned her head to deliver a snotty retort but then she quickly covered her outrage. "I have no idea what you're talking about." She turned back to making the coffee.

"Yes, you do. I am talking about Kyle. You called him."

"I can't call my own son-in-law?" Marynell always managed to make her tone sound deeply offended in conversations like this.

"Not when I'm involved in a divorce action with the man. You told him I was seeing Luke. You are never, ever to speak to him about me again. Got it?"

"Too late for that." Marynell's tone became full-blown hostile now. She turned from the coffee. "I've done nothing but talk to the poor man about you for two days. In fact, he's here."

"What?" Frankie jumped up from her chair. "You should have told me that when I called!"

"You can't keep avoiding him. I wanted you to have to face up to what you've done. He's very hurt, Frankie. You have twisted this thing all out of proportion. Having him arrested, for God's sake. And by that man."

"Where is he?" Frankie looked around the small farmhouse kitchen with a genuine sense of panic.

"He's out to the hay barn with P.J. He's been here ever since he got out of jail. He turned his practice over to his partner for a few days. He's been helping us out a lot. He asked to stay here so he could find some peace and quiet. Poor man. You know his own family has never been close."

It was Kyle who had alienated his family, but Frankie didn't say so because Marynell pressed on. "But I know he's really been hoping to see you. You think your husband is the first man in the universe ever to stray? Stop acting like a child, running around with a man you hardly know, and put your mind where it belongs, repairing the life you built with your husband. Think of your history together."

"You know nothing about our history." Frankie knew she sounded angry and threatened. And she was. Why hadn't she seen Kyle's Mercedes?

"We put his car in the shed," her mother supplied as if reading her mind. "Kyle doesn't want it to get coated with ice if there's another storm. And he doesn't want any trouble on account of that silly protective order you got yourself. Honestly, Frankie, I know you are out to punish him, but must you insist on humiliating us all publicly in the process?"

"You should have told me he was here, Mother," Frankie repeated as she gathered her purse and jacket. "I don't want to see him now."

"You've made that all too clear." The voice was Kyle's. He stepped through the doorway from the mud porch. P.J. was behind him, looking hangdog and apologetic, as always.

After she cut Kyle a steely look, Frankie said, "Hi, Daddy."

"Hello, sweetheart."

Marynell made an annoyed little *pfft* sound, and P.J. stepped over to appease his wife.

"I'll be going now." Frankie tried to maneuver around Kyle but he blocked her path, grabbing her arm.

"Let go of me," she said calmly, though inside she was starting to quake. Surely he wouldn't do anything in front of her parents.

"Frankie, I admit I made a mistake, but we have got to talk."

"No. We don't. Now let go."

Kyle dropped her arm as if it was contaminated. "You see how it is," he said, turning his gaze to Marynell and P.J. "She refuses even to let me apologize. I'm afraid your daughter is becoming one bitter, angry woman." He backed into the doorway and braced a hand high on the jamb.

"She has always been headstrong," Marynell offered. "Stubborn as an old boot."

"Shut up, Mother."

Marynell gasped. "You will *not* talk to me—"

Frankie ignored her and faced Kyle. "Get out of my way, Kyle." She was going out that door even if she had to bodily knock the man aside.

"Frankie." P.J. came at her peripherally, extending his arms in placation. "Maybe it wouldn't be a bad idea for you two to talk this thing out. Divorce is a terrible thing. Sometimes you gotta bend in a marriage."

"Bend, yes," she tossed over her shoulder at her father. "Get trampled on, no." Her eyes locked on Kyle's again. "I said, get out of my way, Kyle."

"Or what?" He stepped up and grabbed her arm, twisting the flesh viciously. "Or you'll call the…*cops?*"

"Good idea," Frankie said through clenched teeth. She wrenched her arm free, daring him with her eyes to try anything more in front of her parents. She flipped her cell phone out and punched a speed dial number before Kyle grabbed the back of her hair.

"Kyle!" P.J. and Marynell both cried at once. "You let her go!" P.J. added.

Frankie twisted her head away and Kyle released her hair, but kept a grip on her arm. She managed to keep the phone pressed to her ear. *Damn.* It was Luke's voice mail that picked up. "Luke?" she spoke urgently as if the conversation were live. "It's me."

Kyle thrust her arm away.

Frankie kept talking. "I'm at my parents' and Kyle is here. And he refuses to let me lea—"

"Oh, go on then." Petulantly he flipped the fingers of one palm up at her. The gesture might as well have been a single finger.

Finally, he stepped aside to let her pass.

Frankie left without looking back. She felt bad for walking out on Daddy, but the other two could go to hell in a handbasket for all she cared.

"KYLE HAS BEEN staying over at Mother and Daddy's place," she told Robbie the minute she stepped into the old Victorian on Cypress Street. Robbie was walking the baby in the entry hall and the boys were glued to the blaring television set. The place still smelled like the pizza Zack had probably brought over before he took the boys to the game.

Tonight, Frankie found Robbie's ordinary life really comforting.

"You're kidding!" Robbie marched over to Frankie, her attention riveted.

"He's been over there sucking up to Mother and Daddy."

Danielle fussed and rooted into Robbie's shoulder. "She's teething, I think. Walk with me." They paced with the baby.

"So he *can* rearrange his precious schedule when he wants to. And now he's out there trying to drum up sympathy from our parents. What an absolute a-hole."

Frankie smiled, despite her shaken emotions. "That's what Markie always called him, even back when she was a teenager. His true character is becoming plainer to me with each passing day," Frankie sighed. "I wish I'd seen it before I married him and wasted half my life on the man."

"Better late than never." Robbie stopped pacing and faced her. "Can I tell you something, sister to sister?"

"Sure. No secrets here." Frankie reached up and patted Danielle's tiny back and the squirming warmth of the baby reassured her, too.

"Well, I never liked Kyle. My boys never liked him. And Danny could hardly stand to be in the same room with him."

Frankie smiled again. "I only wish you'd told me sooner."

"Would you have listened?"

"No, probably not. But until recently, Kyle has never gotten physically abusive with me."

Robbie frowned. "Did he pull something else?"

"Yeah. He grabbed me by the back of the hair."

Robbie's eyes went wide. "Whoa, Sissy! Have him arrested."

"I thought about it. But really I just want him gone. I called Luke but got his voice mail. I'm gonna try again." She dialed, got Luke's voice mail once more. This time she hit the button without leaving a message.

She snapped the phone shut and frowned at Robbie. "He said he'd be stuck to me like glue, but now when I need him, where the heck is he?"

LUKE KNEW what his old Uncle Beecher would have to say about his nephew's involvement with a woman caught up in the middle of a messy divorce. *Rescuer complex.*

Beecher loved to issue cautionary statements about all things relating to women. "Women with troubles'll make you forget your own troubles," Beecher would warn in his blunt way, "But only for a little bit. Then one day you wake up with a whole new set of troubles—their troubles plus yours."

Luke himself had to wonder about his entanglement in this situation. Except that he'd had a certain feeling about Frankie McBride from the get-go, before he'd ever known she was extracting herself from the clutches of an abuser. He'd only had that feeling once before. For just enough brief years to know that when a relationship was right, you knew. And once you knew, nothing was ever going to change it. He wasn't going to wake up one day and want out of this relationship for this reason or that reason.

The question wasn't what he wanted out of this relationship, it was what did *she* want?

Putting thoughts of Beecher and Frankie together caused Luke to dig out his cell phone and flip it open.

"Beech? Luke. Can you hear me okay? Cell phones don't work worth a crap up in these hills.... Yeah, I'm still in Five Points, and I'm gonna be up here for a while longer, it turns out. Listen. I need a couple of favors. Find out what you can about a guy named Kyle Hostler for me. He's a surgeon. See if he's got any kind of record. Tail him for a while, if you can. I'll get back to you. How's Philo? Being good?...I was thinking about bringing him up here with me. I bought a house.... Yeah. Imagine that. You can come up and stay, too. It'll be like our vacation place....No. I just like the town, the area. It's—...What do you mean, have I got me a woman up here or something?"

After they hung up, Luke imagined the old guy was

probably telling Philo that Luke had lost his mind, buying a Sunday house way up in the hills.

Back to the case. He dialed the number Brandon Smith's dad had given him. "Brandon? Listen, turns out I can't leave Five Points right now. I hate to ask you to drive up when the roads are so bad—"

"I have a Jeep. No problem." Brandon's youthful voice was eager. "I'm anxious to get to the bottom of this story."

And Luke wanted to know what the kid had seen. "All right. I'll meet you. But not in town."

"I know a place out on the highway," Brandon supplied. "It's called the Store."

THE STORE, Luke decided, should have been called the Hole.

He figured the name had originated as a way for the local bar flies to snooker their wives. As in, *Honey, I'm going to the store.*

He nearly missed the turnoff, save for the moonlight reflecting off the tattered marquee near the road. The parking lot was a washboard, jammed with pickups. The building itself was a tin-roofed shack, pulsing with honky-tonk music, dark except for a winking blue beer sign and a rim of light leaking under the door.

He flipped his cell phone open to call the kid, the light illuminating the cab of his pickup like a pale candle. *Great.* No signal.

He went inside. Smoke hung in the dim air, punctuated by pounding music and the occasional expletive. There were probably more strung-out meth addicts in place than in the holding cells at Huntsville.

At 10:00 p.m. the Store was just getting warmed up. At the bar a wall of backs in a variety of jackets sat stooped over cold drafts in tall mugs. In the corner, a pool table was the focus for the entertainment now and the fights later. The few ladies present were anything but.

Luke found an empty stool at the bar and kept his hat pulled low. This was no place for a good clean cop. "A draft," he told the bartender.

Eventually the door opened again and a clean-cut young man wearing a flak jacket over a white fraternity T-shirt slipped inside. Luke gave the kid a flicker of eye contact and the kid nodded.

When Luke picked up his beer and walked to the one empty booth near the bar the kid angled his way across the room. "Mr. Driscoll?" he said above the music.

"Yes," Luke said quietly despite the din. "Nice to meet you, Brandon, even in this dive."

"I can pick 'em, huh?" The kid slid into the booth. "This place is like my Mecca or something. The last time I was here, it was broad daylight and it was deserted." He surveyed his surroundings. "I actually think it looks a little less creepy in the dark."

"Maybe it's the cozy crowd."

"Yeah. That's gotta be it. They were packed in like this when I was here one night last summer, too."

Somebody over by the pool table yelled, "Sink it, Bubba!"

A man with a barbed-wire tattoo ringing his biceps made a corner shot. His triumphant smile revealed a missing front tooth. "He looks a lot like a guy that made me eat grass outside of gym class once," Brandon mumbled.

Luke chuckled. He liked this kid.

"I think I cried and wet my pants. I used to be a skinny dork." Now the kid looked like he worked out in his sleep.

"So you gave up nerddom and became a frat boy?"

"Huh? Oh. This T-shirt. My roommate's. It's like some kind of mortal sin to wear Greek insignia if you're not actually one. I'm on my way to hell, I guess."

Luke smiled. But his delight in the kid was tempered by a tiny subliminal wave of sadness that he'd grown accustomed to over the years. Bethany would be in her teens now. She had been so bright, so independent. Luke imagined she would have entertained him with this kind of banter. He had stopped mentally aging his daughter about three years into his private hell. But on occasion it would sneak up on him—like when he was talking to a brash college kid.

The bartender brought another beer. Luke aimed his index finger at Brandon and the guy plunked the mug down in front of him. "Do you drink?"

"Like a fish. Thanks." Brandon picked up the mug and took a long pull. "So, I guess my dad told you I'm a P.K."

"P.K.?"

"Preacher's kid."

"Oh, yeah. Your father seemed very proud of you. Said you were doing really well at U.T. What's your major?"

"Journalism. I'm a general assignment reporter for the *Daily Texan*. Which basically means I don't get paid any money yet." Brandon hunched forward. "I smell a big story, with the congressman at the heart of it. You show me yours. I'll show you mine."

Luke smiled again. "You first."

"Okay, here's the shrinky-dink version. Last summer I did an internship here in Five Points for Doug Curry. The guy who ran for congress against Kilgore and got his ass kicked? One night a couple of my buddies on the campaign thought it'd be a hoot to go slumming in the country bars. We were in here," he tapped the table, "when I overheard some rough-looking Mexicans talking—Chiapan dialect. Maybe Jalisco. High-mountain people, anyway."

Luke's eyebrows went up. Few knew the difference.

"I did time as a missionary."

This kid was full of surprises.

"I heard them talking about Kilgore. Anyway, I listened in, thinking it would be so cool to catch the congressman doing something hinky with illegals, and you know, use it against him to help Curry. They were talking about looking for some *stuff* that the congressman had. And they were talking about Juan and Julio, like they knew where the *stuff* was and like, you know how machismo Mexicans can talk, like they'd kill them if they didn't fork it over.

"I told my dad, my birth dad, about it at the time. I didn't know he was my dad then, of course. He told me he was worried about the Morales brothers. They had just disappeared. I guess he had good reason to worry, huh? I mean, I hear their sister's been murdered."

But Luke didn't tell the kid the Morales boys had contacted him about Maria's death. He didn't tell him about his pictures of the shaft into a gutted Mayan tomb in Chiapas. He was here to find out what the kid knew, not spill his guts to some cub reporter.

"If you ask me it all goes back to those caves. I actually caught the congressman in there one night."

Luke's eyes widened over the rim of his beer mug. This was what he wanted to hear. "So I heard. From your parents."

"Really? I didn't tell them anything about it. My mom would have a cow sideways if she knew I'd had a gun pulled on me."

"I meant your birth parents."

"Oh. Markie and Justin."

Luke could tell the kid had no more attachment to them than he would to a distant aunt and uncle. Luke wondered how the couple had recovered from losing a kid like this. Letting him go. Finding him. Letting him go. One thing for sure, there was plenty of brokenness to go around in this world.

Brandon pulled a face. "I've been investigating the whole deal ever since the old guy threatened to kill me, but I'm getting nowhere." Evidently he didn't think of the congressman as a grandfather, either. "Then I saw on the news about some Coyote suspected in the murder of a girl down on the border, and her name's Morales. I wondered if there was a connection. Juan and Julio are her brothers, right?"

"You get an A."

"I like to pretend I'm a real reporter, even without the paycheck. It's not like this stuff hasn't been thwacking me in the face. Now what?"

Luke sat up straight, leaning in on his elbows. "I think the Coyotes you overheard in this bar might be the same Coyotes who killed Maria, the same Coyotes I saw out at the sinkhole."

"I think so too, sir." Brandon planted his elbows, too, straining to hear over the pounding music.

"I think they were out there trying to find a way into the caves short of dropping themselves down into that sinkhole. A way that you stumbled on when you followed the congressman. The question is, what are they after? I intend to answer that question."

Brandon gave him a small nod. "I'd like to answer that one too, sir."

"Think you could show me that other entrance?"

"I can sure try. I want to find out what's in there as bad as you do. This is the kind of story that might actually get me *paid*."

If Luke's suspicions were confirmed, it was the kind of story that would launch Brandon Smith's career. "Good. We'll go in, but we'll have to wait for this weather to clear. There's too much ice on those rocks for us—or them—to scale that limestone now."

"Yes, sir."

Luke looked around the bar. "Another thing. Do you remember what those guys looked like?"

"One looked like your typical Mexican. Smallish. But the other one stood out. Huge. Big scar." Brandon traced a finger from his eye to his mouth.

Luke unsnapped the breast pocket of his cowboy shirt and fished out a paper. He unfolded it and spread it on the table. "Like this?"

"Wow." Brandon stared at the picture. "That's him."

"Izek Texcoyo." Luke folded the paper away. "Did this guy talk about the congressman?"

"Oh, yeah. Fatso was doing most of the yakking. About how they'd be stinking rich when they found the *stuff*. The little one just kept saying *bueno*."

This was the thing Izek Texcoyo had lusted for, killed for. This *stuff* in the caves. Of its potency, Luke had long since been certain. Now its monetary value was established as well.

There were a few Hispanic-types scattered around the bar right now. "You don't recognize anybody in here tonight?"

Brandon looked around from face to face, then shook his head. "No."

A scowling man caught Brandon's gaze and swayed unsteadily on his barstool, listing heavily in the direction of their booth.

"Uh-oh," Brandon said under his breath. "I sense a disturbance in the Force."

About that same time the drunk bellowed, "What're you lookin' at, kid?"

"Nuthin'," Brandon said with a nerdy squeak that would have made any ectomorph proud.

The guy growled and made to stand up.

"Time to go bye-bye." Luke tossed a ten spot on the table and they were gone.

CHAPTER TWELVE

P. J. McBRIDE was a patient man, but at the moment he was fed up with Marynell and her harping and her endless meddling. For the first time in their forty-three-year marriage, he was mad enough to confront his wife about her behavior.

But what really had him riled was the way his son-in-law had just treated Frankie. Kyle had always been a little too big for his britches anyway. P.J. believed in being respectful, and he expected the same from Kyle, an educated man and all.

He knew they'd had their troubles, and that, excepting for him and Marynell, all couples fought. But what had just happened had been especially ugly. What if Frankie's claims were true? What if it wasn't at all like Marynell said?

After all, Marynell had been wrong about things before. Look how wrong she was about Markie and Justin. The boy did love Markie, it turned out. He would have wanted that baby, even though they were young. Thank God they were happily married now. Yes, Marynell had been wrong about all of it. So wrong. He considered all of these things before he spoke.

"Kyle, I know you claim Frankie can push your buttons,

but you should not have tried to keep her here against her will just now."

Kyle was rummaging in their refrigerator. "You still have no wine?" He addressed this with genuine irritation to Marynell.

"There's beer," she said meekly.

Kyle drank a little too steadily, P.J. had noticed.

"Nobody tried to keep anybody from going anywhere, Pops." He added the last word pointedly before he took out a beer and twisted off the cap.

P.J. didn't like that habit of Kyle's, calling him Pop or Pops as if P.J. were old and addled. It dawned on him that this was disrespect of the kind that Kyle had probably dished out to Frankie. But he was not going to be deflected by a little bit of high-handed talk. With a determination he'd never felt before, he returned to the matter at hand. "No, Kyle. I'm sorry. I saw what you did. And I heard everything you said. The way you asked her if she was gonna call the cops or what was a threat, like you was daring her to—"

"Oh, for heaven sakes," Marynell interrupted. "Stop blaming Kyle for this mess. Frankie is just as much at fault as he is. He was only trying to talk to the woman. He's trying to get his wife back, to save his marriage *and* the secure life he built for her."

Marynell was hinting again, in her not-too-subtle way, at the fact that the life P.J. had built for *her* had not been all that secure at times, and P.J. was sick of her harping. He really was. He felt his face growing warm.

"This is between me and Kyle, Marynell, and I'm asking you to…please be quiet."

"I will not be silenced in my own kitchen!" Marynell took two tense steps across the space until she was right in P.J.'s face. "Your spoiled daughters," she hissed, "can treat me like dirt, but I will be damned if I take it from my own husband in my own house."

"It's *your* house, all right. And that's just the beginning of the problem, ain't it?" P.J. felt his ire rising along with his color. "It was your idea to invite this man to stay here, no matter what I thought."

"He is our *son-in-law!*" Marynell gaped at P.J. as if he were some kind of monster, talking that way in front of Kyle.

But Kyle seemed not to care what was being said. He had slumped into a dinette chair, and was sucking down the beer with a detached expression on his face.

"And it was also your harebrained idea to try to get them back together. Why are you always interfering like this? You don't know everything about people's lives, Marynell. You don't know what's happened between people."

"What nonsense are you talking now?" She coiled her skinny arms into a twisted rope across her belly. "Kyle has been out here for two whole days, licking his wounds—"

Kyle emitted a disgruntled, "Hmph," then just kept on drinking as if the three of them weren't even in the same room.

"And in all that time I haven't said so much as one word to the girl. It took her this long to come out and see me, I expect, because she felt so guilty about our last conversation."

"What conversation was that?" P.J. jutted his neck, well aware that with Marynell he was always in over his depth. He felt an uncomfortable pulse of dread beating at his temple. But by George, this time he was not backing down.

"For your information your daughter, Miss Frankie, said some very hurtful, very hateful things to me a few days ago in Robbie's store. You are the one who doesn't know everything, old man."

"*Frankie* was hateful to you?" That didn't sound like the daughter who always kept her cool, who was always ladylike and gentle-spoken. But he had to admit that lately, in the wake of this separation from her husband, Frankie had been changing.

"Yes. She called me an ugly name. I won't repeat it, but it hurt my feelings. It was all I could do to keep from crying until I got to my car."

"Why would she do that?"

"I have no idea. I was only trying to talk sense into her about—" Marynell's voice grew hushed, shamed "—about seeing that man."

"Are you talking about Luke Driscoll?" P.J. refused to whisper in his own kitchen because of Kyle. The man could dern well get up off his arrogant ass and go into the living room if he didn't like what was being said. But instead of leaving, Kyle had gotten up, gone to their fridge, and extracted another beer for himself.

Marynell pursed her lips and cut a cautious glance toward the table where Kyle resumed his steady tipping of the second bottle to his lips. "Yes," she hissed at length. "The two of them have been—" she lowered her voice "—seeing each other."

"Well if they have, is that any of *our* business?" Again, P.J. did not bother to lower his voice.

"It *is* our business when she's humiliating this family in front of the whole town like some teenaged tramp!"

P.J. felt the flush rise all the way to his bald pate. Marynell was a fine one to call her own daughter that. "*Now* who's calling names?"

"Well it's true. If she thinks running around with that man—"

"Marynell, maybe you better just shut up!"

"Oh!" She puffed up instantly. "Where did you get that kind of talk?"

She had a point there. It was not like P.J. to tell anyone to shut up, least of all her. They had never allowed rudeness in their home, and he felt wrong to start it now. He took a deep cleansing breath. "I am sorry."

Marynell ignored the apology and shook a finger in his face. "I can tell you exactly where all the hatefulness started in this family. It started back when your ungrateful, spoiled daughter Markie got herself pregnant!"

P.J.'s attempt at calm vanished. "Don't bring Markie into this! The harm you did her can never be fixed!"

"The harm *I* did her?" Marynell exploded. "What about the harm she did to this family? Do you realize Robbie signed over her farm, *our* farm, *my father's farm, my grandfather's farm*," she jabbed a bony finger into her birdlike chest as her voice rose to the ceiling, "to protect Markie's dirty little secret?"

"You don't give a big green bean about that farm," P.J. accused. It felt good to be speaking the truth. *Great,* in fact. "You just wanted to rub Kurt Kilgore's nose in it one more time."

"How dare you bring up that man's name in my house!"

"It's my house, too, Marynell. You keep forgetting that.

And this is *my* farm, humble as it is, not some extension of your father's. This land has been in the McBride family, *my* family for longer than that rocky strip over by the river had been in yours. You only wanted to get that piece of no-good hilly crap back because Kurt had finally become the Kilgore heir and you didn't want him to have it." He paused for breath and to collect his courage.

This next part was hard. This next part would cost him plenty probably, but after forty-three years, it was high time to slap the cards on the table. He had held them close to his chest for far too long.

"You never got over him did you? Or the way he dumped you? Some part of you has always thought that you should have been the congressman's wife. I was just a poor substitute, wasn't I, Marynell?" *Good God,* this truth thing did feel good, it really did. Even if it was making him a little short of breath. "You always wanted to take a little piece out of Kurt's hide, and you used Markie's misfortune to do it."

"Her *misfortune?*" Marynell's coloring was flaming as high as his was now. "That child was screwing Kilgore's son! Kurt was the one who didn't want his precious son dragged through the mud. He was only too happy to offer up the farm for our silence—"

"*Our* silence? Wasn't no *our* about it, woman. You never told me a thing about any of it. Not Markie's condition. Not that low-down deal you made for the farm. None of it. I have to find out I have a grandson eighteen years later when I am looking the boy right in the face."

"You couldn't have handled the truth if I'd told it to you!

You never could. I did what was right for this family. Robbie and Danny needed a place to live. And Danny was never cut out for anything but farming."

"Oh, now you're going to try and lay it on poor old Danny, may he rest in peace. It wasn't about helping Danny, Marynell. It was about what *you* wanted. It's always been about what you wanted."

"You don't know what you're talking about. Kurt asked me to name anything. Anything I wanted, anything Markie wanted. I got my grandfather's farm back, yes, but I also got Danny and Robbie a place to live in the process. And I would have kept the whole thing too, had it back in the family intact where it belonged, if Markie hadn't popped up with this boy—" Marynell stopped abruptly.

"What are you talking about, woman? Robbie signed that farm over because she couldn't afford to keep it."

"I know *I* certainly never approved of Markie's loose behavior." A disembodied voice floated up from the vicinity of the table. "Or of that deception with the maternity home in Austin that she and Frankie tried to pull."

The couple stared at their son-in-law as if he'd materialized out of thin air. Having polished off a third bottle of beer, Kyle was sitting stupefied, with a slack, bitter expression on his face.

"You stay out of this," P.J. warned.

"What is your problem, Pops?" Kyle came suddenly alert. He bolted out of the chair, swayed and burped. "You got some kind of hair up your ass of a sudden?"

Marynell blinked. The refined surgeon couldn't have shocked her more if he'd picked his nose.

"My problem is with you, fella." Between this little prick and Marynell, P.J. had had just about enough. "I think you'd better leave my house and get your sorry butt back to Austin and abide by that protective order."

For one instant Kyle adopted an aggressive stance with fists balled, but then he went all slack again. "I'll be more than happy to get out of here." He cast about for his coat, which was on a hook by the door. "I only came to this dump in the first place hoping I might get a chance to see Frankie."

"Don't let the door hit you in the butt on your way out." P.J. stomped to the hooks and grabbed the coat, flinging it overhanded at Kyle's head.

When he lowered his arm, a flood of bottled-up anger and agitation hit him like a sledgehammer in the chest. He wanted to belt Kyle, but instead found himself sinking into the nearest chair. All of a sudden he couldn't talk. He couldn't think. He couldn't breathe.

"P.J.!" It was Marynell's shrill command. "P.J.! What's wrong?! *Look* at me!" Her frightened voice seemed far, far away.

"Do something!" he heard Marynell scream.

And then everything went black.

"HE HAD a major heart attack." Zack, one of the firefighters who answered Marynell's distress call, was explaining things to the McBride sisters in the hallway of the hospital where Kyle was on staff in Austin. "If Kyle hadn't been there to give him CPR, he would have died."

"Thank God for that," Markie breathed.

Frankie wasn't so sure. Markie still didn't know the

whole story of what Kyle had done at the farm, so she couldn't be blamed for her reflexive gratitude. But Frankie was wishing anybody but her estranged husband had been the one to save her father's life.

Here they were, called to Austin in the middle of the night, and Kyle lurking over there at the nurses' station like some white knight, waiting for her to come and express her appreciation. No telling what emotional blackmail he would wring from this. Or Mother.

Frankie needed to know what happened. How long after her abrupt departure had the heart attack occurred? Was this her fault? Her father had looked awfully flushed when she'd left.

She went over to Kyle to get details. Before she could stop him, he had clasped her in an emotional hug. "My poor baby," he said. The nurse looking on probably thought Frankie was the luckiest woman in the world. "I'm so sorry this happened. Especially now…" he glanced at the nurse, who buried her nose in a chart "…when you won't let me be with you."

How dare he act the role of the rejected but loving husband! "Kyle, I…" Frankie put a palm on his chest as if patting him, but with the last pat she subtly levered him away.

He let her go.

"Thank you for…being there," she said because she felt she had to, but she quickly added, "For Daddy."

"I'm just glad I was. Hell of a thing," he said. "One minute your parents were arguing about Markie, about, you know, the, uh, adoption." Kyle gave her a look that said he'd always known *that* would come to no good. "I didn't pay attention to everything they were saying—I admit I had a couple of beers in me, though I'm not anywhere near impaired, of course."

"Of course not." He seemed sober as a judge. How well he could disguise his drinking. Frankie was suddenly wondering if Kyle had ever done surgery while he was "not anywhere near impaired."

Her attention refocused as Kyle started going on about how Marynell had apparently had a romance with Kurt Kilgore when she was young and how that was apparently a sore point with P.J.

"Mother and…and Kurt Kilgore?" There was never a more unlikely match.

Kyle seemed intrigued by the idea. "Yeah. Imagine. I guess you could have been a congressman's daughter, if things had gone differently."

"Perish the thought." Frankie couldn't stand Kurt Kilgore. The pompous ass hadn't even come to his own son's wedding.

"Well, your dad seems to think Marynell still hasn't gotten over him. They were really going at it. And then all of a sudden he just collapses into a chair. But really…" Kyle drew her to the opposite side of the corridor as if wanting to speak confidentially. "Your dad was already pretty upset over their argument about this Luke guy. The man is nothing but trouble, Frankie, waving a gun and trying to come between us like that."

Frankie closed her eyes. If she could only open them knowing that she would never have to look at Kyle Hostler again…. "Kyle." She kept her eyes on the floor. "I think I need to go in with the others and talk to the heart doctor now."

"Maybe I should go with you." He tried to tip her chin up with his finger but she jerked away.

Honestly, had the man not one single honest bone in his body? "No." She was not going to allow Kyle to use her father's close call as a reason to insinuate himself back into the family. But even so, as she walked off she felt guilty and conflicted for all of her spiteful thinking.

It was nearly midnight, but the cardiac surgeon wanted to go ahead with open-heart surgery. So, they waited on stiff green vinyl couches in an empty waiting room with harsh fluorescent lights and industrial gray carpeting. Frankie let her sisters console and control their mother by turns. She just couldn't do it. Her anger and guilt seemed too vast.

When Marynell finally went to sleep with a hard hospital pillow and a waffle-weave blanket, the McBride girls withdrew to a tiny adjacent family conference room to pow-wow and come to a decision.

"Kyle admits he was drinking," Frankie started in, "so he wasn't paying real close attention, but he told me enough." After Frankie told them the abridged version of what had happened that night, Robbie spoke first.

"Wow. Mother and Kurt Kilgore were sweethearts? That's just too weird. Well, maybe she was different back then."

"You mean maybe *he* was," Markie said. She had no great affection for her pompous father-in-law. "Or…maybe that's what made her so hard."

"She married the wrong man," Frankie said. *Was* she like her mother?

The three sisters exchanged looks. "Poor Daddy," Robbie said. "Mother will be upset if we try to interfere."

This from Robbie, the peacemaking middle child, who still had to battle the impulse to placate her mother at times.

"Nevertheless, we have to think of Daddy's health and make arrangements to protect him," Frankie insisted. "He doesn't need more of her rejection now."

"And Mother won't be able to hold her temper for long," Markie agreed. "Daddy won't have a moment of peace. She'll kill him for sure."

"He's got a few more days in the hospital. Why don't we wait and see what Daddy wants to do?" Robbie suggested.

P.J. SURPRISED THEM ALL when he came to a couple of days later. First, with stiffened lips, he asked Marynell to please leave the room.

She pressed a tissue to her mouth and did so without argument.

"I don't have much strength, so hear me out. I've had a narrow escape here, girls." P.J.'s voice was weak and quiet. All three daughters gathered around his ICU bed, clutching at his hands. "And I realize now, more than ever, that life is too short to put up with the rasp of a contentious wife. I don't intend to patch things up with your mother until she gets herself some help."

"Help?" Robbie leaned in. "What do you mean, Daddy?"

"Counseling. I may be a stodgy old farmer but I know about counseling and such. And your moth—" he coughed dryly "—needs some."

Frankie held the cup and straw so he could take a sip of water. "She loves you, Daddy," Robbie said while he drank. Frankie didn't contradict her. Somewhere in her training she dimly remembered some research that showed heart patients fared better when they felt genuinely loved by their spouse.

But P.J. shook his head. "Nope, she doesn't. I do not believe the woman knows the meaning of that word. Maybe she did at one time, when she was very young, but it wasn't me she loved back then." He seemed submerged in deep thought as he caught his breath.

His daughters looked at each other uncomfortably. This was not their complacent father talking.

"I am not even sure why the woman married me, looking back, except probably for security. And she claims I never gave her near enough of that. For years I tried to make her happy, stayed out of her way, but I tell you I am fed up."

"Daddy—"

"Let me say my piece. Even at this late date in her life, I am gonna insist that your mother change her ways. She's an unhappy woman who's been critical and just plain mean all her life, even to you girls. It has got to stop. Counseling is the first step, as I see it. I should have made her go and get some a long time ago. And another thing. I refuse to stay in the same house with her until she agrees to it."

This was as much as the three girls had heard P.J. say of a piece in their entire lives. And it was far more decisive than anything their mild-mannered father had ever said before. By the time he was done, all three of his daughters were looking at each other with tears in their eyes.

WHEN THEY SOUGHT OUT Marynell in the waiting room she was standing, rigid with defensiveness, her arms tucked around her middle, staring out a window.

"How is he?" She turned when they came in.

"He took a sip of water," Robbie supplied. "And talked a little."

"You blame me for this." Marynell bit her lip, seeming truly contrite.

"Nobody blames you," Markie said.

"Yes, you do. All of you." Marynell pressed the shredded tissue to her mouth. She had cried so much her eyelids were swollen. Frankie could almost believe her mother genuinely loved her father. The fear in her aging eyes was real. "I can't believe he sent me away like that!" She drew a shuddering breath. "I suppose he told you we were having a terrible argument when it happened. But it wasn't all my fault. Kyle blew up at him, too."

"Kyle?" Frankie stepped forward.

"Yes. Kyle was drinking and being surly, and P.J. threw his coat at him and told him to get out. That's when he collapsed."

This was not the story Kyle had told her. In some perverse way, Frankie felt vindicated for her suspicions of his motives earlier.

"And I'm sure all this *other* stress didn't help." Over the tissue Marynell shot Frankie an accusing look, clearly indicating that *she* was the main source of that other stress. "I am amazed I haven't had a heart attack myself."

"Mother, listen," Frankie said, seeing her opening. "It

might help you cope with all of this if we can get you a little counseling."

"Counseling?" The tissue came down. "Counseling? For *me?* Oh, that's very funny coming from someone who's made a complete mess of her own life! I am not the one who needs counseling! At least I have stuck by *my* husband."

"And I think when it comes time to bring Daddy home—" by an act of will, Frankie kept the focus off herself and went on calmly "—I'll come out to the farm with you. You have been under a great deal of stress lately, with the strange incident out at the caves and all. And you are going to need a lot of help."

"We'll all take turns and come out and help you," Markie jumped in.

"That way, you'll never have to take care of him by yourself," Robbie reinforced.

Marynell held the tissue away from her mouth, suspended in midair as if having a sudden insight, then she gripped it to her bony bosom. "You all don't want to leave him alone with me, is that it? You don't trust me to take good care of him!"

"No, Mother," Robbie protested, hands stretched forth. "It's just that it's hard, taking care of someone who's just had open-heart surgery."

"By George, P.J. is *my* husband." Marynell's color was rising and her voice with it. "And I can take better care of him than any of you selfish girls."

"Mother." Frankie tried to sound reasonable, but with Marynell that could always backfire. "Let's keep our voices down. We're in a hospital."

"Oh, we wouldn't want to embarrass the big doctor's wife, is that it?"

Frankie felt her gut tightening as it always did when her mother's anger escalated. "I don't care what anybody in this place thinks of me." That was so true that saying it aloud actually made Frankie's heart light for one instant. "We just wouldn't want to disturb the patients."

"Oh, Miss Noble Nurse, are you?" Marynell said sarcastically. "How *dare* you come to me now, of all times, and suggest that I need counseling!"

"It's what Daddy wants," Markie blurted. Markie was the one who had never been intimidated by her mother's underhanded tactics.

Marynell practically staggered backward. "*P.J.* wants me to get counseling?"

"Yes." Markie seemed willing to be blunt. "In fact, he said he doesn't intend to patch things up with you until you get help."

"Well, just let him stay mad then. I am not going to any counselor."

"Mother," Frankie said calmly, though her heart was pounding, "he said he is not going home with you until you agree to see a counselor."

"*What?* That is just plain ridiculous! He's pumped full of drugs. Doesn't know what he's saying. Who will take care of him, way out there on that farm, if I don't?"

"Frankie's a nurse." Markie's tone remained brisk.

Frankie shot Markie a look that said her hard attitude wasn't helping. Markie never did know how to handle Mother short of taking out the flame thrower.

"Frankie hasn't practiced nursing in twenty years! And she doesn't give a fig about P.J.'s needs. Everybody knows all she can think about is chasing after that Ranger." Marynell's rage erupted into the attack Frankie had dreaded. "And you—" their mother turned her thin, tense frame on Markie "—you and Kurt Kilgore's spoiled brat of a son, out there on that ranch with your silly so-called humanitarian work. Only a couple of miles down the road, and do you ever come over?"

"And you—" Robbie was next "—you and your stupid craft store and your gah-gah romance with that firefighter." She slapped a bony hand at the trio. "Every one of you! So wrapped up in your own doings that you've hardly had time to notice that that farm out there—" Marynell stabbed a finger in the general direction of Five Points "—is falling down around our ears. Your dad has to almost die of a heart attack before you pay any attention to the parents who raised you, even if it wasn't in fine style."

"None of us has a problem with the way we were raised," Frankie countered. At least not materially, she added in her own mind. Emotionally was another matter.

"Mother," Markie chimed in, "we care about you and we care about the farm."

"Oh, bah! You couldn't get away from it fast enough when you were a teenager."

That comment was so cruel it didn't deserve a response. The reason Markie had left the farm was to have her baby in secret.

Red-headed Robbie, usually the most soft-hearted of the three sisters and the one most likely to be hurt by Marynell's tongue, actually called her mother on her baiting. "Mother, stop it," she said forcefully. "This isn't about *style* or how much money you and Daddy had, or what anybody did as a teenager. It's about the way you treat Daddy *now*. It's disrespectful. And you are accountable for that."

"I always did my level best with the little we had!" Marynell blasted on as if Robbie hadn't even spoken. "It is not my fault P.J. was such a poor provider."

"That is exactly what I am talking about!" Robbie's fiery side boiled over. "Daddy did as well as other farmers in his day. You have no right to attack him."

Frankie stepped up, assuming the leadership mantle of the oldest sister. "All right. Let's just let the counselor handle this. Mother, you are going to try some counseling and see what happens. It might make you a happier person."

"*You* try a little counseling," Marynell said, fuming at her. "You're the one who's bound and determined to mess up her life. I will not sit here and take any more of this." She gathered up her purse, coat, a thermos from home. "You girls want to take care of your father? Have at it." And with that, their mother was gone.

MARYNELL LEFT Austin in a blaze of anger, burning up the road to the farm in her little minivan. She returned to the outskirts of Austin in the night, the girls later learned from Ardella, where she took up residence with her sister-in-law Roberta, retired and living in luxury with her golf-addicted husband in a white stucco mansion at the crest of a hill.

P.J. surprised his daughters again by taking the news of his wife's departure from the farm with stoicism.

"She'll be right at home in that *mons-shroshitty* Roberta and Don built for themselves," he said. "Place gives me the creeps. Five bathrooms! Maybe Marynell'll finally have enough shitters for all 'er crap!" He chuckled at his own slurry joke.

P.J.'s bravado was drug-induced, but for the girls it was better than watching his poor old surgeried heart break to pieces. After that he settled in peaceably and let his daughters take care of him. Things got unnaturally mellow in the McBride family, at least for the remaining days of P.J.'s hospitalization.

But then the weather warmed up.

CHAPTER THIRTEEN

I have little to do here in the coronary care waiting room except write in my journal and read Robbie's stash of romance novels. The novels are fun, but they make me miss Luke all the more.

I go and tend to Daddy when he's not sleeping. We've done a lot of talking. He told me he was so glad I've gotten away from Kyle. I told him I can't imagine why I stayed so long. The only way I can explain it is that it was some kind of sick habit. Like a rotten old security blanket. But my head is clearing more day by day. And I am getting stronger, day by day.

The only pain I feel now is from never having a child. I told Daddy that this divorce means I probably will never give him grandchildren. I got a little emotional then, I'm afraid. Daddy doesn't need that, not in his condition. But he was great about it. He patted my hand and told me we would see all of those babies in heaven.

He told me he still has Great-Grandma McBride's diary and that I should read it when we get back to the farm. (I hope Mother didn't throw it out. I hate to say it, but that would be just like her.)

Anyway, Daddy said that Great-Grandma went through some of the same things I have. This amazed me. She lost several babies, back in those hard pioneer days. He said she wrote about looking forward to seeing a baby named Claire in heaven. He patted my hand and said it would help me to see how she turned out, with a house full of kids and all.

I can almost see the pages turning and turning in the Texas wind, like the endless days in the endless cycle of life.

Yesterday, when Daddy woke up from his nap, he seemed a little blue. But he looked out the window and said that soon spring will come to the Hill Country, as if he was holding on, waiting for the wildflowers to bloom.

As for myself, even though I have no idea what the future holds, I am actually looking forward to spring, to change, to seeing Luke again.

THE WARMING WINDS of change blew into Five Points the day Frankie took P.J. home from the hospital. A strong winter sun and the promise of spring pushing up from the ground seemed to melt the last patches of ice from within.

The checking-out and last-minute instructions and loading up at the hospital had seemed endless, and indeed, it was now already late afternoon. Small herds of cattle, barns and scattered horses in the fields cast long shadows, but not another car or truck or human was in sight.

The farm was quiet, too. Marynell had put her kitchen

in perfect order. One last time? Frankie wondered. And in the puritanically appointed quarters of the downstairs bedroom that P.J. had shared with Marynell, the drawers were all closed, though some were empty now, and the bed was neatly made.

Frankie got her dad settled in his recliner for a nap, and went upstairs to the dormitory-style attic room to unpack her things, all the whole while worrying, worrying, about her father's emotional state.

What a mess their family had become. Markie with a son she did not know. Robbie widowed by a hideous act of arson. Herself divorcing, with a nasty protective order against her estranged husband. And now their dad, recovering from a close call with death, left all alone, abandoned by their shrewish mother.

She sighed and went to one of the tall, narrow dormer windows. The vast black-soil fields of her father's farm, lying fallow now in the last dregs of winter, came alive with fall color in her mind's eye.

Her mother had been outside, ready for church in a sky-blue polyester pants suit, tapping her Hush Puppy-clad foot on the boards of the back porch. "Don't be such a poke!" she had yelled at P.J., who was inching the Sunday car out of the narrow shed at the end of drive.

Twenty-one-year-old Frankie, home from nursing school for fall break, came up beside Marynell.

"You're not going to church dressed like that?" Marynell eyed Frankie's baggy sweatshirt and leg warmers.

"I'm not going to church at all. I have to study."

"You really should attend church when you're home and

make it clear that you are still practicing, or Pastor might not be willing to marry you when the time comes. He's made Robbie and Danny jump through hoops, you know."

Frankie remembered thinking this might be a good opportunity to tell her mother that she and Kyle were getting married at the courthouse without the big church wedding Marynell had been hoping for. Money was tight; Kyle needed to study for the MCAT.

But before Frankie could broach the subject, a big white car rounded the corner at the base of the hill, pulling slowly into the driveway, bumping over the cattle guard and through the gate. Frankie squinted at it. It was a big old Cadillac El Dorado.

"Who is *that?*" When she'd turned to look at her mother, Marynell's mouth was pinched up like a persimmon and two spots of crimson had stained her cheeks.

"How *dare* he!" Marynell whispered aloud before she realized her daughter was looking at her.

"Who is that, Mother?" Frankie repeated.

Marynell stared at Frankie. "Go in the house," she snapped. "And tell Markie and Robbie to stay in there with you."

She had obeyed, bounding up the narrow stairs to the attic room where her sisters were still getting ready for church.

The two older girls had peered out this very dormer window and watched while Markie sat on one of the twin beds, hugging her waist.

"Wow. That's sure a big car. What is it?" Robbie had said.

"A Cadillac," Markie mumbled from her perch on the bed.

"Huh?" The older sister glanced back at the teenager.

"How does she know?" she mumbled to Frankie. "She's not even looking."

Frankie shushed her. Something was really not right here.

The Cadillac rolled to a stop, blocking P.J.'s way just as he was righting the family Ford to point down the driveway.

Marynell marched up to a tall man in a three-piece suit as he was unfolding himself out of the Cadillac, while P.J. sat idling the engine of the Ford, his frowning face partially obscured by the glare on the windshield.

The tall man held out a sheaf of papers to Marynell and Marynell snatched them from his hand.

They exchanged sharp words, their voices briefly raised, then lowering again to an inaudible level.

"Who is he?" Robbie asked.

"Kurt Kilgore," Markie muttered glumly from the bed.

"The congressman?" Robbie looked at Markie again, who sat motionless, staring as if she'd just been given the death sentence. "My gosh! That's Congressman Kurt Kilgore?"

"Hush!" Frankie poked Robbie.

"Why?" Robbie breathed in a whisper. Then she peered out the window again. "It looks like they're fighting. I wonder what the trouble is."

By that January Frankie had discovered what the trouble was. Her seventeen-year-old sister Markie was pregnant.

She suspected, though Markie would never confirm it, that Justin Kilgore was the father. And it was nineteen years before she learned that her mother had traded the promise of an abortion for the title to the farm where her sister Robbie had settled.

A ball of orange evening sun backlit the old windmill that

in her mind had always stood for her father. Decent and kind, he deserved none of the past, none of this. The live oaks that hugged close below the old windmill were dripping with melting ice, each droplet like a brief streak of peace as it fell to ground. The stock tank had dark circles of water where Zack, who had been taking care of the animals for P.J., had chopped holes in the ice with his firefighter's ax.

Would this place deteriorate if Mother never came back? Marynell had sent word, through poor shocked Ardella, that she would not return. How could a wife of forty-three years leave her husband in his worst moment of crisis? But Frankie knew that in Marynell's mind she was the one who was being wronged, the one shoved away. It was so ironic it made Frankie's head hurt.

But at least now spring was pushing through and when the bluebonnets bloomed, Zack and Robbie would marry and move onto the farm next door to P.J. That would help. He was crazy about those three boys.

As her galloping thoughts settled down, she found herself looking out on the mellow twilight scene and missing Luke again. He had come to the hospital once, but the nurses wouldn't let him into the ICU unit because he wasn't family. So she had missed seeing him in person, though they had talked on the phone every day.

Kyle, on the other hand, came by every time he was in the building for rounds. She did nothing to enforce the protective order, which she had come to realize was nothing but a piece of paper. If Kyle was going to do her harm, he would. Physically, emotionally, financially, he would.

Maybe, she had begun thinking during their long days

apart, it would be wiser not to see Luke again. At least not until the divorce was final.

But that evening Luke showed up, bearing a Western paperback novel for P.J. and fresh flowers for Frankie. With Brandon Smith at his side.

FRANKIE WAS STRUCK AGAIN by how handsome Brandon was. Well, so was Justin. So was Markie. Wouldn't they automatically produce a beautiful child?

"Hi." He smiled with orthodontically-straightened teeth. "We met at the wedding. I'm Brandon and you're my Aunt Frankie."

"Yes," Frankie breathed. *Aunt* sounded so strange, coming from the mouth of this adult child. "Come in."

As Luke came in behind him, his eyes looked so understanding, so beautiful beneath the brim of his Stetson that she wanted to kiss his mouth right then and there. "Hi," she said.

"Hi." The minute Luke stepped inside he pulled her into a tight hug. He wasn't hiding anything from anyone, evidently. But P.J. had only met him on two occasions. She hoped he was mindful of that.

"How's your dad?" he asked.

"Doing real well. About ready to get up from his nap, I expect. Come on in and sit down."

"I just wanted to see my grandfather," Brandon explained. "You know, one more time."

"I see." Frankie looked from man to man, unable to reconcile why they were here together, but she knew Luke would explain it eventually. "I'm cooking dinner. Do you guys want to stay?"

Texas men rarely turned down a meal.

She led them into the commodious, well-lit, well-scrubbed, rigidly appointed kitchen of Marynell McBride.

P.J. appeared in the doorway in flannel robe and slippers with a sleep whorl smashed into what little hair he had in the back. "Thought I heard company."

"Luke Driscoll." Luke stood and extended his hand.

"I remember. The Ranger." P.J. shook his hand.

"I hope you're feeling better, sir." This was Brandon, also with his hand out.

As they shook hands P.J.'s face became emotional again, as it had by constant turns since his brush with death. And again, Frankie worried.

She set the table, checked the roast and pronounced dinner a half hour away, so they went into the living room and talked while the slow cooker finished its work.

Luke finally got around to the reason Brandon was here. "In the morning, Brandon and I are going to go out to the caves and look around."

"Really?" Frankie sat up straighter. "Is that safe? Going down in the caves without professional guides?" Frankie didn't want one more thing to happen to one more loved one, Luke especially. When had she started thinking of him as a loved one?

"There is no other way right now. The local judge won't issue a search warrant. Without a piece of paper, I can't justify the expense of spelunkers."

"Ah." P.J. flapped a hand. "I expect that old judge is in Kurt Kilgore's pocket. All of 'em are." He had always spoken of the congressman bitterly this way. Now Frankie knew why.

"Don't worry." Luke squeezed Frankie's hand.

"So, you're still tryin' to figure out what those varmints were up to out there?" P.J. said cheerfully.

"Yes sir," Brandon answered instead of Luke. "I'm an investigative reporter. Well, hoping to be one, anyway. I think there's a story in those caves. I started looking into it when I was in town last summer. I overheard some men talking in a bar, that Luke here thinks were Mexican Coyotes."

"Really now?" P.J. perked up even more.

"Yes, sir. A long time ago, Congressman Kilgore was investigated for irregularities in his campaign funds. He weaseled out of it at the time. But he was definitely up to something that night when I followed him into the caves. He claimed he was in there because he'd had trouble with kids trespassing and he saw my headlights. But that's bull. I followed *him*. Whatever he was looking for, or hiding or what have you, I think it's all related."

"And so do I," Luke put in. "But you must not let anyone know you know anything, Mr. McBride. These Coyotes are dangerous men."

"Oh, I wouldn't do that," P.J. vowed. "Don't have nobody to tell except Frankie here anyway."

"What about your other daughters?" Luke reminded him. "And your son-in-law? And Zack Trueblood? It's his land, even if Kilgore has kept control of it."

"Kurt Kilgore controls all kinds of people in this county. If he got any inkling that Luke here was closing in," Brandon put in, "he could cover it up. There's something big and nasty underneath all of this and even if he is my birth grandfather, I intend to get to the bottom of it."

"Atta boy!" P.J. was flushed with the intrigue of the whole thing now, and Frankie didn't like to see him so excited. "Somebody needs to bring old Kilgore down a notch or two!"

"Where will you be staying, Brandon?" Frankie changed the subject.

"I told him he could bunk with me," Luke said.

"Over at that torn-up Sunday house? It isn't even finished yet."

"I've got a mattress on the floor. All I need is a sleeping bag."

And probably not even a pillow, Frankie thought. Luke really was a cowboy in so many ways. "Stay out here." She turned to Brandon. "Daddy doesn't mind. Do you, Daddy?"

"Why, no!" P.J. beamed at his grandson. "I would flat enjoy having the company. Use the place for a base while you research your story."

Brandon smiled. "You're sure it won't put you out?"

"You're welcome in my home anytime."

Frankie smiled. It was the first time she had ever heard her father call the farm "my home."

THE NEXT MORNING Frankie saw Luke again when he came to get Brandon. They had coffee together before the men left for the caves. The thought of her recent experience among those rocks made Frankie nervous. What if somebody showed up while they were out there?

But by lunchtime the men were back with an unsettling report.

"Well, we found a way in," Luke told Frankie as he pulled off his muddy boots on the porch.

"And right away we came to that room-like area," Brandon chimed in, tugging at his own boots. "You know, where the congressman pulled a gun on me that time? At least I think it was the same place. But then we dropped down and it got to be really rough going. A lot of stalactites and stalagmites. High flowstone cutting off the passageways, some pretty deep-looking formation pools, and then we had to stop when we came to a really steep streamway."

"Brandon's been studying up on caves," Luke answered Frankie's puzzled look. He stood up.

"Did you find anything?" Frankie came up beside him.

"Evidence that we weren't the first ones there."

"Evidence? What kind of evidence?"

"Some busted-up wooden crates—empty, of course— some old wooden pallets."

"Did you collect this…evidence?"

"No. Didn't touch a thing—"

"We even dusted away our boot prints," Brandon put in.

"I don't want anyone to know I've been in there. Yet."

"But Luke got some pretty decent video of it all on his Treo," Brandon piped up again, "and e-mailed it to Austin."

Frankie frowned. Brandon was young. Of course he was excited, but Frankie wasn't sure he needed to be involved in something so dangerous.

"What could have been in those crates? Weapons? Drugs?"

Luke shook his head. "No idea. We need to get cleaned up a bit. Then we're headed over to the Light at Five Points."

"To see Markie and Justin?" Frankie cut Brandon a concerned glance.

"It's cool," Brandon offered. "I want to see them again."

"You guys want some lunch real quick?" Cooking for Robbie's boys had taught Frankie how to slap food on the table pretty fast.

"I'm starving." Brandon, who had the ravenous appetite of a typical nineteen-year-old, was already heading to the kitchen.

"I'd appreciate that." Luke stepped up close to Frankie, facing her. He looked in her eyes and bracketed her shoulders with his big hands, which made her feel paradoxically aroused and secure. "Don't worry about Brandon. He wants to be with me when I interview Yolonda and that pregnant girl, Aurelia. They know more about the Morales brothers than they're telling, I think. I want some answers. I don't care if I have to track somebody clear to Mexico to get them."

MARYNELL CALLED the farm that afternoon. "He's home then?" she said without preamble when Frankie answered the ancient wall phone in the kitchen.

"Yes."

"No problems?"

"No. He's doing fine. Mother, when are you coming back home?"

"Tired of taking care of the old coot already, are you?"

Frankie could no longer be deflected by this kind of talk. "I think Daddy deserves some closure. You just up and left."

"Closure?" Predictably, Marynell adopted a hostile, defensive attitude. "*He's* the one who started all this! *He's* the one who tried to make me out to be crazy! And then my own daughters ganged up on me. What have I done to earn this kind of treatment?"

"Mother, calm down." Marynell was getting worse, Frankie decided.

"I want to talk to my husband," Marynell huffed.

"All right." Frankie went in the living room where P.J. was parked in his recliner and handed him a portable phone. "It's Mother." Then she went back to the kitchen to give him privacy.

But she could still overhear a little bit of her dad's side of the conversation—"Phoenix? Now, Marynell"—and before long she couldn't help carefully lifting the wall phone again. If Marynell was upsetting P.J., Frankie vowed, she would interrupt and tell her mother that Daddy needed his rest.

"…if you can learn to live in peace." She heard P.J.'s voice, sounding calm and not at all upset. "Otherwise, I want to spend my remaining years having some measure of happiness with my daughters and my grandchildren."

"*Your* daughters!" Marynell exploded. "You had nothing to do with raising them except to coddle them. That is why things have turned out all twisted up. It all started with *you* letting them run wild on the farm, undermining me every time I tried to instill some discipline, some order, teaching them to keep secrets in those damned diaries. Families should not have secrets!"

Because she was on an extension right in the next room, P.J.'s sigh sounded particularly heavy to Frankie.

"Marynell, I'm going to hang up now. My grandson is here and I want to get a shower before he comes back from Markie and Justin's."

"Markie and Just—*What* grandson? For heaven's sake, you aren't talking about—"

"Brandon, yes. He's a very fine young man. The best."

"You want to talk about crazy? *This* is crazy! Getting all cozy with that child when Markie should never even have given birth to him in the first place. The whole thing should be over and done with, in the past."

Frankie could well imagine that her mother wanted it *over and done with,* after what she'd pulled nearly twenty years ago.

"He is Kurt Kilgore's grandson, too," she overheard Marynell adding spitefully. "Have you thought about that?"

Frankie knew she should hang up, but she just couldn't bring herself to do it. Her cheeks were blazing as she listened for more.

Such a long silence followed that finally Marynell said, "P.J.? Are you all right?" She sounded uncertain, as if she was worried that she'd gone too far.

"He is simply Brandon, Marynell. Just Brandon. And I love him, and I am glad to have the boy in my life. I really don't think you should come home right now. You need to think about everything you've done…to all of us."

"What *I've* done? That tears it! Don't you worry, P. J. McBride. I never intended on coming back to Five Points anytime soon, if ever. I'll be going to Phoenix to take care of my ailing brother. At least he will appreciate my caring." Marynell hung up.

Frankie returned the phone to its cradle gingerly, as if it might shatter to pieces in her hand. Uncle Louis was ailing? The elderly uncle was childless, had never married, and didn't associate with his sister Marynell much. Frankie wondered if her mother's motivation for going to Phoenix didn't have more to do with inheriting Louis's large home than with compassion.

Everything had blown up in their faces: the past about Brandon, Danny's death, her father's health, her parents' marriage. Her own marriage. The only happy thing, the only thing halfway normal in this family was Robbie and Zack's coming wedding.

She went into the living room where her father was watching a basketball game.

"Daddy?"

"Mmm-hmm."

"You okay? I...I listened in a bit, there at the end."

He lifted the remote, muted the sound and gave her a pained look.

"She's never gonna change," he said at last. His voice sounded weak with defeat. And sorrow. But then it got stronger as he went on. "But unfortunately for Marynell, I *have* changed. I've learned that you don't have to let people walk all over you, even if you are married to them. I learned that from watching you."

Frankie lowered herself to the edge of the couch, dumb-struck. "From *me?*"

"Yessirree. From you, my daughter. Look how you had the guts to just up and leave your life in Austin to find a new life here, to find peace. And you may not realize it yet, but I believe you have made the right choice. You're going to be a lot happier in the long run. Heck, you're a happier person already. I can tell it all over you, just by looking at you."

"Thanks, Daddy." Frankie smiled. "I really am a lot happier these days." But she had to wonder if the changes her father saw in her weren't more the result of her raging infatuation over Luke Driscoll than her wise choice.

CHAPTER FOURTEEN

THE NEXT DAY, a Saturday, P.J. asked Frankie if she was aware that the following Monday was Valentine's Day.

"I know it is, but that's okay, Daddy," Frankie said, setting a bowl of beef and vegetable stew before him on a TV tray. "Robbie can handle the store just fine without me."

"That ain't what I'm talking about." P.J. held his spoon perpendicular to the tray like Moses's staff, as if he were going to make an important pronouncement. "I was thinking about you and your Ranger. I bet you haven't had yourself a happy Valentine's Day in a long time," he observed quietly.

"*My* Ranger?" Frankie had to smile.

"You know what I mean. You spent all that time with me while I was laid up in the hospital and now you're cooped up out here on the farm on account of your mother has checked out. I just thought you two might like to go out and have a nice time together. You know, continue with what you've started."

"We haven't started anything!" Frankie protested, but she had to wonder how long she was going to persist in this denial. "Besides, I don't think you're ready to stay out here alone just yet."

"That's why you got to do it now, while Brandon's here." P.J. frowned like a little boy trying to get his way. "He has to go back down to U.T. tomorrow. Him and I already talked about it. I'm gonna teach the boy how to play a little dominoes. There's plenty of stew in that pot and all. So. You gonna call Luke or not?"

"Oh, all right," Frankie said as if he were twisting her arm. "If it will make you happy, I'll call him."

It was a hard call to make for some inexplicable reason, and Luke didn't make it any easier.

At first, his voice sounded concerned. "Everything okay?"

But then it became teasing when she explained why she was calling. "Dad says I should get out of the house while Brandon's here to babysit. I thought we might go to dinner and a movie or something." She wasn't about to mention Valentine's Day.

"Are you buying?"

"Sure. There's a great burger joint and a dollar-a-show theater down in Deep Springs." She wasn't entirely joking. She hadn't gotten any settlement money yet and Kyle had been annoyingly lax about sending the spousal support mandated by the separation agreement.

"Okay. Deep Springs it is."

BUT WHEN Luke picked Frankie up at the farm, he was dressed in his best and carrying a dozen roses. And a box of expensive chocolates. And a card. And a small gift in a red foil sack.

"Monday is Valentine's Day," he explained casually as he handed her the stuff.

"Oh really?" Frankie winked at P.J.

She put the flowers in one of her mother's nice vases, broke the seal on the chocolates to share with Brandon and P.J. But she held the card and the gift bag close. "I think I'll wait and open this later."

When they got out in his pickup, Luke announced he had plans to take her to a nice place over at Wildhorse, but Frankie didn't want to be that far away from her dad. "I left my cell number with Brandon."

"Oh. So is it the Aggie then?"

"That or Dixie's."

Dixie's was on the order of a countrified tea room with pink tablecloths and a collection of china plates on the wall.

"The Aggie," Luke said.

But he hadn't driven a half mile onto the highway into town before he pulled into a ranch-road turn-out.

He left the engine idling, jerked the parking brake on. "I've missed you so damn much." His voice was low, emotional. "I can't keep my hands off you another minute. Please come here."

"I've missed you, too!" Frankie cried as she threw herself into his arms and they kissed.

"I don't want to go to a town," she mewled when they finally pulled apart.

"Me either."

He drove them to the top of a lone hill that was unfamiliar to Frankie, but that had a view like none she'd ever seen. He pulled into a small gravel clearing, doused the headlights and lowered the truck's electric windows. Cool air that held the promise of spring poured in and when

Frankie tilted her head to look out, the stars were so numerous they made her dizzy.

"You ever gone parking before?" His voice floated to her from the darkness, deep and sexy, like a physical embrace.

"No." She raised her head and stared at him solemnly in the darkness.

"Smile," Luke teased. "I won't tell."

She didn't smile. She looked down. "You don't understand. I…never mind." She wasn't going to allow her ex-husband anywhere near this moment. She wasn't going to talk about how the first time they'd made love it had been because Kyle had insisted he wouldn't be able to concentrate in the OR the next day if they didn't. She wasn't even going to tell Luke that Kyle was the only man she had ever made love to.

Seeming to note that her mood wasn't exactly light, Luke said, "Let's see if I can find us a good song."

But instead of searching the backlit menu of his XM monitor, he picked up the small gift sack off the seat and held it forth. "First you'll have to open this."

She ripped the tissue paper out quickly. Inside was a CD. *Classic Country-and-Western Love Songs.* Without asking, he took the jewel box from her hands and opened it.

He slid the disc into the player and hit the select button until he found the song he wanted. The harmonized voices of Kenny Rogers and Dolly Parton singing "Islands in the Stream" filled the cab.

As the ballad rose up around her, Frankie felt sudden tears sting her eyes. Had he actually remembered that was the first song they'd ever listened to in the cab of this pickup?

"Where did you come up with that?" She swallowed. Were they that much in love? Like the song? She knew *she* certainly was.

"Wal-Mart," he said, as if she were being literal. "I figured this has got to be our make-out song."

She had to smile, tears or not. "So, are we going to make out now?"

"Absolutely."

He reached for her, starting, to her surprise, by gently kissing her hand. Not in the way some dandy in the French court might. But in a way that was far more tender. Far more possessive. And far more devastating.

His hot breath fanned her skin in a controlled but hungry arch that made Frankie think he would take a bite of her if not for restraint. And she probably would have been thrilled if he had. By the time he pressed his soft, firm lips to her skin and held them there, reverently, she found that she was already aching with a need she'd never felt before.

He raised his head, and did not look at her, but kept his gaze steady, trained straight ahead, as if he was looking at something over her shoulder, far off out there in the dark hills. Slowly, absently, he flipped his free hand over until it was palm up, capturing her wrist. He encircled her wrist with his strong fingers, pressing the pads of the two middle ones to her pulse. "You smell so good." His voice was hushed.

Still moving ever so slowly, he lifted her fingers to his mouth again. His lips felt soft, yet firm as he touched them to her skin, again reverently, but with an underlying possessiveness. His breath was hot, moist, as he crushed his mouth to her hand for the count of several excruciating heartbeats.

As he did, she involuntarily curled her fingers over his forearm, gripping him with sudden need. Evidently this was the response he wanted because he groaned approval, and she felt his lips briefly tip up into a smile while the singers sang, "No one in between."

He worked his grip up her arm, turning it up, kissing the soft underflesh. Frankie took in the sight of his bowed head—by the CD player's pale-green lights she could see that his eyes were closed. She drew a deep breath and released it on a ragged sigh. Her eyes went wide and she swallowed when his tongue made a tiny circle on her flesh.

"Frankie," he said in a low, achingly sincere voice, "I've been waiting for you. Dying to be your lover."

"Oh, Luke," was all she could manage.

"Is that a yes?"

"Yes."

"Well then," he growled with his hot lips hovering over her skin, "We'd best get started."

"Here?" Frankie was astonished to discover that despite her extreme arousal she was very nervous.

"Right here." He pulled the hand he had taken command of around to his back while he moved his athletic body over hers. "Right now."

His mouth hovered over hers as she gave the weakest argument, "But I've never…*done it* in the cab of a pickup."

"Well, we're not going to *do it*." He smiled as his lips teased at hers. "We're going to make love."

"Sail away with me," the singers wailed as Luke's mouth fully assaulted hers.

And Frankie was gone, sailing away in a grapple of arms

and legs and sweet lips and hot hands and pounding pulses. Of clothes pushed up and opened, hungry mouths seeking whatever needy areas of skin they could find access to.

She was awestruck by how sensual and desirable he made her feel. Was it this setting? The cab of the pickup with the night crickets and the stars and the new spring air outside the windows? The creak of leather as they struggled for *more* of each other? The seductive rhythm of the music and the fogging-up of the windshield? All she knew was, it had been a very long time since she'd felt this young, this sexual. No. She'd never felt this sexual, even when she was young.

She heard the pop of the last snaps of his cowboy shirt and looked down to see that he'd given her full access to his bare chest. She ran her fingertips over his warm, taut muscles, through the springy, masculine hair. He was so fine. So solid and real. So Luke. She could feel his heart thudding beneath her palms.

"Oh." He seemed to come to himself suddenly. "I guess you're concerned about protection." He reached across her, bringing his skin and the scent of him devastatingly close. From the glove box he retrieved the necessary item.

She took it and closed her palm on it. "That's thoughtful, but with the long dry spell we've both had…"

"Shh." He touched his fingers to her lips. "No arguments. We're doing this right. Think of the babies."

"What babies?"

"The ones we don't want to make until we're ready."

Frankie's heart was already pounding, but now it pounded harder. How could she tell him? There would be no babies, most likely. That was her sorry fate. But at least fate had seen fit to gift her with this man. And if she could make of herself a gift to him, if she could somehow make him glad he had survived the pain of his past to find her, she would count herself fortunate. She wanted to be the one to tell him first.

"I love you, Luke," she whispered.

"Oh, Frankie." His voice had dropped to a low growl. "If only I could really show you how I feel about *you*."

"Show me."

He kissed her again, fiercely, while his hands peeled her clothes free so that they could be flesh to flesh.

"You are so beautiful," he whispered reverently as his admiring eyes, his touch, his ungoverned mouth sent her where she knew she probably should not go. But yet, in her heart she knew she should, she would. This man was it. The right one. She closed her eyes and tilted her head back with the glory and the freedom of knowing it.

"Open your eyes." Luke's whispering breath felt hot while his mouth traveled down her neck.

Somehow she knew, with a sense of inevitability, that once she looked into his eyes, at this moment, there would be no turning back. Not ever.

He was right. They weren't just "doing it." They were making love. And, oh, the astonishing difference for Frankie.

Thrill after thrill shot through her as his eyes, alive with an animal fire, connected with hers and held them captive while they shoved the last remnants of clothes out of the way.

He used his hands to awaken every womanly inch of her,

to leave her with no defenses, no secrets. She used hers to call him forth even stronger, for sweeter torment.

He angled himself under her and she, lithe as a kitten, molded to fit around him.

Frankie didn't know what had been missing in her marriage, knew only that she'd been cheated, despite all their athletic straining and clever tricks. But when Luke entered her fully while looking into her eyes she knew what it was. It was *meaning.*

For him, this moment meant everything. He didn't have to tell her so. She read it in his eyes.

He grasped her hips and moved them together at first. Then they found their rhythm. And they kept looking into each other's eyes.

Driven by a kind of need she'd never imagined possible, she cried out, then surrendered to the impact of his increasing thrusts. With cry upon cry, part anguish, part rapture, her first explosions came while his hands raked and framed her body like a prize he was holding up to the stars outside.

Anguish because suddenly she was desperate for more of him, all of him. It was not humanly possible to merge with another person as fully as she suddenly needed Luke.

Rapture because she felt herself giving over to something she'd never experienced before.

Luke's way was easy and natural, one thing flowing into another but so intense. So compelling. A demand, an unstoppable invasion. An eye-widening surprise that pushed her higher. To the next level. Higher. Out of control.

And once the surges of climax fully gripped her, she felt as if they would never stop. *This,* she thought as Luke's eyes continued to drink in the pleasure he read in her gasping mouth and astonished eyes, *this is what it is supposed to be like.* When she could no longer stand the intensity, she turned her head, eyes squeezed shut again.

"No," he commanded, "Look at me."

She did, but barely. She was gasping harder now, biting her lip, wanting to scream. To cry.

And tears did come. Tears of relief. Tears of disbelief. Tears of joy.

"It's okay," he whispered as he turned her face to his, with his strong thumb bracketing her jaw and his fingers brushing at her tears. "Just keep looking into my eyes." His were radiating both tenderness and triumph now, as if he could see the passion and surrender that had at last gripped her, as if he could see how part of her had fought it, and how powerless she was now to resist it as, once again, she came, contracting around him.

"Baby, baby," he coaxed, his voice growing more fierce with each wave.

When her body finally collapsed from the throes of climax upon climax, he held her to his chest like a fragile doll.

"I won't always make you look at me," he was speaking to her so quietly now that to Frankie his voice seemed far away. Far, far away from where she was now. Floating. She was vaguely aware that her body was splayed open, poured out, spread helpless on top of him. And that he was still hard.

"Not always. But this time." He stroked her hair back possessively as he tilted her sideways and brought one of her thighs up high on his side for his greater access and satisfaction. He moved purposefully in her this time and his voice grew husky as finally his own waves of release started. "This time, I just had...to...see...your eyes."

CHAPTER FIFTEEN

I am losing my mind. All I can think about is Luke. How to get away with him. How to get to bed with him. Everything I ever held dear, everything I ever worried about, every petty upset, every rigid compulsion in my life has flown out the window. All I want is one thing. Is it normal to think about sex morning, noon and night?

Ah yes. Sex. I'd almost forgotten. Or, rather, it's more like I'd never really known.

We go to his house, even though it's not quite finished yet and still smells faintly of paint and varnish. We make love on his mattress, which is still on the floor. With candles all around us, like hippies. I lie there afterward, inhaling his scent and feeling his warmth and listening to the rhythm of his breathing, and I just want to leap up and dance around the room. This, *this* is love!

Heavens. Why do I keep writing this stuff down? Is it because I don't believe it's happening? Maybe I'd better write down those instructions for Robbie to burn this journal should I die, too.

The truth is, the person who should really have

this journal, should anything ever happen to me, is
Luke Driscoll.

FRANKIE AND LUKE were glad they had taken Brandon
and P.J. up on the offer to have some time together,
because it felt as if they saw precious little of each other
for the next few weeks.

All they had were *stolen moments,* as one of Luke's
country-and-western songs might have put it. Frankie
thought she might lose her mind for wanting the man. She
wasn't sure she'd ever understood the meaning of lovemak-
ing before, and she had the constant urge to keep testing
their chemistry, to see if it was real.

But the things that kept them apart were real, too. Luke's
investigation dragged on with legal setbacks and frustrat-
ingly few leads while he and Zack finished up the Sunday
house, also with some setbacks. In the meantime, P.J.
slowly got well and the weather warmed up faster than
usual. Record rains followed by sunny days would have the
wildflowers blooming exceptionally early. Robbie was
suddenly frantic for help with her wedding.

It was during one of those stolen moments at Luke's
Sunday house that it dawned on Frankie that they had,
after all, forgotten about the condom that night under the
stars in his pickup.

His personal supplies were in his freshly remodeled
master bathroom, which he kept in military order. They
were both brushing their teeth at the pedestal sink, and
when he reached into the medicine cabinet in front of her,

pulling a package off a neat stack in the corner, Frankie paled and said, "Oh gosh."

"What?" He closed the door and met her eyes in the antique-framed mirror he'd mounted on the cabinet only days before.

"Nothing."

"No. It's something." He stared at her. "You're white as a sheet."

"I just realized. We forgot...you know...the first time."

He wrapped his arms around her waist from behind and brought his chin down to her shoulder, speaking to her reflection.

"I know, but don't freak out, okay?" He smiled reassuringly into her eyes in the mirror. "I'm probably a bigger health nut than that silly surgeon you dumped. You have to be careful when you go undercover in some of the places I've been. Tested and retested, that's me. Flat paranoid. Okay?" He nipped at her shoulder.

But his face fell when he raised his eyes back to the mirror and saw tears in hers.

"Darlin'." He turned her to face him. "I'm just kidding. Really, I am very firm about protecting my health. It's the Ranger way," he tried to joke again. "Perfectly sound in mind and body." When she regarded him solemnly, he sobered. "And don't worry about the other. If you get pregnant it will be a flat miracle. It was only that one time, okay?"

"I doubt I will get pregnant," she whispered. "It has always taken exactly that—a miracle—for me." Her tears spilled over. "In vitro fertilizations, the whole bit. I lost them all. Four babies."

He loosened his arms, holding her more lightly, more tenderly. "I didn't know." He seemed truly at a loss for words.

Frankie sniffed and told herself to stop this crying. Hadn't she shed enough tears about this issue already? What did it have to do with her and Luke? "I would have thought you uncovered that when you were digging around about my family."

"No. We can't get into medical records without a subpoena."

"It doesn't matter now." She tried to pull away, but Luke held her captive, hugging her to him. "I'm getting a little old for baby hunger."

"You are?"

"Will you stop that?"

"Stop what?"

"Repeating everything I say in the form of a question." It was annoying her so much it had dried up her tears.

"I am?"

She rolled her eyes, but he only gathered her closer in his arms and kissed her cheek. He turned her to face him. "If you could turn back the hands of time, you wouldn't really want to have a child by a jerk like your ex, would you?"

"There you go again."

He backed away enough to look in her eyes. "That's a real question."

She sighed. "I would have wanted a child in my life, no matter how I got the child, no matter how things turned out."

"Is this an iteration of ''tis better to have loved and lost,' etcetera?"

"Yes, I guess it is. Here I am, forty. And I'm realizing…it's not gonna happen, Luke."

"You don't know that."

"Be real. The chances of getting pregnant after forty go way down, even if you haven't always had the kind of problems I have."

"Well, I'll do everything I can to help." He ran one hand down over her bottom while he twiddled the packet between two fingers of the other. "We can always send this guy back to his little corner."

"You don't mean that." She had to smile at his teasing. "Come on. Just be a sport and let me get all angst-ridden and weepy without trying to fix it for a change."

"Okay." He smiled at her as he tucked a stray strand of her hair behind one ear. "I guess you've earned it."

He took her by the hand and led her to the mattress that sat on the newly laid carpet in the bedroom. They settled, facing each other cross-legged on the rumpled sheets.

"How do you imagine your life would be different if you had had a baby?" Luke toyed with her fingers. "I mean beyond the obvious stuff like the pitter-patter of little feet and soccer practice and facing a massive college bill."

Frankie looked down at a nail, picked at it. "I don't know. It would be less…*sterile*, I guess. There comes a point when…when if you're childless, you can get weird and not even know it. When everything in the house becomes too perfect, you know? Kyle and I had a giant portrait of ourselves where most people hang the pictures of their kids. At one point he wanted to add a smaller portrait of us holding Charm. Like it'd be okay to have multiple versions of ourselves if we added the dog between us, like some surrogate child. Like something had really changed between the old portrait and the new. It was creepy. I wouldn't let him do it."

"Smart move. That would have been really bad for the decor. Charm is so homely. Now Philo, there's a handsome dog. I can imagine his portrait right smack in the middle of the wall." He leaned back on his palms as if satisfied with the vision.

"Stop it. Don't pretend you don't know what I mean. Haven't you ever felt like you're on the outside looking in, with your nose forever pressed to the glass, wanting something you'll never have? Don't you suspect that people feel sorry for you sometimes because you don't have kids, but that they're hiding it? I could almost *feel* women with kids avoiding the whole subject with me after a while."

"People probably do feel sorry for *me*," Luke said offhandedly. "But what other people think doesn't change anything, Frankie."

"Don't you ever get tired of being single?" she pressed on.

"Is that a proposal?" He leaned forward and grinned.

"No." She frowned at him, annoyed.

He shrugged. "Suit yourself. But I would've said yes."

"I'm serious, Luke. How do I deal with this? With feeling like I've been cheated of something vital and important?" Now the tears welled up again, damn them. Frankie had battled these emotions for so long, with no support from Kyle. It was Luke's kindness that made her cry so easily. But she had forgotten how to let someone help her instead of feeling like she had to hide or justify

her feelings. "And please don't tell me life's not fair.
Nobody gets how I feel!" Her voice grew higher with
emotion. "You get judged when you don't have children.
People think you're *selfish*. They assume it's a choice, especially when you have plenty of resources the way Kyle
and I had. Well, it was not my choice at all!"

"I understand," Luke said calmly. "I do. You're disappointed because you wanted to be a mother—"

"My whole life!" Her voice broke.

He gave her a moment to recover her composure before
he went on. "Look. Is this really about wanting to *be* a
mother, to do the little things that mothers do? 'Cause my
understanding is, the job is not all that thrilling, most days.
And if you really want to do all that stuff, the diapers, the
spit-up, the sleep deprivation, you've had a chance to experience it with Robbie's baby, haven't you?"

"You know good and well that's not what I'm talking
about."

"So, what *are* you talking about?"

She could see then that his goading was a device to get
her to clarify her own feelings out loud. "I guess it's about
having a legacy. Having a child with someone you love.
Watching that child grow and develop into a wonderful
human being— Oh, gosh, Luke. I shouldn't even be talking
like this. Not after…not with all you've been through."

"It's okay. Your pain is just as valid as mine. And I want
to help you with it." There wasn't a shred of self-pity in his
attitude. "Look, I think any rational person would say that
if you really wanted to be a mother all that badly, why didn't
you just adopt? But it's more complicated than that, isn't it?"

She nodded, like a child admitting to a guilty offense.

"It was about wanting to have *your own* child with someone you love, wasn't it?"

Again, she nodded. She added quietly, "I did love him at one time, you know. But I don't now. He killed any feeling I had for him. I want you to understand that, too."

"I do. And I also understand that you can't exchange one dream for another just because it's the rational thing to do. In other words, if you wanted with all your heart to get pregnant and have a baby, even adopting a child wouldn't quench that desire entirely. A part of you would still be wishing for something you couldn't have. But no matter how you look at it, the upshot is you're grieving over something that can't be changed. Don't go there, Frankie. Believe me, I know what that kind of looking back will get you." He fell silent, looking as if he were allowing himself, for the moment, to remember.

"Luke Driscoll," Frankie chided, hoping to keep him from slipping into melancholy as well, "you amaze me. I don't think I've ever heard you say that many words in a row before."

"This is important to me. *You* are important to me." He gathered her in his arms. Immediately, Frankie felt herself melting against the full heat of contact with him.

"I love the way you smell," she whispered into his neck.

"Oh yeah?" he murmured. "Tell me what you like about it."

"I can't describe it. You smell…so safe." She drew a deep breath, drinking in more of his scent.

"Safe?" The word came out a disgusted growl. "You are

not *safe* with me, lady. In fact, I intend to have my way with you right now."

"Your way. Yes." Her voice dropped, hushed with the gravity of desire. "I do so love your way."

BY THE TIME the wildflowers bloomed in mid-March, Frankie was beginning to suspect she'd made a terrible mistake on Valentine's Day. In the past her periods had often been irregular, so she tried not to panic, but now it had been over a month and there was nothing for it but to do a test and face the crazy truth.

Fearful that someone in Five Points would run into her in a checkout line, she drove all the way to a neighboring town to a busy Wal-Mart to buy a home pregnancy test kit. She stuffed the box down in the bottom of her oversized tote, not trusting herself to leave it anywhere around Robbie's place for the boys or her sister to see. Life was wild at the Tellchick house these days.

Wedding preparations, full speed ahead.

Robbie had chosen a simple satin dress. Zack was going to wear his firefighter's dress blues. The boys had been outfitted in chinos and navy blazers that might serve them well for other special occasions. Danielle would be decked out in a fairy-princess-style dress with layers of lace and tiny seed pearls. Ardella, who had developed an affection for the baby whose life she had helped to save, would fashion Danielle a baby's breath headpiece herself. And, in a magnanimous gesture the likes of which the town had never seen, she offered to donate the other flowers.

But it wasn't these wedding ceremony concerns that had

thrown Robbie into a tizzy. It was the party itself. Robbie and Zack were planning a bona fide old-fashioned German-style wedding.

After the outdoor ceremony in the field of wildflowers at 5:00 p.m., there would be a picnic dinner at the farmhouse. Eating and drinking and dancing to a live band under the stars until everyone collapsed. The guest list had grown week by week until practically all of Five Points was invited. Frankie knew she couldn't face Luke throughout the entire long affair without knowing the truth.

Was she or was she not pregnant? She was hard-pressed to find even fifteen minutes of privacy to run this test.

And if she was, oh, if she was. How was she ever going to tell Luke?

CHAPTER SIXTEEN

I can't believe it's already the morning of the wedding.
I haven't had a moment alone with my journal in days.
I finally had to barricade myself in the tiny bathroom
at Robbie's farmhouse to run the…test. No sooner had
I locked the door than my dear little namesake Frank
had to pee. He was hollering through the door, saying
he had to go *now*. There is only one bathroom in this
old farmhouse, and I hated to make the child wait, but
I held my breath until I saw what the little strip said.

Positive. That's what it said. No mistake. I've run
a billion of these things over the years, hoping,
hoping, hoping to be able to say that word *positive*
to myself. But more times than I could count, my
heart would sink because the test was negative.

But now my heart was sinking because it was
clearly positive.

Why now? I collapsed to my knees on the rug
while Frank kept pounding on the door and yelling,
"Aunt Frankie!"

Why now? All I ever wanted was a baby, but not
like this.

A baby. Oh, God. But just like all the others, I'll

probably lose her. Him. Him, her, whatever. I simply can't let myself start thinking about this baby as real.

I shouldn't be scribbling in a journal like this! And writing about it isn't helping. I've got to talk to somebody. I'll die if I don't. Now. Today.

Robbie's outside. I can't lay this burden on her on her wedding day, for heaven's sake.

Markie! She's been in this predicament herself, albeit as a teenager. Maybe she can help me sort this out.

A baby. Luke Driscoll's baby.

WHEN FRANKIE opened the bathroom door and little Frank shot past her, she stepped into the narrow little farmhouse hallway feeling disembodied. She skittered into the little back bedroom where her things were and stuffed her journal in her bag.

She opened the door and spotted Markie, darting across the hallway from room to room like one possessed.

"Markie! Could I talk to you?"

"I'm kinda busy, here." Markie looked down at something in her hands. "As soon as I get these untangled, I've gotta go to the farm and make sure Daddy's dressed right, then bring him back over here, then run back out to the Light and help Aurelia transfer the food trays to the van. She's way too far along to do any heavy lifting." Aurelia, past her due date, had begged to do the cooking for this wedding. It was her chance to show off her skill to townsfolk who might give her a job after the baby came, a job she would need if Julio Morales never showed up.

Frankie should have been equally focused. Her tasks were to string tulle along the serving tables outside, help Ardella place the centerpieces and to feed and dress Danielle. Not to mention assisting the bride when it came time to prepare Robbie. Maybe she should have waited until tomorrow to run the test.

"Please?" Frankie stepped forward and grabbed Markie's arm. "It's kind of…urgent."

Markie froze, looking at her face. "Has something gone wrong? Is Daddy all right?"

"No, Daddy's fine." Frankie pulled Markie along until she was in the tiny bedroom at the back of the hallway. She shut the door.

The room, a fussy little cell with country wallpaper, lacy curtains, homemade quilts, and an antique rocker, was very small-town-girl Robbie. Markie would have hated it except that she'd spent her wedding night here and that made it sentimental for her. Frankie pulled her down to sit beside her on the saggy bed.

"Well?" Markie urged as Frankie bit her lip. "I gotta hurry."

Frankie disliked this finger-snapping aspect of Markie's personality, a holdover from her career in politics. It was so ungracious, really.

As if to confirm Frankie's judging thoughts, Markie actually snapped her fingers. "Spill."

"I'm pregnant," Frankie blurted.

Markie couldn't have looked more stunned if Frankie had whacked her upside the head with one of Robbie's lacy pillows.

"You're *what?*"

"I just did the test in the bathroom."

"Oh, crap." Markie sank back. Then she sat upright, jutting her chin forward and hooking a thumb in the direction of Austin. "Please tell me it's not Kyle's?"

"Don't be ridiculous. I haven't had relations with Kyle in a year."

"Thank God." Markie wilted with relief, then sucked in a long breath of comprehension. "It's Luke's?"

Frankie nodded.

"Oh, *Frankie.*"

"Don't *Oh Frankie* me. You did the same thing."

"I did not! I was seventeen and stupid. And Justin and I were in *love.* You are a grown woman and you barely know this man!"

"I don't need this." Frankie jumped up.

Markie grabbed her arm. "This is unbelievable!"

"Ironic, isn't it? After all those years of infertility treatments, suddenly, here I am. All knocked up, without even trying. Luke and I only did it without protection once."

"Amazing. How far along are you?"

Frankie sank back down on the bed. "About a month." She hadn't felt the urge to cry until just now. She supposed her irritation at her little nephew and all that furious scribbling in her journal had distracted her. But now a great lump rose up in her throat and the backs of her eyes stung as reality set in.

Markie patted her hand. "Now, Sissy, it'll be okay. The first thing you have to do is tell Luke."

"On Robbie's wedding day?"

"Don't put it off. I know what I'm talking about here.

The longer you keep this secret the worse it will be. No good can come from hiding it. He has the right to know, to help you make a decision."

"A decision? In all likelihood, I'll lose this baby, just like I lost all the others, and the whole thing will be moot."

"Moot?" Markie mocked her choice of words. "Frankie, you are rationalizing. This is Luke Driscoll's child. Fathers have rights. Legal rights. Don't put it off."

LUKE SHOWED UP for the wedding in a fresh white Stetson, a laundry-starched long-sleeved white shirt cinched at the neck by a distinctive club tie printed in muted tones of wheat, black and Texas red, tan trousers and black boots. The only thing that kept his look from being a uniform was the absence of the modest round silver badge of a Texas Ranger over the breast pocket.

When he touched the wide brim of his Western hat in salute to Frankie, she saw that his face was clean-shaven! Her jaw dropped as he flashed her a grin of straight white teeth, far more stunning now that his salt-and-pepper goatee was gone.

"What have you done?" she said as she walked up to him. She had not realized how perfectly square his jaw was, how deeply etched the lines that made parentheses down the planes of his cheeks when he smiled.

He swept off the hat, leaned down and gave her a feathery kiss on the lips. The delicious scent of his rich aftershave instantly had her senses singing. "Seems like I rubbed your face a little raw the last couple of times," he said confidentially. "I thought this might be gentler on your skin. You know, later."

"Later?" Instantly, she could feel a certain heat rising within. Her heart drummed with the anticipation of it.

"You will come back to the Sunday house with me when the festivities are over?" He resettled his hat as he said this, his voice low.

"How can I not? You look…so handsome." She was genuinely short of breath now. Would their baby inherit Luke's good looks? Hope began to beat in her chest. Maybe she wasn't going to lose this baby. Maybe the miscarriages had not been entirely her fault. Maybe it would be different with Luke. She would tell him. At the Sunday house. Later.

People had parked around the farmhouse and the former barn site, assembling in little clusters under the trees or on the screened porch, visiting while they waited. When it was time for the ceremony, they walked as a group, slowly, up the rutted drive to the top of the hill where the little stone house sat empty, but clean. Zack and Robbie led the procession. She minded the hem of her cream-colored dress. He carried the decked-out baby on his arm like a prize. The trio of dressed-up boys followed close behind.

They gathered around, so many people they threatened to spill over the sides of the hill. Over two hundred in all. Zack's extended family. Robbie's. Nattie Rose and Earl and kids near the front. All of Zack's firefighter buddies and their wives and girlfriends. Old Parson and his dear, smiling wife, their sable countenances beaming and chins tilted high as if it were their own girl who was getting married. Robbie had insisted her former boss attend the wedding as an honored guest and not cook any of the food, except for the elaborate Lone Star-shaped groom's cake, which he'd made the evening before.

Robbie and Zack stood at a high point on the grounds. Behind them, the sun was low and ripe in a bright spring sky and the meadow below the little hill was replete with Zack Trueblood's loving tribute to his new wife. Acres of bluebonnets created an undulating sheet of blue and in the distance bright patches of yellow showed where the tickseed was already starting to bloom. Beyond the sea of flowers, twin dark live oaks and a rickety barbed-wire-and-post-oak fence framed the new spring green of a wide pasture where a smattering of fat, white-faced cattle grazed. Beyond all that lay the endless rolling hills, turning leaden green in the slanting evening light.

Zack and Robbie stood clasping hands, stating their vows with all that glory as a backdrop. A priest presided, but their solemn words to each other were all that mattered. No music, save the song of a pair of mourning doves, perched on the roof of the old house, saying goodbye to the day's light.

It was all so beautiful and moving, especially after all Robbie had been through. Many were dabbing at their eyes.

Frankie tried to concentrate on her sister's wedding, though she felt as though she was carrying a guilty little secret that caused her cheeks to stay pink and her movements to be nervous. She dropped her bouquet in the dirt; she twisted her ankle on a rock; she stared off in the distance one time too many. When they walked back down the hill, Luke finally asked her, in a quiet voice, what was wrong.

"Nothing." She smiled up at him. "Just some sympathetic wedding jitters for Robbie."

"Your mother's here. Are you going to talk to her?"

Frankie swiveled her head toward the crowd walking behind them. "She's here?" She hadn't even noticed.

"She arrived late." Luke would have observed the arrival of every attendee, Frankie realized.

"Maybe later."

The spring weather held, with a full moon rising and stars peeking out in the evening sky. They ate at long picnic tables Zack and his buddies had built, the newly ripped wood still fragrant.

Aurelia's chicken enchiladas and green mesquite brisket were so delicious that several people suggested she should open her own Tex-Mex place in town. Markie promised to pass along the compliments.

Nattie Rose had made the wedding cake because no one could find a way to tell her no. After all, she had made Markie's cake, the waitress boasted, and it had turned out *gorgeous*.

So Robbie got more of the same. That is, hideous. For this occasion Nattie Rose had gone extra creative. She'd cast small white ceramic figures of birds, a big one for Zack, a medium one for Robbie, three smaller ones for the boys, and a teeny tiny one for Danielle. The eyes she painted on them were crooked and splotchy, but it was the sentiment that counted. She crowded these bird figures onto an elaborate icing "nest" on the top layer, complete with sticks and leaves, spray-painted silver. The other three layers, done in graduating shades of pink, were buttressed with lumpy clusters of what were presumably bluebonnets fashioned from sugary frosting in an otherworldly blue. The thing was big enough to feed Caesar's legions.

P.J. led the toasting. Each of the Tellchick youngsters followed their grandpa's example with a shy sentence or two that had obviously been coached beforehand. Robbie couldn't drink the champagne, of course, and had to retire to the house once to nurse the baby. Frankie had never seen her sister happier.

A guitar-and-fiddle combo called the Smallwoods provided live music that was part country, part Celtic and pure joy to dance to.

Luke stayed glued to Frankie's side. He danced with her, a knight in a white hat and a white shirt who smelled of fresh starch and clean aftershave and pure Luke. When he skillfully dipped her backward Frankie wanted to swoon.

Marynell was sour as ever, except when pasting on a smile for the benefit of the camera. After the meal, she seated herself in a lawn chair, facing the musicians, and did not speak to anyone unless *they* approached her throne.

P.J., on the other hand, laughed and danced and had a blast. He even took his baby granddaughter out for a light spin around the boarded deck area beside the house.

After they'd tired of dancing, Luke got himself and Frankie each a cold beer and guided her over to a secluded spot at a table under the trees, where paper lanterns swaying in the night breezes provided a soft glow. He straddled the bench, framing Frankie's backside with his legs. She rested her back against his chest and smiled up at the lights.

"Man. This wedding was a lot of work," he noted. "Who got the job of stringing extension cords way out to here?"

"Zack, I'm sure. All of this was Robbie's idea. She's full of it." Frankie smiled. "Creativity, that is. Hard work doesn't bother anybody in this family. It's the McBride way to just get things done."

Frankie tilted her head and studied Luke's face in the soft light as the music seemed to recede and the rising rhythm of chirping crickets rose up around them. They were alone now. It was quiet.

"Luke. We never did get back to the subject of your family the other night. You never told me how your wife and daughter died."

"I really don't like to tell people, right off."

Right off? They'd been sleeping together for weeks now. "When are you planning to tell me?"

"Now, I guess."

He was so astonishingly direct, a man who showed an utter absence of guile, that she had to forgive him.

"Did they die at the same time?"

"In the same moment," he said in a whisper.

"Oh my God. How?" And why, oh why, hadn't she asked him about this before? Frankie was suddenly aware that she had been monstrously selfish. She had lost the dream of a child, over and over, but Luke had actually watched a child develop and grow…and then had lost that beloved child. On the night when he'd been so understanding about her infertility troubles, she had completely bypassed his mumbled comment about people feeling sorry for him. She should have known there was much more to his story. And now, apparently, she was about to hear it.

LUKE TOOK a cooling sip of beer before he started in. "My wife was...she was a very compassionate woman. She spoke Spanish fluently, just like me, and almost every summer she went on a mission trip to Acuna, right across the border. That year, she took our daughter, who was six at the time, along with some other church families. She kept insisting it was all completely safe, and it usually was. The group had made this trip year after year, stayed at the same mission. The children always fared well, learning about another culture, making friends with the Mexican children."

The band struck up a toe-tapping fiddle piece, wholly incongruous with this heavy conversation. Frankie wanted to scream at the musicians to *stop,* to play something sad and quiet, that the man she loved was telling her about his broken heart. "What happened?" she asked gently.

"Liana wanted Bethany to see me while they were down there. I had been working undercover across the border for several months. Liana had this idea that we would all meet up in Acuna for a week, and then they'd go back to Austin and I'd go back to Chiapas."

"What were you doing all the way down there?" Chiapas, Frankie knew, bordered on Guatemala.

"Investigating reports of robbers stealing artifacts from Mayan tombs and smuggling them into Texas. The Mexican government was cooperating with us in tracking down these guys.

"I was obsessed. I had tracked one dangerous *hombre* in particular all the way north to San Antonio and back to Chiapas."

"The one with the scar," Frankie said, suddenly understanding Luke's reaction when they'd seen the man that first day out on the river.

"His name is Izek Texcoyo. Now you know." Luke looked down, which hid his face behind the brim of his hat. "The point is, Liana had been patient about my bulldogging, about my need always to get my man. But she was determined not to let our little family suffer because of my pigheadedness. She thought she'd found a safe way to bring my daughter to see me in Acuna."

"How did they...how did it happen?"

Luke's expression closed. After a long silence he said, "It was a long time ago, Frankie. Six years. I'd just as soon lay it to rest."

"Except you haven't. You're tracking Texcoyo still."

"Only because he's bad. Only because he deserves to die."

"Luke." She clutched his arm, completely forgetting her own troubles for the moment. "Don't you see? Your whole involvement in this case is about *them,* about avenging their deaths." She realized now that that was the thing holding him back despite the fiery passion in this relationship.

"No, it's more than that. I'm not some bitter man out for vengeance. What about the girl they murdered on the border? What about the guy they shot out by the caves? What about countless others we don't even know about? Texcoyo is evil, Frankie, and I'm so close to putting him away I can taste it. After dogging him for six years, I've come to this, a small town in the Texas Hill Country, where back in those caves, I would bet the farm we're gonna find those artifacts." He looked off in the distance, where the caves lay.

"But I promise, once I get these guys I mean to settle down. I'm getting a little long in the tooth for this cloak-and-dagger stuff anyhow. And you can't be a Ranger past the age of fifty regardless. I hadn't planned on risking my heart ever again."

With one gentle finger he turned her face up to him, and in his eyes she saw how much he meant his next words. "But since I met you, I've really started to think about a future, about how I'd like to settle down and be happy again. For good. Right here." His hat tilted at the ground.

"In Five Points?" Did he mean that? Her heart lifted with hope.

"Yeah. I kinda like the place, actually. But I'd have to convince Beecher to move up here. I can't exactly boot the old coot out on his ear. Something about this place, something about *you*, makes me want to start my life fresh."

"Oh, Luke," she whispered as his lips came down on hers.

It was as close as he'd come, except for the very telling way he made love to her, to admitting to Frankie the depth of his feelings for her. But suddenly a cloud passed over that ray of hope. She began to doubt her earlier plan to tell him about the pregnancy tonight. Now she understood why Luke had sealed a part of himself off. After all he'd been through, Luke, of all men, would be doubly devastated once, *if*, she lost the child. How could she tell him about the baby when she knew she was going to lose it? Her feelings—driven by hormones?—seemed to be on a roller coaster.

When he raised his head from the kiss, she ducked hers, trying to hide her conflicted feelings. "Luke, I—"

But he cut her off. "Come on. We need to do our part on that monstrosity of a cake."

The party was still in full swing when a battered old pickup came barreling up the rocky drive.

"*¡Señor!*" Jose Ramos, a resident at the Light at Five Points, left the engine running and the door ajar as he ran toward the men assembled near the keg. "Señor Justin! Come quick. Bad things going on." Jose had been learning to read English under Markie's tutelage, but he did not speak it all that well, especially when he was upset, which he clearly was at the moment.

Luke snapped to immediate alertness. "Stay here." He left Frankie and jogged over to Jose, with Justin and Zack at his side.

"Julio," Jose explained between rasping breaths, "he come back tonight, on account of the baby. Aurelia, she due now."

"Julio Morales," Justin explained to Zack, then encouraged Mr. Ramos in Spanish. "Just tell us what's wrong."

"The Coyotes, they come too. Follow Julio, I tink."

"How many?" Luke demanded.

"Four. One very bad one."

Jose slashed a finger from his mouth to his eye. "He shoot at us. Then he takes Julio."

"Where?"

"Don't know. They all got guns. We do what they tell

us. Aurelia, she crying and screaming so much that now the baby coming fast! It coming *now!*"

"Let's go," Luke said to Justin.

"Right," Zack said. "My emergency kit's in my truck."

"You can't leave," Justin argued. "This is your wedding."

"You gonna deliver this baby, sport?" Zack threw the comment to Justin over his shoulder as he jogged toward his truck.

Hearing that last comment, Frankie stepped up and grabbed Luke's sleeve. "I can help Zack." Her nursing skills were rusty, but back when she had practiced, she had been the best. Cool and calm and efficient. "At least I can be another pair of hands."

"Okay." Luke took her hand and she dashed to his truck with him. Zack was kissing Robbie goodbye as the wedding guests murmured uncomfortably.

AT THE LIGHT AT FIVE POINTS, emotions were high.

Several men were posted on the veranda, guarding the barn door after the horses were out, so to speak. And without weapons, to boot. Guns weren't allowed at the Light.

As soon as Justin and Markie got out of his truck, the men started yelling in overwrought Spanish.

Juan Morales was there. He was vowing, in high-macho style, to go after the men who had kidnapped his brother and slit their throats.

Frankie, Luke and Zack trotted to the porch where someone said Yolonda was crying hysterically, wanting Luke. They dashed inside.

The children from the various families had already been

herded upstairs. Someone had called 911 for Aurelia, but she was already pushing, with Mrs. Ramos, Jose's wife, planted stoutly at her side ready to catch the newborn.

Zack and Frankie took over. At one point Frankie had to go out on the veranda and tell the men to take their loud voices away from the house.

The baby was birthed without incident, even though Aurelia was a first-timer. Markie stationed herself at the mother's head to coach and praise the girl in soft Spanish.

Zack's performance was skillful and confident. This time, unlike that night when he had delivered Robbie's baby, his very own stepdaughter now, he had his kit, complete with all the sterile supplies he needed.

The baby needed no encouragement to cry as, with steady hands, Frankie peeled back the corners on the package containing the sterile cord clamp. Zack applied the clamp, then winked at Frankie. "Nothin' to do now but wait for the placenta."

Frankie nodded. All of her nursing skills had come back to her in a strong, confident rush. She had missed this. Helping people. Being of service.

After the sisters showed Aurelia the baby Frankie took him off to the side to check him. That's when her emotions finally kicked in.

As she toweled off the vigorous, howling baby, she felt so flushed with conflicting feelings—envy, longing, joy, terror—that she wondered if her chest would explode.

A newborn. Fresh from the womb. Her eyes teared up as she dried his firm, muscular little body.

Terror. Yes, underneath all the other emotions roiling inside of her, Frankie could not push down the real terror.

Because a new life had started inside her, as it had so many times before. And as so many times before, she feared her baby would never reach this stage. She always imagined them, tiny, silent, dead inside her. Sleeping, as it were. But already gone. She bit her lip, blocking the thoughts. No. She could not tell Luke. She could never put him through anything so hideous. The promise of having a child again, only to lose it.

"Ooo," she crooned despite the lump in her throat, more to distract herself than the baby. "What a big boy we are." There was too much emotion in her voice, she was sure. Markie had glanced up at her, alert, no doubt, to her distress. "Let's get some little clothes on that little body. You're gonna be okay, little one."

Finally the ambulance arrived from town. When mother and baby were bundled up and transported, Zack left to rejoin his bride.

And Frankie went straight to Luke's arms.

He was in the kitchen with Justin and some of the immigrants and when he saw her in the doorway, he opened his arms.

She ran to him. As he hugged her tightly, clutching her back, she wrapped her arms up around his neck, flattening herself to his trunk, not caring if others were watching.

"What now?" she whispered, pressing her cheek against his chest, letting the muffled *thud-thud* of his heart comfort her own.

"I'm going to Mexico," he said against her hair.

She tilted her head back. "When?"

"Tonight. I can't let the trail get cold. Yolonda found her courage. She'll testify against Texcoyo." Frankie looked to a corner where skinny young Yolonda, still weeping, was being comforted by the macho Juan. "My guess is the Coyotes are taking Julio back to Chiapas with them."

"Why there?" It was Justin's voice. He had been trying to find out everything he could on Aurelia's behalf. He and Markie had been standing to the side, waiting for Frankie and Luke to notice them.

Luke relaxed his hold on Frankie, but kept one arm draped around her waist as he turned to face Justin. "Without papers, Mexican immigrant farm workers do not have the means to open bank accounts, so they typically keep large amounts of cash on their persons. But these guys didn't even rob anybody.

"The way they just busted in here and nabbed Julio— if Juan hadn't been in the barn, and Yolonda hadn't hidden upstairs, they would have gotten them, too—makes me think they've been watching the place, waiting for Julio to return because of Aurelia and the baby."

Over at the table in the corner where Mrs. Ramos was comforting Yolonda now, Juan let fire with a burst of Mexican expletives.

"Maria Morales was bringing her brothers a map of sorts. A vest with a very specific pattern woven into it. The design of some ancient Mayan wall carvings that were pillaged from a tomb in Chiapas. It's complicated, but half of the design represents male, half of it represents female. Only a female can carry the female part."

"Thus the sister."

"Yes. This…carving would have greater value on the black market in Europe if the two parts—male and female—are sold together. Trouble is, the original tomb raiders only took out half of the mural. That much I have confirmed with some architects who are experts on the area. I believe the Morales family has the rest."

"Still hidden in Chiapas?"

"I think Juan and Julio were looking to recover the other half the night before Danny Tellchick was killed."

"In the *caves?*" Markie breathed. "So that's what's in there. Stolen artifacts."

"Yes." Luke turned his head in the direction of the table in the corner. "Are you ready to come clean with me now?" He raised his voice, speaking to Juan in Spanish.

The broken man, his anger spent, now sitting at the table with his head on his arms, croaked out, *"Sí."*

Luke walked over, his heavy boots thudding on the rough-hewn wood floor, punctuating the tense atmosphere.

Frankie could not understand the conversation, of course, but when it was done, Juan was sobbing and Luke looked determined.

Juan had stood up, yelling, but Luke had shouted back, gesturing with a flat-handed *no*. In a lower voice, Luke spoke to Justin for some moments.

When they finished, he crossed the room and took Frankie aside. Before he spoke he kissed her tenderly. "I have to leave now. Julio's life is at stake. I won't have a cell phone signal for much of the trip, but I will see you as soon as I get back. Remember what I said, about what I want when this is over. I mean it, Frankie. You see, I forgot to tell you one other thing, and that is that I…" His eyes searched hers. "I love you."

CHAPTER SEVENTEEN

FOR SOME LONG MOMENTS after Luke left, Frankie stared after him, eyes watering up, heart thudding.

And her sister and brother-in-law stared at *her*.

"Sissy?" Markie said, reaching out to touch her. "Are you okay?"

"No, I am not," Frankie said harshly. "The man I love has just walked out that door, to face God knows what. What did that little man—" she pointed accusingly at Juan, who had resumed his defeated pose with his head on his arms "—say to him?"

"Let's go in here." Markie guided Frankie into Justin's office, which jutted off the back of the kitchen.

The rectangular stone cell had formerly been the cooking room, back in the days before air conditioning. With a massive hearth and a slanting shed roof, it was designed to allow baking and slow cooking without heating up the rest of the house. The tall windows, black now in the middle of the night, would have presented a stunning view of the Kilgore ranch in the daylight.

After she closed the door, Markie sighed. "Sit down, Sissy." She fanned a hand at two leather desk chairs. "I've got a lot to explain."

Frankie sank into a chair. She didn't know if it was the pregnancy or what, but she had started feeling hot and cold, weak and jittery.

"Your Ranger's sharp," Markie started in, pacing. "He pretty much guessed right. I only wish we could have found Juan and Julio sooner. Juan confirmed everything Luke theorized. It all started when their father came to the States years ago and sent their mother the sign of the star."

"The sign of the star?" Frankie knew nothing about this.

"It's a way for crossers to let their families know they've made it this far into Texas, to Five Points. Any kind of Lone Star symbol. A drawing, cheap jewelry, a scrap of fabric. They send it home and the message is clear. So the Morales family knew their father had made it here. But then it seems he disappeared."

"I don't mean to sound jaded, but wouldn't that be a common occurrence? A father who just abandons the family and starts a new life in *el Norte?*"

"No. Not this family. They had a plan. They had dug up the pieces of an ancient mural, far out in the jungle. Luke has pictures of the trench they dug into a tomb chamber. Robbie saw those pictures. By the way, let's not tell Robbie about all of this just yet. Let her enjoy her honeymoon, okay?"

"Okay." But Frankie felt a little clutch of resentment. Let Robbie enjoy her honeymoon, while she, Frankie, was enduring absolute agony. But she quickly scotched those spiteful thoughts. They were too Marynell-like for her comfort.

"Anyway, it seems an old Mayan medicine man told them of the mural's power, or more to the point, its value.

He drew the completed pattern, what it is supposed to look like, according to the ancients. The male side he gave to the father, the female side to the mother. In this village, they have a little network that has regularly smuggled artifacts as far north as Five Points for years, apparently because they have a source, someone willing to pay good money for these items."

"A source? Here? In Five Points?" Frankie was thinking of art smugglers, even highbrow antique dealers. There wasn't anyone like that in Five Points.

"Who has all the power around here? Who spends money like water on politics? Who can't account for the high-rolling way he lives?"

"Your father-in-law?" Frankie couldn't believe this.

"This is very painful to Justin." Markie stopped pacing and sank into a chair as well. "Luke was really grilling Juan about other people missing from his village. The senior Morales is the only one."

"Surely Kilgore didn't—" Frankie could hardly say this next part— "kill people?"

"Luke says it can never be proven without the bodies. Even if Kilgore's caught red-handed with the artifacts, he'll claim he was only collecting them, that he bought them legally from their rightful owners. The Coyotes he engages will take the fall for any murders. Kilgore has got himself some great hit men, all right. Ruthless killers who do what they're paid to do and then disappear to the highlands of Mexico."

"But why would he kill these people? Why wouldn't he simply buy the artifacts and make his profit?"

"The Mexican government wants these things back, and rightly so. Kilgore has to wait a long time before unloading them, sometimes decades. He has to find the right buyer overseas. He has to cover any connection to himself. There's a lot of potential for somebody talking, even if they're going to do their talking in Spanish."

"It's all so much to absorb." Frankie felt sick.

"Yes. Back to this mural. When Juan and Julio got old enough to handle themselves, the brothers came north, hoping somehow to find their father and to recover the priceless half of the Mayan mural that he brought with him.

"Turns out they are very brave boys. They're stone masons, as skilled as their Mayan ancestors, so they carved and aged a fake half of the pattern and left the real one in that tomb in Chiapas. They're not afraid to go into deep, dark places…like those caves. Anyway, they brought the fake to the States with them, sent out word, through Coyotes, that they wanted to make a deal with this buyer."

"The congressman." Frankie felt clammy.

"They sold him the fake and then followed him to the caves. This is the part that made Juan start crying out there." Markie angled her head toward the kitchen. "The night Danny came upon them, they had found the mural pieces, the real half and the fake half they'd just sold the congressman, and crates and crates of other artifacts, too. And…their father's knife. Juan described it in detail. The blade had rusted, but they could still make out the elk-horn handle, carved by a Huichol artisan who is a friend of the family. One of a kind. No mistake. Juan said their dad would never have parted with it. Fortunately, they had the cunning to leave it where they found it. But Danny saw it all, too, and Juan thinks he heard them talking about the congressman."

Frankie could hardly breathe. "Kurt Kilgore didn't...?"

"Danny must have blackmailed him. You know how desperate he was for money. You should have seen the farm's books.

"By now the congressman has discovered the fake and is plenty mad about it, Juan figures. He wants the real half, the one that's still in Chiapas. The one being guarded with magic by a Mayan medicine man. Luke figures the Coyotes will kill Julio as soon as they get it."

"But why did the Coyotes kill their sister, Maria?"

"It was all a set-up. The congressman wanted the pattern to assemble the pieces, and she was to bring it, woven into the vest. Superstitions die hard down there, and a girl has to carry the pattern. But the Coyotes took matters into their own hands and killed her to get the vest and to draw out Juan and Julio, who, of course, knew where the real half was down in Chiapas."

"Oh, this is all so sickening," Frankie said. "And right here under our noses."

"For decades. The congressman thought he was pretty smart, I expect, when he made that dirty deal with Mother, selling that land for a song to a lazy bumpkin like Danny. He knew Danny would let the rocky area around that sinkhole go to weed and lie fallow forever and his secret would be safe."

"Until Danny caught the Morales out there that night. My Lord. He killed Danny for blackmailing him?"

"We can't pin Danny's death on the congressman." Markie was talking about her father-in-law as coldly as if he were one of her old political enemies. "Technically, Mestor set the fire. But Mestor is just an old torch who was hired by the Coyotes."

"Who were hired by the congressman," Frankie said, finishing the chain.

"See why it's going to be hard to nail the old man?"

"Lord, yes. So, when the fire happened, Juan and Julio got scared and ran?"

"Yes. Since they'd had a run-in with Danny, they thought they would be blamed for his death. Of course, all this time they were the only ones who knew the way in to the artifacts, except for the congressman himself."

"Well, Brandon came close the night he followed Kurt."

"That must have been a real scare for the congressman. It was a nightmare for me, I'll tell you."

"I can't imagine. Did you have any idea Kurt was so…immersed in evil that night?"

"No. But I knew he was covering something up. I thought maybe it was just more of his dealings with Mother that he didn't want exposed."

"You have no feeling at all for the man, do you?" Frankie was just checking. Her sister was being amazingly strong about all of this.

"None but scorn. And I can't believe our mother ever had a relationship with him."

"That is just too ghastly to think about. Do you think she has any idea about any of this stuff? About the caves? The artifacts?"

"I think she knows what Kurt is capable of, but I doubt she knows how far gone he is."

"He's got to be stopped!" Frankie bolted upright. "Why don't we contact Joe Pultie right now and have that Juan kid—" she pointed toward the kitchen excitedly "—have him show the sheriff the way into the caves and confiscate that stuff?"

"Not cool. Luke figures the congressman owns good old Joe. And besides, then how would we connect that stuff to the congressman? Just because it's hidden on his former land, doesn't mean he knew about it. You can be sure he'll claim that he didn't. Luke has to catch those Coyotes. They'll have to testify against their boss."

Frankie buried her face in her hands. "Why does he have to go down there," she choked back a sob behind her palms, "all alone?"

"Sissy." Markie dropped to one knee in front of her. "You'd better get some rest. You're under a lot of stress—"

"Stress? Really?" Frankie's beleaguered eyes snapped up to Markie's face. "You think? I mean, I'm forty and not married and pregnant and the father of my baby has just split for Mexico—" her voice rose, threatening hysteria "—where he's probably going to get himself killed!" Frankie buried her face in her hands again and broke down into full-fledged sobs this time.

"Sweetie, sweetie." Markie's arms were around her instantly. "Luke's not abandoning you. I heard him say that he loves you. Did you tell him about the baby?"

Frankie shook her head no. "And I'm not going to."

Markie bracketed Frankie's shoulders with her hands. "For heaven's sake, why not?"

Frankie sniffed and raised her head. "Because. He's already lost a child once. He had a daughter who died. A little g-girl." Frankie started to blubber again.

"Oh, my goodness. Here, sweetie." Markie handed her a tissue from a box on Justin's desk. "When? How?"

"He was running down these same Coyotes across the border in Mexico. There was a shootout and his wife and daughter were killed. You're a news junkie. Do you remember hearing about that?"

"About a Ranger's family getting killed down on the border? Seems like I do. I *thought* the name Driscoll rang a bell. That was Luke?"

"Yes. So, you see, I'm not about to tell him the happy news. And don't try to convince me otherwise. Since I'm probably going to lose this baby anyway, I refuse to put Luke through that pain again."

"That's just fatigue talking," Markie said confidently. "Too much has happened today for you to even think straight. You just need to go home and get some rest." She pulled Frankie up by her elbows. "Justin and I will take you back to Robbie's place in town. We need to go and check on Aurelia and the baby at the hospital anyway. I'll make you some herbal tea when we get there."

"Thanks, Sissy." Frankie tried to dry her eyes one last time. "I can't believe my life is falling apart like this."

Markie gave Frankie a shoulder-to-shoulder hug as she led her out the door. "There was this aging hippie chick that lived next door to me in Austin. She was full of beans, but I remember she had a saying: *Falling apart is coming together.*"

"That makes absolutely no sense." Frankie sniffed.

"I think it means sometimes things get worse before they get better. You know, like sometimes you have to have surgery in order to get well?"

That metaphor resonated for the nurse in Frankie. But how could she get well, she wondered, when there were surely more grievous wounds to come?

Sometimes a person just had to give it up. Just surrender and let their loved ones take care of them. And so Frankie, the oldest sister, the strong one, the one who always had a plan, the one who always took care of the others, allowed her baby sister to lead her home.

ROBBIE'S WEDDING NIGHT was the beginning of a long dark period for Frankie. She cocooned herself in Robbie's old rental house on Cypress Street where, feeling as if she had no place in the world to call her own, she would sit every evening and listlessly pet her finicky little poodle.

She had known for certain that she would never go back to Austin, to Kyle. By June the divorce would be final and she was glad. There was no guilt in her heart when she thought about it. The marriage had died long ago, if in fact it had ever begun.

But even though she was thoroughly finished with her life in Austin, she couldn't figure out where she fit in here in Five Points.

Much to her amazement, her father was progressing merrily with his life and seemed to have no need of a spinsterish daughter taking up permanent residence out on his place. Not that she wanted to step into Marynell's shoes in any case.

Brandon Smith was making plans to spend a few days with P.J. when the hay-baling started. He said he enjoyed the break, the physical labor, and wanted to spend more time with his long-lost grandfather. Cooking for a couple of bachelor farmers was not her style.

Markie wanted her to come and apply her nursing skills out at the Light. The immigrants had plenty of little health problems that needed tending to and they would be grateful, Markie insisted. But Frankie saw through that ruse. Her proactive sister thought the answer to all of life's problems was work, work and more work. Frankie knew her problems wouldn't be resolved by staying busy and pretending to be the missionary she clearly wasn't.

Robbie still needed her help at the store, of course, especially with the tourist trade picking up during wildflower season. But without Luke coming by to distract her, Frankie had the entire place as orderly as a surgery suite inside a week.

The newly formed Tellchick-Trueblood family tended to use the store as their in-town base. Robbie, Zack, the boys, the baby, all of them were always coming and going, being picked up or dropped off, connecting with each other. One day Frankie went back into the storeroom and caught herself staring at a row of Zack's firefighter shirts, hanging where Robbie had left them after she'd picked them up at the cleaners. That was when she realized she was starting to feel like an interloper at the store as well.

Still, she ricocheted from Robbie's store to her dad's farm to the Light at Five Points and back to the catacombed rooms of the big old house on Cypress Street, waiting to lose the baby, so she'd be done with that and could decide what to do next.

She spent hours scribbling in her diary and took to talking to Charm as if she were human. The tiny poodle was a good listener, cocking her head with a little doggy frown as if she understood weighty words like *miscarriage* and *ultrasound* and *commitment.*

All Frankie knew for sure was that she did not feel rooted. She didn't know where Luke was, or even if he was alive. She didn't know how she was going to make a living once the separation period ended. She didn't know if she was still going to be pregnant from one day to the next.

A week passed. A month. With a mixture of amazement and dread, she realized she needed prenatal care. She couldn't bring herself to go back to her obstetrician in Austin, and certainly not to that new fertility specialist Kyle had scared up. So she made an appointment with Robbie's doctor in Five Points.

Dr. Jenna, as the town called her, wasn't a fancy specialist, only a family practitioner, but she cared deeply about her patients and Zack seemed to think the world of her. She was Zack's best friend Mason's little sister, and Frankie had met her briefly at the wedding, so she was somewhat comfortable with her.

"Everything looks hunky-dory," Jenna chirped after Frankie's first exam was complete.

Frankie tucked the paper drapes around herself as Jenna

gave her a hand up. "I can't understand it. By the time I've entered the second trimester, I have always miscarried." Frankie had shared her complete history with the doctor.

"Your ex-husband is not the father this time, I take it?"

Frankie's cheeks flamed, an annoyingly regular occurrence of late, and shook her head. "No. Thank God."

"Hmm." Jenna's dark eyebrows raised. "I see. Well, medically I can't explain it, but sometimes a different daddy…" Jenna shrugged. "Sometimes it's just plain good chemistry."

Chemistry, Frankie thought. Such a cold, scientific term for the amazing physical, emotional and *spiritual* bond she had developed with Luke Driscoll. Her head came up. "Are you saying it's not all my fault I miscarried all those times?"

Pain and resentment, and finally a righteous anger, welled up in Frankie's chest as she realized the blame wasn't all hers. "My ex-husband blamed me for the miscarriages, even though our doctors couldn't find anything wrong with me."

"Not very scientific for a surgeon. Sometimes a couple miscarries over and over because the same genetic defect pops up. That's a combo thing. And you've certainly got a healthy pregnancy going now…like I said, with a different daddy."

Frankie picked nervously at a nail, sensing what was next.

"So, I take it you've told the father?" Jenna asked.

Here we go, Frankie thought. Did she *look* like some mixed-up teenager here? "No." Short. Sweet. None-of-your-beeswax. To the point.

"Have you decided if you *want* this baby?"

Frankie rolled her eyes toward the acoustical tile ceiling. Did she want this baby? What a question. When she tipped her chin back down she felt the tears sting. *Did she want this baby?* She braced her palms on the edge of the exam table, elbows locked. How much did she want air? Her very life?

"So you're okay with this?" Jenna pressed. "Having a baby alone?"

Frankie knew Dr. Jenna wasn't being unkind to ask these questions, that she was doing a bit of small-town-doctor therapy. She swallowed, tried to sound in control. "I'm mature. I'm forty. When my divorce settlement is paid, I'll have some resources."

"That's not what I meant. I'm talking about your emotions, Frankie. You've been through a lot, you and your family, in the space of one year. Wouldn't it be easier if you shared the strain with the baby's father instead of going it alone?"

Frankie sighed. "No. I have made up my mind on that. For reasons I'd rather not explain, I prefer to wait and see if I keep this one."

Jenna pressed a thoughtful finger to her lips as she studied Frankie's chart again. "Well," she said at length, "so far everything looks normal."

Even as the doctor had reassured her, Frankie had held on to her doubts. But sure enough, her body tricked her yet again this time, but in a new way. This time, she was glowing with health. Formerly slim to the point of thinness, she started to blossom, to show. Her breasts grew larger and excruciatingly tender. If she stood on her feet too long working in the store, her ankles puffed up.

And then one day she felt it.

A flutter. Like butterflies in the stomach, only much lower. Unmistakably lower, in a place where she knew a life lay, growing.

The instant it happened she sucked in a breath, stopped in her tracks, flattening a palm between her navel and pubic bone.

She was alone and Main Street was caught in the doldrums of mid-afternoon quiet. She stared out the display window and had the crazy urge to dash to Ardella's screaming, *My baby just moved!*

Instead, she caressed her lower abdomen in a slow, gentle circle, testing. Willing it—her—him—to move again. *Please.* Let me know you're real. She felt a little pouch of tummy there, something new for her. She stood still for a long time, with an adrenaline rush of hope surging through her, but at the same time putting the brakes on her feelings, not letting herself surrender to them.

All afternoon she seesawed in that state of conflict.

Elation at feeling that first sign of movement. Fear that that's all she would ever feel of it.

Weirdly enough, that was also the day Luke's Uncle Beecher showed up at the shop. She was kneeling behind the counter, putting away bubble wrap, when the bell at the door tinkled.

Frankie popped her head up and said, "Be right with you. Oh, I'm sorry." She straightened, then angled a hip around the counter, moving toward the man and the massive German shepherd at his side. "We don't allow pets in the store. However, he's perfectly welcome to rest

outside on the veranda while you shop." She smiled her
best shopkeeper's smile.

"This here's Philo." The man returned her smile, and immediately after he spoke, Frankie recognized his resem-
blance to Luke. The same deep-set brown eyes. The same
compelling handsomeness and ramrod-straight body, even
though this gentleman was clearly in his seventies, maybe
even in his eighties. She couldn't help wondering if Luke
would look like this as he aged.

"And you're Luke's Uncle Beecher?" she said.

"Yep."

"I, uh…" Frankie was unprepared for this. She stepped
toward him, extending her hand. "It's nice to meet you."

He took her fingers lightly in his rough, calloused ones.

"I apologize for just showing up like this. Luke plowed
through Austin on his way to Mexico. He needed a few
things for the trip. Side arms, mostly. And he told me about
you. He gave me a key to that house over there and said I
should come up and have a look and maybe get myself accustomed to it."

He was talking about the Sunday house. "Oh," Frankie
said, still mystified by his sudden appearance. "I'm so
glad you came."

"Bit slow about it, but here I am."

"So, how do you like it? The house?"

"Fair. I think Luke is determined to make this town his
home, once he has got Texcoyo dealt with."

Frankie tried to keep her face from showing her anxiety.
"That doesn't scare the hell out of you? Your nephew off
chasing Coyotes, alone in Mexico?"

"He's a Ranger."

"Luke told me you were one also."

"Oh, yes. *Was*. Out to pasture now. Are you hungry?" he said abruptly.

She was. Constantly these days. Unlike her other pregnancies, this one had little accompanying morning sickness. Frankie ate all day long. Everything tasted good.

Beecher took Philo for a walk until it was time to close the store. Then they went over to the Aggie. Frankie had a feeling Beecher would love Parson's chicken-fried steak as much as his nephew did.

They tied Philo's leash onto the leg of the newspaper dispenser outside and the dog settled on the sidewalk like a statue of a sphinx, paws flat in front of him.

"He's very well-behaved," Frankie commented.

"Luke won't have it no other way. My nephew's a strict devil." There was a note of warning in Beecher's voice.

"Mr. Driscoll—"

"Beecher to you."

"Beecher." Frankie smiled as he opened the diner door for her. "Something you should know about me. I'm a pretty straight arrow myself. Your nephew and I got along just fine."

"I'm aware. He told me all about you."

After Nattie Rose took their orders, Beecher said, "Luke never talked about a woman the way he talked about you. He makes you sound like a cross between a Dallas Cowboys cheerleader and a Mensa recruit. Kinda took me by surprise, after all this time of him being single."

"He never had another serious relationship? I mean, except for his wife, of course."

"Oh, Luke's never suffered for the attention of women. After he was widowed, the ladies from Liana's church, especially, were all over him. Brought him covered dishes for a solid three months. But then they quit it when he stopped attending services and got himself a motorcycle."

"He has a motorcycle?"

"Not no more." Beecher waved a palm. "He ditched it after a couple of years. He's wantin' a horse now. What that boy really needs is a family, if you ask me."

Frankie's cheeks flamed at the secret knowledge that, unbeknownst to Luke, he had already started one.

Nattie Rose showed up with their dinners, dumped them with a smile, and was off. Frankie was glad it was tourist season and the diner was too busy for Nattie Rose to indulge her curiosity about Beecher.

"I wasn't sure old Luke would ever get back in the harness again," Beecher continued conversationally as he sprinkled Tabasco sauce on everything. "He has taken up with various ladies over the years, but he always finds a way to end it eventually."

There must have been something distressed about Frankie's face because he stopped shaking the small sauce bottle and studied her.

"If it makes you feel any better, I never heard him say those gals' names the way he says yours."

Frankie swallowed, wanting to say, *Bless you.* How she'd needed to hear these words! "I wish he'd just come back," she admitted as Beecher studied her with his kindly brown eyes. It seemed pointless to maintain a front with him. She'd never met anyone so thoroughly disarming, unless it was his nephew. Maybe it was genetic, this calm acceptance, this straightforward strength. That got her to thinking about the baby.

"Something you need to understand about my nephew, young lady, if you are going to insist on getting all involved with him. That boy has always been one to get his man. But after Liana and Bethany were killed, Luke became the kind that would charge hell with a bucket of water. He is hell-bent on revenge. He will not be back this time until Izek Texcoyo is dealt with."

Without Beecher having to say it, Frankie knew Luke would see it to the death. She just prayed that death wouldn't be his own.

BEECHER'S PRESENCE in town somehow made Frankie's life more tolerable. She felt as if she had a living connection to Luke.

The Sunday house, though still sparsely furnished, felt more like home to her than the rambling place on Cypress Street. The final renovations had ended up being much to her liking. Beecher allowed as how he might consent to "camp" there without too much strain.

Luke had chosen a warm ochre for the outside trim that emphasized the native rock. The porch boards shone glossy aqua and the authentic period light fixtures were already taking on a coppery green patina. She loved Luke's taste.

But that first night when she flipped on the light in the great room that angled off the back of the house, the sight of some new furniture beneath the bow windows arrested her breath. Luke enjoyed the town's antique stores, she knew. What she hadn't realized was that he'd bought a child-sized mission table with two tiny chairs.

Looking at it brought tears to her eyes and paradoxically gave her hope. Suddenly, she wished she'd told Luke about the baby before he went to Mexico. What if he never came back? He would die without knowing he had a child on the way. She had to stop thinking like this or she'd make herself sick.

So, Beecher became her lifeline. A means to stay sane while she waited to see what her future would hold. They spent many an evening together, getting to be friends, playing cards, talking about Luke. Frankie couldn't get enough of that. But when she pumped Beecher for details about Luke as a child, as a baby, the old guy became suspicious.

"You haven't taken a shine to the idea of having children with this man now?" he said. Beecher was blunt-spoken, like his nephew.

"Is that such an outlandish idea?" she hedged.

"Well, there needs to be some kind of a wedding first, don't you think?" Beecher, she had also learned, was conservative, religious.

"I suppose." Frankie hid her blushing face by taking a sip of Coke, a rare indulgence now that her weight was climbing.

"Even if you can get him to marry you, little sister, there's a part of Luke's heart is sealed off tighter'n an armadillo's ass."

Frankie's cheeks flamed and she frowned at her Coke. She was glad that Beecher's crude language gave cover for her awesome secret.

Beecher cleared his throat. "Pardon my French. But

you'd understand it if you'd been there to see him after…"
Beecher frowned at his cards, his grizzled face set like
flint. "I don't really like to think about it myself."

Frankie clutched her cards to her chest and leaned forward.
"It should be obvious to you that I'm in love with Luke."

Beecher swallowed and put down his cards. "It's not my
story to be telling. And there's a lot of sorrow in it."

"I am not afraid of sorrow." Frankie was glad that she
could say that about herself now. Glad that she could accept
life, and people, for what they were instead of always
trying to pretty things up, always seeking approval. All her
life she'd strained for control, thinking that would make her
safe and secure. Only recently, thanks to Luke, had she
learned that acceptance was sometimes the higher way.
From him she had learned to let go and just *live* each day,
each moment, doing your best. More than anything, she
wanted to hear how the man had come to such a place.

"Let's go in here," Beecher said. They went to the twin
leather recliners that Luke had had delivered from Austin a
couple of weeks earlier. They were the lone furnishings in the
great room, save for that little mission table. Frankie looked
at it and swallowed as she lowered herself into one of the
chairs, canted to face the dark hole of the stone fireplace.

"Want me to light that thing?" Beecher asked.

"Please." It was a spring night, not overly chilly, but
Frankie had a feeling she was going to need the fire's
warmth before Beecher's story was over.

After he raised the flames, Beecher settled into the other
recliner and started in. "Before he ever becomes a Ranger
a man has to prove he can handle himself without direc-

tion from higher authority." Beecher puffed up a bit when he said this, but Frankie understood. Beecher was the real deal, like Luke, and a man could be forgiven for being a little prideful of such things.

"Luke had the required eight years of experience in law enforcement, of course, before he became a Ranger. He got good at running down leads in questionable deaths, unidentified bodies and missing persons, stuff like that. That's how he got involved in this business down on the border.

"Families of illegals claimed their relatives were missing. It was Luke's wife, really, who first made him listen to those people. She had a heart in her, that girl. She had done missionary work down there before they were married, and some after, too, as she was able."

"She sounds exceptional."

"She was." With that one past-tense verb, all of Beecher's sorrow about Luke's deceased wife came through.

"So what happened? That night in Acuna?"

"Luke traced the missing persons to the hands of a ruthless Coyote named Izek Texcoyo. That was the first link. All of the missing persons, Luke discovered, had paid this one Tex character for passage."

"Rangers maintain a lot of contacts—in Texas and nationwide—but even so Luke knew he would have to go into Mexico to nail this guy. He tracked Texcoyo, undercover, with unofficial sanction. It took a long time, and Luke went far, disappeared most thoroughly. No one would have ever known he was down there if Liana hadn't had the bright idea to meet up with him briefly in Acuna. She missed her husband and she wanted Bethany, only six at

the time, to see her daddy for a few days. Unfortunately…"
Beecher cleared his throat as he stared at the flames.

"Luke uncovered some strange things in Mexico. Mayan
tomb raiders and such. Texcoyo and his boys grew suspicious
of the gringo Luke. They followed him up from Chiapas
when he went to Acuna. Luke figures the gang must have seen
him in the mission with his family, and figured out he was
not what he claimed to be—an American ex-con on the run."

"Later, Luke figured out one of the Mexicans in the
mission must have talked to Texcoyo's boys. Told them
Luke was really a Ranger. Texcoyo staged a border gang
shoot-out—a common thing down there—but the real
purpose was to eliminate Luke. But instead, when the
shooting died down Liana and Bethany and two Mexican
children from the mission were dead."

"In the years since, Texcoyo has only become more
dangerous. And Luke has never let go of the hunt. He
formed a sort of triangle in his mind—" Beecher slashed
the air with his finger "—that town in Chiapas, Texcoyo
and this here place."

"He kept saying he couldn't make the dots connect. But
then you all got shot at out by those caves, and there was
Texcoyo, bigger'n Dallas. He knew he had a genuine hot
tamale then. So, you see," Beecher finished up, "for Luke
this is far more than solving a case."

"It's catching the man who murdered his family."

"And the man behind the man who murdered his family.
Luke won't stop until he exposes the whole chain, top to
bottom. Until he does that, part of my nephew will be
stuck in the past—"

"With his family." Frankie had started to weep.

"I guess I should'na told you all this." Beecher's tone was regretful.

"No." Frankie dabbed at her eyes as she placed the other palm on her quivering stomach. "I'm glad you did," she whispered, deciding again that it was for the best that she hadn't told Luke about this baby.

CHAPTER EIGHTEEN

TWO MONTHS flew by, then three, all while Frankie endured her private limbo and her body continued to change and grow. It became obvious that she was not going to lose this baby, and it also became harder to imagine how she was going to tell Luke, now that she was so far along. He would surely be angry over her deception.

No word came up from Mexico, not so much as a phone call.

"He's deep undercover this time," Beecher repeatedly explained. "Texcoyo knows what he looks like, too, you know."

Beecher became Frankie's anchor. During the pleasant spring evenings, he would often walk Philo and Charm over to the shop together and then the trio would walk Frankie home.

Ardella often came out on the sidewalk to pet the animals. Frankie suspected it was Beecher that Ardella was really of a mind to pet.

"You like her?" Frankie asked as they walked the dogs into a glorious sunset one evening.

"That flower woman?" Beecher said. "Why, she's wound up tighter'n a rusty old spring. And she's a nosy one. Asked me if you weren't gaining a little weight."

Frankie hoped that the crimson rays from the hills hid her furious blushing. "What a strange thing to ask."

It wasn't, of course. She was showing so much that she would soon have to transition into maternity clothes.

Markie was merciless in her pestering. She felt she had the right, given her experience in these matters. "Tell everyone," she urged Frankie, "so they can get busy and help you."

But each week Frankie put it off while life in Five Points moseyed along. She made a conscious choice to enjoy the small-town rhythm. There was no point in making herself sick worrying about Luke. The anxiety couldn't be good for the baby, and she didn't want her—or him—to look back and see her mother as weak. June came and she disguised her tummy as best she could under oversized T-shirts.

Markie threw a barbecue out at her dad's farm when Brandon came back for the hay-baling. She wanted him to get to know his blood relatives without too much pressure. Frankie found a big denim shirt and took Beecher along because he was like family to her. The party had gone on well past dusk, with the dogs barking and children playing and the babies sleeping, when Jose Ramos again sounded the alarm.

"The Coyotes!" He roared up in the same battered pickup and yelled from the cab in a way that Frankie found sickeningly déjà vu. "I seen 'em at the caves!"

Zack and Justin trotted up to the door of the pickup.

Jose sputtered out the details—three SUVs; four Mexican guys, one of whom he thought might be Julio, plus the one with the scar; a heavyset white man; boxes being loaded.

Justin made a command decision. "Everybody stay

calm," he said. "We are calling the sheriff. Everybody go into the house."

"Julio!" Aurelia cried as Yolonda pulled her back. "I go to him!"

"Nobody is going anywhere," Justin ordered.

But before anyone could stop him, Brandon lit out for his Jeep.

"Where is he going?" Markie demanded, as the Jeep's headlights flared on. "Stop him!" she yelled as Brandon roared up the drive, tires spraying gravel as he turned off toward Robbie's place.

"He's chasing down his dang story!" This from P.J. "He showed me he's got a camera and a gun in that Jeep."

"A *gun?* He'll get himself shot!" Markie practically screamed. "Stop him!" She clutched at Justin, who circled calming arms around her.

Zack and Robbie were already herding their family into the house. But amidst the chaos, Frankie felt frozen in place. The Coyotes? Here? Now? Was Luke out there somewhere?

LUKE KEPT a pair of binoculars smashed to his face as he lay prone on a slab of rock on the ridge above the river. The battered pickup that had downshifted and slowed on the ranch road to the south some moments ago worried him. If someone had seen the activity, they might call the law, and that would not be cool. Incompetent—or worse, corrupt—locals running around out here would interfere with his plan. Like any Texas Ranger, Luke really did prefer to work alone. It would be nice to have all the evidence to hand.

He adjusted the binoculars, straining to keep tabs on the busy figures below, limned in the light of a full moon, with the headlamps of the vehicles making silhouettes of them. Four Mexican men. One definitely Texcoyo. One possibly Julio. Even for as long as Luke had tracked the gang in Mexico, he had never managed to see the boy in person. But who else would they have forced into the caves at gunpoint? The well-dressed portly man with light reflecting off his spectacles was the congressman.

He wanted to wait until they were all outside, hands lugging the crates before he got the drop on them.

He cursed when he heard another vehicle approaching. He dropped the binoculars long enough to observe headlights coming up that south ranch road again. He made out a Jeep just before all went black as the car undoubtedly stopped short of the padlocked gate. Who could this be?

The figure of the congressman stalked toward the gate, then disappeared into the gloom. The large man reappeared with Brandon Smith in tow. He yelled at his thugs and everyone followed as the fat man and the boy disappeared into the crevice in the wall of rock.

Luke cursed under his breath. Now he would have to go back into the caves.

When he did so, blindly, groping from boulder to boulder without a flashlight, he hoped he was following the route Brandon had shown him last winter. He had not felt his way far inside the first chamber before he heard voices deeper in.

He edged around a curtain of stalactites and looked toward the light illuminating a cluster of shouting men in the larger chamber. This was obviously the place he and

Brandon had not been able to find before. And no wonder. Across the gaping hole of a vast streamway, the congressman and his thugs had erected a collapsible steel walkway.

Above their heads Luke recognized the tall black shaft that led up to the sinkhole. This is what the spelunkers would have found if the congressman had not used his influence to stop Luke from getting his search warrant: a cavern the size of a barn, with water dripping off grotesque rock formations lit now by two enormous halogen lights. Against the walls, in every niche, were boxes and crates. The congressman's wire-rimmed glasses shone like silver dollars on a dead man's eyes.

"Lad," he was saying to Brandon, "I don't know what your problem is, but you desperately need to learn to mind your own business. I thought I ran you out of here once before."

Brandon's sweat-soaked, blanched face was clearly lit. One of the Coyotes was holding his arms behind his back. "I'll tell you what my problem is, sir," he breathed. "*It's you*. I don't know what all you've done in here, but when I get to the bottom of it, the whole state, the whole country, is going to know about it."

"The only thing you are going to get to the bottom of is that pool down there."

Luke saw Brandon's eyes grow wide as he stared where the congressman pointed, to the precipitous edge of a dark streamway.

"Down there," the congressman continued, "you will be very quiet, along with a few dozen unfortunate Mexicans."

The Coyotes, standing in a small circle with guns raised now, cackled like a pack of nasty hyenas. All save one.

Julio, Luke thought. How could he get Julio *and* Brandon out of here alive? Julio, he hoped, knew his way around these caverns as well as Brandon. Luke checked his options and saw the shadow of what Brandon had called a drapery, something that looked like a wave of surf frozen as it dropped. Just big enough, Luke decided, to do the job.

"Why?" Brandon was saying in a voice strained with fear. "Why, man? Money?" The word *money* echoed off the chamber's walls like a filthy curse.

"These artifacts are of no use to peasants like these," the congressman spat. "These people don't know what to do with money when they do have it." He stepped over and jerked on a flashy gold chain at the neck of one of the Coyotes as if it were a leash.

The man shook him off with an evil glare, but the congressman only laughed. "For years I funded my campaigns with this junk. It was a tidy little nest egg. But this last piece, this entire wall of carvings…once completely assembled, it is worth far more than I ever imagined in my wildest dreams. It is being shipped, flown out under the radar, so to speak, to Europe. Tonight. And then I will become one very, very wealthy man. After that, I will be dead. My plane will disappear in the waters of the Gulf. Sad, no?"

Brandon didn't answer. He was looking at Luke, who had shown himself around the curtain of rock.

"*¡Suelten las armas!*" Luke said. *Drop the guns,* which was enough to draw the Coyote's fire.

Luke dived beneath the drapery while bullets sprayed and Brandon and Julio broke free. He did not waste shots on the Coyotes right away, but took out the lights. *Ping! Ping!* Pitch blackness.

From under his protective curl of rock, he yelled, "Run, boys!" Twice. Once in English for Brandon. Once in Spanish for Julio.

THE THREE SISTERS, anxiously waiting for the deputies Justin had summoned, heard the sound of gunshots in the distance as one.

"Brandon!" Markie cried as she jumped to her feet.

Aurelia and Mrs. Ramos were already herding the kids into the back room.

"By God, I will not leave my grandson to fend for himself out there." P.J. stomped up the narrow stairs to his spare attic room, and while the other adults were all still arguing about what to do, he came back bearing his shotgun and two loaded side arms. Zack and Justin grabbed the pistols and then everyone was yelling at once.

"We can go too!" Markie cried.

"Daddy, have you got any more guns?" This was from Robbie.

"I've got one in my truck!" Beecher yelled.

"No!" Zack cried out.

"You will all get in the back of the house with the children!" Justin demanded.

The roar of an approaching vehicle shut them all up.

They looked out as Brandon's Jeep fishtailed in on a cloud of dust. Markie ran out onto the porch, heedless of the fact that another vehicle was in close pursuit. Robbie and Frankie ran after to stop her.

For that one fateful instant, Frankie thought of her sister instead of her baby. But only for that instant, because in the next a rain of gunfire broke out and Frankie was hit.

FROM INSIDE the Jeep, Luke saw Frankie fall. As he clawed to get out of the vehicle, then dodged from tree to tree to get to her, he could only think how he had chosen wrong. Making himself a decoy for the Coyotes, he'd led them to P.J.'s place, though Robbie's was closer, thinking he could not put the Tellchick children in harm's way. From the snake incident he knew that at least the old farmer had a gun.

All around him Luke heard the rapid frizzing pop-pops of automatic rifles.

Inside the house, the men kept up an exchange of covering fire while, with a nightmarish horror that threatened to choke him, Luke crawled up the porch steps to Frankie's prone body.

His mind, his heart, everything that was in him swore when he got to her and saw blood. *It was like Liana and Bethany all over again.*

Frankie's sisters had flattened themselves on their bellies at either side of her.

"Get inside!" Luke waved them away as he threw himself over Frankie's wounded body, clutching her, blinded by the terror that for the second time in his miserable life the woman he loved had been killed because of him.

He pressed the butt of his hand to a seeping wound in her back. He scooped her into his arms, and the next thing he knew they were all in the house and he was laying her limp body on her parents' kitchen floor.

She was still breathing. The amount of blood he could immediately see wasn't excessive. But that didn't mean there weren't internal injuries.

Please God, he prayed, *don't let me lose her.*

Robbie, who was crying so hard she could hardly get the words out, pleaded with her husband. "Zack, help us!" Then she got to her knees and crawled toward the kitchen wall phone.

Zack handed his gun off and threw himself to his knees beside Luke while Markie grabbed some kitchen towels for a pressure dressing.

Between them, Zack and Luke marshaled every last one of their skills to stop Frankie's bleeding. But they couldn't wake her.

"It's this head injury. A concussion, maybe." Zack moved her head carefully to the side so Luke could see the bump.

"I believe that girl's pregnant," Beecher called out over his shoulder.

Luke had a moment of disorientation as he stared up at his uncle. "Beecher?" He hadn't even noticed him before.

"Glad you made it back alive, son." Beecher kept shooting. "Just wish you hadn't brought these *hombres* with you."

Luke stared at Frankie now. From her face to her slightly rounded abdomen and back. "Pregnant?"

Markie, kneeling again at Frankie's other side, nodded with tears in her eyes. "She is."

Luke stared at her, his jaw slack as if the wind had just been knocked out of him. "Why didn't she tell me? Unless…"

"Oh, it's yours," Markie said, very quietly, lest the others hear. "She just…" Markie was on the verge of tears.

Luke grabbed Markie's arm. "No. She will wake up."

"The ambulance is coming," Robbie announced to all. "Hope the law gets here fast."

"Why didn't she tell me?" Luke pressed Markie for an answer.

Markie leaned over Frankie's deceptively peaceful face. "She wanted to, but she's lost so many babies, she was just sure she'd lose this one, too. But…"

She glanced at Frankie's rounded tummy and Luke followed her gaze, then closed his eyes. *Don't let her lose this one, too,* he prayed. *No matter what happens between us, just let Frankie keep her baby.* "Keep pressure on this." He rejoined the shooting. That ambulance would get through.

The county deputies finally arrived, sirens blazing and in chase as the Coyotes took off down the drive and spun back out onto the highway, almost colliding with the ambulance on their way past.

FRANKIE'S TINY BABY, *his* baby, had a heck of a heartbeat, Luke thought. He had been at her bedside for hours, days maybe. He didn't know. He had urged the nurse to come in so many times with her Doppler and let him listen to his child's heartbeat, she was surely sick of him.

"When do you think she's going to wake up?" he asked when the nurse came in to check Frankie's pupils again. He noticed she had brought the Doppler without being asked this time.

The nurse, a heavyset lady with kind, coal-black eyes and a wide, peaceful face, smiled at him patiently. He had asked this question every time.

"The concussion from the fall will probably not cause permanent damage," she reiterated. "It's a matter of waiting for the brain swelling to resolve. But like the doctors told the family, it might take her a bit longer to come out of her fog because with the pregnancy we are limited in the drugs we can use to bring the swelling down."

Luke nodded, reassured for the hundredth time, though never enough.

"She's lucky to be alive," the nurse commented quietly as she checked the dressing on Frankie's shoulder.

"Yes."

"They caught those guys, I heard."

"Yes." Luke did not take his eyes off Frankie's closed ones.

"*Umm-mmm.*" The nurse shook her head. "Those Coyotes are sure bad. And imagine old Congressman Kilgore behind it all!"

"Yes." Luke didn't really care about any of this anymore, not like he used to, anyway. It grieved him that Frankie's family had been through this ordeal, but they were strong people. Sweet people. And now there was going to be another member of the McBride clan. He slid a protective palm over Frankie's abdomen, something he couldn't seem to stop himself from doing.

"Well then, shall we?" The nurse took the Doppler out, smeared blue gel on its tip, gently lifted Frankie's gown and expertly found the heartbeat.

At the loud, steady whooshing sound, Luke's eyes got watery and Frankie's fluttered open before falling, hooded again with semi-consciousness.

"Frankie? Baby?" Luke leaned over her. "Do you hear your little one?" He couldn't keep the emotion out of his voice. Didn't even try. Let the nurse think what she would. "We're going to be a family. And we're getting married as soon as you wake up. Wake up, darlin', so I can marry you."

The nurse smiled just like she had the other ten times she'd heard him say it.

But this time Frankie struggled, coming more alert. "Oh Luke," she said drowsily, "You *are* here. I thought I was…dreaming."

With sudden tears, Luke squeezed her hand, kissed her forehead. "You aren't dreaming, princess. I'm here. And we're getting married just as soon as you say yes. We're going to raise this miracle baby together, as man and wife over in that Sunday house. That is, if you'll have me."

After the nurse checked her level of consciousness, Frankie said, "Oh, Luke," her voice dry and slurry as if she might drift off again, and he wanted to kiss her before she faded. But he waited until the nurse had helped her take a sip of water.

When she'd swallowed, Frankie tried to talk again. "Luke, I'm sorry. I should have told you—"

"Shh. Just let me kiss you."

When he'd finished giving her the gentlest, most reverent kiss he could place on her mouth, Frankie opened her hooded eyes a little wider. "And Luke?"

"What, my darling?" He stroked her hair back with two tender fingertips.

Her eyes fluttered closed, and he had to lean down very near to her lips to hear what she was trying to say. The one word she said came out in the faintest whisper, but for tonight, it was enough. For tonight, it was the only word Luke needed to hear.

"*Yes.*"

* * * * *

*Experience entertaining women's fiction
about rediscovery
and reconnection—warm, compelling stories
that are relevant
for every woman who has wondered
"What's next?" in her life.
After all, there's the life you planned.
And there's what comes next.*

*Turn the page for a sneak preview
of a new book from* Harlequin NEXT.

CONFESSIONS OF A NOT-SO-DEAD LIBIDO
by Peggy Webb

*On sale November 2006,
wherever books are sold.*

My husband could see beauty in a mud puddle. Literally. "Look at that, Louise," he'd say after a heavy spring rain. "Have you ever seen so many amazing colors in mud?"

I'd look and see nothing except brown, but he'd pick up a stick and swirl the mud till the colors of the earth emerged, and all of a sudden I'd see the world through his eyes—extraordinary instead of mundane.

Roy was my mirror to life. Four years ago when he died, it cracked wide open, and I've been living a smashed-up, sleepwalking life ever since.

If he were here on this balmy August night I'd be sailing with him instead of baking cheese straws in preparation for Tuesday-night quilting club with Patsy. I'd be striving for sex appeal in Bermuda shorts and bare-toed sandals instead of opting for comfort in walking shoes and a twill skirt with enough elastic around the waist to make allowances for two helpings of lemon-cream pie.

Not that I mind Patsy. Just the opposite. I love her. She's the only person besides Roy who creates wonder wherever she goes. (She creates mayhem, too, but we won't get into that.) She's my mirror now, as well as my compass.

Of course, I have my daughter, Diana, but I refuse to be the kind of mother who defines herself through her children. Besides, she has her own life now, a husband and a baby on the way.

I slide the last cheese straws into the oven and then go into my office and open e-mail.

From: "Miss Sass" <patsyleslie@hotmail.com>
To: "The Lady" <louisejernigan@yahoo.com>
Sent: Tuesday, August 15, 6:00 PM
Subject: Dangerous Tonight
Hey Lady,
I'm feeling dangerous tonight. Hot to trot, if you know what I mean. Or can you even remember? ☺ Look out, bridge club, here I come. I'm liable to end up dancing on the tables instead of bidding three spades. Whose turn is it to drive, anyhow? Mine or thine?
XOXOX
Patsy
P.S. Lord, how did we end up in a club with no men?

This e-mail is typical "Patsy." She's the only person I know who makes me laugh all the time. I guess that's why I e-mail her about ten times a day. She lives right next door, but e-mail satisfies my urge to be instantly and con-

stantly in touch with her without having to interrupt the
flow of my life. Sometimes we even save the good stuff for
e-mail.

> From: "The Lady" <louisejernigan@yahoo.com>
> To: "Miss Sass" <patsyleslie@hotmail.com>
> Sent: Tuesday, August 15, 6:10 PM
> Subject: Re: Dangerous Tonight

So, what else is new, Miss Sass? You're always danger-
ous. If you had a weapon, you'd be lethal. ☺
Hugs,
Louise
P.S. What's this about men? I thought you said your
libido was dead?

I press Send then wait. Her reply is almost instantaneous.

> From: "Miss Sass" <patsyleslie@hotmail.com>
> To: "The Lady" <louisejernigan@yahoo.com>
> Sent: Tuesday, August 15, 6:12 PM
> Subject: Re: Dangerous Tonight

Ha! If I had a *brain* I'd be lethal.
And I said my libido was in hibernation, not DEAD!
Jeez, Louise!!!!!
P

Patsy loves to have the last word, so I shut off my
computer.

* * * * *

Want to find out what happens to their friendship
when Patsy and Louise
both find the perfect man?

Don't miss
CONFESSIONS OF A NOT-SO-DEAD LIBIDO
by Peggy Webb,

coming to Harlequin NEXT
in November 2006.

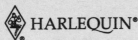

HARLEQUIN®

NeXt™

**Entertaining women's fiction
for every woman who has
wondered "what's next?"
in her life.**

Receive $1.⁰⁰ off

any Harlequin NEXT™ novel.

Coupon expires March 31, 2007.
Redeemable at participating retail outlets
in the U.S. only. Limit one coupon per customer.

5 65373 00076 2   (8100)0 11266

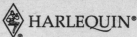

HARLEQUIN®

NeXt™

Entertaining women's fiction for every woman who has wondered "what's next?" in her life.

Receive $1.⁰⁰ off

any Harlequin NEXT™ novel.

Coupon expires March 31, 2007.
Redeemable at participating retail outlets
in Canada only. Limit one coupon per customer.

RETAILER: Harlequin Enterprises Ltd. will pay the face value of this coupon plus
10.25¢ if submitted by customer for this product only. Any other use constitutes
fraud. Coupon is nonassignable. Void if taxed, prohibited or restricted by law.
Consumer must pay any government taxes. Void if copied. Nielson Clearing House
customers submit coupons and proof of sales to: Harlequin Enterprises Ltd., P.O.
Box 3000, Saint John, N.B., E2L 4L3. Non-NCH retailer—for reimbursement submit
coupons and proof of sales directly to: Harlequin Enterprises Ltd., Retail Marketing
Department, 225 Duncan Mill Rd., Don Mills, Ontario, M3B 3K9, Canada. Valid in
Canada only. ® is a trademark of Harlequin Enterprises Ltd. Trademarks marked
with ® are registered in the United States and/or other countries.

52607178

nocturne™

HER BLOOD WAS POISON TO HIM...

MICHELE HAUF

FROM THE DARK

Michael is a man with a secret. He's a vampire
struggling to fight the darkness of his nature.
It looks like a losing battle—until he meets
Jane, the only woman who can understand his
conflicted nature. And the only woman who can
destroy him—through love.

On sale November 2006.

Christmas comes to

In November 2005, don't miss:

MISTLETOE MARRIAGE
(#3869)

by Jessica Hart

For Sophie Beckwith, this Christmas means facing the ex who dumped her and then married her sister! Only one person can help: her best friend Bram. Bram used to be engaged to Sophie's sister, and now, determined to show the lovebirds that they've moved on, he's come up with a plan: he's proposed to Sophie!

Then in December look out for:

CHRISTMAS GIFT: A FAMILY
(#3873)

by Barbara Hannay

Happy with his life as a wealthy bachelor, Hugh Strickland is stunned to discover he has a daughter. He wants to bring Ivy home—but he's absolutely terrified! Hugh hardly knows Jo Berry, but he pleads with her to help him—surely the ideal solution would be to give each other the perfect Christmas gift: a family....

Available wherever Harlequin books are sold.

REQUEST YOUR FREE BOOKS!

2 FREE NOVELS PLUS 2 FREE GIFTS!

HARLEQUIN®

Super Romance®

Exciting, emotional, unexpected!

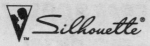

SAVE UP TO $30! SIGN UP TODAY!

INSIDE *Romance*

The complete guide to your favorite Harlequin®, Silhouette® and Love Inspired® books.

✓ Newsletter ABSOLUTELY FREE! No purchase necessary.

✓ Valuable coupons for future purchases of Harlequin, Silhouette and Love Inspired books in every issue!

✓ Special excerpts & previews in each issue. Learn about all the hottest titles before they arrive in stores.

✓ No hassle—mailed directly to your door!

✓ Comes complete with a handy shopping checklist so you won't miss out on any titles.

- -

SIGN ME UP TO RECEIVE INSIDE ROMANCE ABSOLUTELY FREE

(Please print clearly)

Name _____

Address _____

City/Town   State/Province   Zip/Postal Code

(098 KKM EJL9)

Please mail this form to:
In the U.S.A.: Inside Romance, P.O. Box 9057, Buffalo, NY 14269-9057
In Canada: Inside Romance, P.O. Box 622, Fort Erie, ON L2A 5X3
OR visit http://www.eHarlequin.com/insideromance

IRNBPA06R   ® and ™ are trademarks owned and used by the trademark owner and/or its licensee.

HARLEQUIN®
Super Romance®

Join acclaimed author
Tara Taylor Quinn
for another exciting book
this holiday season!

MERRY CHRISTMAS, BABIES

by *Tara Taylor Quinn*

#1381

Elise Richardson hears her biological clock ticking
loudly and, with no husband on the horizon, she's
decided to have a baby on her own. But she begins
to depend more and more on her business partner,
Joe Bennet, who's also her best friend—especially
when she finds out she isn't having one baby this
Christmas, but four!

On sale November 2006 from Harlequin Superromance!

*Available wherever books are sold including most
bookstores, supermarkets, discount stores and drugstores.*

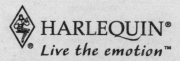

HARLEQUIN®
Live the emotion™